YEARLING BOOKS

Since 1966, Yearling has been the

leading name in classic and award-winning

literature for young readers.

With a wide variety of titles,

Yearling paperbacks entertain, inspire,

and encourage a love of reading.

VISIT

RANDOMHOUSE.COM/KIDS

TO FIND THE PERFECT BOOK, PLAY GAMES,
AND MEET FAVORITE AUTHORS!

Shana Burg

A Thousand

Never Evers

A YEARLING BOOK

Sale of this book without a front cover may be unauthorized. If the book is coverless, it may have been reported to the publisher as "unsold or destroyed" and neither the author nor the publisher may have received payment for it.

This is a work of fiction. All incidents and dialogue, and all characters with the exception of some well-known historical and public figures, are products of the author's imagination and are not to be construed as real. Where real-life historical or public figures appear, the situations, incidents, and dialogues concerning those persons are fictional and are not intended to depict actual events or to change the fictional nature of the work. In all other respects, any resemblance to persons living or dead is entirely coincidental.

Copyright © 2008 by Shana Burg
Frontis photograph © Lance Nelson/Corbis

All rights reserved. Published in the United States by Yearling, an imprint of Random House Children's Books, a division of Random House, Inc., New York. Originally published in hardcover in the United States by Delacorte Press, an imprint of Random House Children's Books, a division of Random House, Inc., in 2008.

Yearling and the jumping horse design are registered trademarks of Random House, Inc.

Visit us on the Web! www.randomhouse.com/kids

Educators and librarians, for a variety of teaching tools, visit us at www.randomhouse.com/teachers

The Library of Congress has cataloged the hardcover edition of this work as follows:
Burg, Shana.
A thousand never evers / Shana Burg
p. cm.
Summary: As the civil rights movement in the South gains momentum in 1963—and violence against African Americans intensifies—the black residents, including seventh-grader Addie Ann Pickett, in the small town of Kuckachoo, Mississippi, begin their own courageous struggle for racial justice.
ISBN: 978-0-385-73470-7 (trade) — ISBN: 978-0-385-90468-1 (glb) —
ISBN: 978-0-375-84893-3 (e-book)
1. Civil rights movements—Southern States—History—20th century—Juvenile fiction.
[1. Civil rights movements—Fiction. 2. Race relations—Fiction. 3. African Americans—Fiction. 4. Mississippi—History—20th century—Fiction.] I. Title.
PZ7.B916259Th 2008
[Fic]—dc22
2007028226

ISBN: 978-0-440-42209-9 (pbk.)

Printed in the United States of America
10
First Yearling Edition

Random House Children's Books supports the First Amendment and celebrates the right to read.

R0452097293

With buckets of love for my father,
Harvey Burg,
who teaches by example
that we're all in this world together

The things that I don't like I will try to change.

—MEDGAR EVERS

Contents

A NOTE TO READERS

Although I spent a whole school year in seventh grade, it's the two minutes when my math teacher stepped out of class that I'll remember for the rest of my life. In those two minutes, the boy who sat behind me took a thick black Magic Marker and drew a swastika on the cover of his math book. I knew that what he drew was a symbol of hatred toward Jewish people, and I had the feeling he knew too. To this day, I can still hear everyone's giddy laughter as he opened the third-floor window and hurled the math book out with disgust. Being Jewish, I felt my heart fall right down to the ground with that book.

Looking back, I'm not surprised it was during seventh grade that I began to ask my father all kinds of questions about his work in the civil rights movement—a movement in our nation to gain equal rights for citizens of all backgrounds, especially African Americans.

Even though my parents are not African American, they wanted to help combat the racism they felt was unjust. It was the 1960s, and my parents believed that in the United States, all Americans deserved the right to vote for their leaders, attend good schools, and go to whichever public parks or public swimming pools they liked best. So my parents moved from New York to Alabama, the heart of the civil rights movement. My dad joined a law firm there. One case at a time, the lawyers in the firm fought so that African Americans could have the same rights as all Americans.

My father told me that although the institution of slavery had ended with the Civil War in 1865, discrimination against Americans of African descent continued in countless ways. Leaders in many states throughout the country actually passed laws to ensure the segregation of white people from African Americans and other people of color. These laws were called Jim Crow laws.

Dad said that according to the Jim Crow laws, African American children were not allowed to go to the same schools as white children. They had to go to older, smaller, more crowded schools with fewer books and desks. And even if there was a school right near their house, they often had to walk for miles to get to the Negro school because the school buses were only for white children. Under the Jim Crow laws, African American children and adults weren't allowed to eat in the same restaurants, use the same restrooms, or sleep in the same hotels as white people.

In addition, racist officials often prevented African Americans from voting by giving them unfair tests and making them pay poll taxes they could not afford. Sometimes African Americans who tried to register to vote were beaten up or fired from their jobs.

My father told me that even in some of the states that didn't pass Jim Crow laws, white people still treated African Americans poorly when they tried to get good work, live in decent houses, and attend good schools.

Then he played me a cassette tape of an interview with the Imperial Wizard of a group called the Ku Klux Klan. This group of white people hid behind masks and robes and terrorized African Americans, as well as Catholics, Jews, and homosexuals. Much to my surprise, Dad said it wasn't just Klansmen who participated in atrocious acts like burning churches and torturing and murdering people different from themselves. Lots of people, including government officials like mayors, governors, and sheriffs, permitted these terrible events to take place.

In response to all this injustice, African Americans organized themselves into what was called the civil rights movement. They moved together to fight racism and demand equal treatment as citizens of the United States of America. And believe it or not, even though so many activists were threatened, beaten, and killed, for the most part they didn't fight with weapons. Instead they used their minds, words, courage, and nonviolent resistance. They bonded together in groups. And they really started to make progress in the 1950s and 1960s when they boycotted shops that didn't treat them fairly, refused to sit at the back of public buses, marched against racial injustice, integrated schools, and registered as many African American voters as they could.

I remember asking my father why he wanted to work for the civil rights movement in the first place. He told me, "It's because I am a Jew." He said, "What happens to one minority group affects us all. There's no place in my America for discrimination because of skin color, religion, or whether you're a girl or boy."

If you believe, as I do, that ninety percent of writing is thinking, then you could say I started writing this book back in seventh-grade math class. I was supposed to be concentrating on negative numbers and equations but was thinking about prejudice and equal rights instead.

After all the thinking I did back in seventh grade, I finished writing the book once I was grown up. As part of my research, I interviewed many interesting people: children and adults who grew up in the Mississippi Delta, vegetable farmers, a hat maker, and an expert on the black modeling industry. I read old newspapers and magazines from the 1960s when my characters lived. I hired my former middle school students to be my first editors. And, oh yes, I also baked butter bean cookies.

A Thousand Never Evers is historical fiction. That means that while I made up most of the story, I also included many facts about where and when it takes place.

Although most of the characters you will read about are fictional, Medgar Evers, Emmett Till, and the four girls who died when their church was bombed were very real individuals whose lives and deaths motivated civil rights workers to keep fighting for equality.

Shana Burg

CHAPTER 1

June 12, 1963

Now get this: there's a boy in Jackson so rich that when he finished high school, his daddy bought him a brand-new car. At least that's what I heard. In my family, we don't have that kind of money, but my uncle gives a whole dollar to any Pickett who graduates Acorn Elementary School. It's tradition.

So here I am, soaring through the sky on my swing that hangs from the oak tree, when Uncle Bump calls out the door of his shed, "Go on. Get your brother. He'll take you." He stretches a dollar bill between both hands and I jump right off. Sure it's not enough for a car, but that dollar can buy a whole lot of good, like twenty Hershey bars.

After my brother graduated elementary school, he bought a baseball. But I'm not going to waste my dollar on something dumb. I want something important, like dye to turn my flour-colored dress new for the first day of school.

"Mama will be proud you're spending your dollar to make a bright impression at County Colored," Uncle Bump tells me.

"It's West Thunder Creek Junior High School," I tell him, and stuff the dollar into my sock. Sure I'm going to the Negro junior high school, but a school's a school. Folks should call it by its proper name and make it sound important.

"Don't dillydally, Addie Ann," Uncle Bump says. He pulls the harmonica out of his pocket and blows a chord. And it's real good to hear him sound those notes, because ever since our boss, Old Man Adams, got the whooping cough, Uncle Bump hasn't had time to play music. "Mama's bringing home some hen tonight," he says. Then he sinks down on the steps of his shed and slides that harmonica across his lips.

I'm heading across the tracks to the white side and I reckon some furry company won't hurt. My cat, Flapjack, and me have a secret code. When I whistle and click my tongue twice, he comes running. *Tweet, click, click. Tweet, click, click.* Other folk think it's magic, but here he comes, dashing across the pine needles, purring as he threads a figure eight round my ankles.

When we pass Brother Babcock's chicken shack, my

stomach growls. And when we get to Daisy's Dry Goods, I kick up the dirt on the path, because I've been itching to buy a real new dress in there, but right about now, we don't have the money.

As always, once we cross the railroad tracks everything seems whiter and brighter, and I don't mean just the people who live here. The fresh-painted shingles and the white picket fences gleam in the late-afternoon sun. Even Flapjack's tan fur lights up a fiery orange. And my feet are glad to walk on pavement.

By the time we get to the edge of Mr. Mudge's place, the sun's diving into the horizon. Flapjack and me pass by Mr. Mudge's greenhouse and his stable full of cows and pigs, on the way to his farm where my brother works. "Now don't squish the squash," I tell Flapjack before we head across the leafy rows to meet Elias, who's bent like a rainbow over the tomatoes. He's been working this land since he was five.

"Uncle Bump says you've gotta take me to get the dye," I say, and hold up the dollar to prove it's true. But Elias stares straight past me like I'm not even here. Mama always says he's "half legs, half smile," but today his grin is gone. His eyes are sad and distant.

"What's a matter?" I ask. He's probably worried up about getting into college, so I tell him, "I bet you'll even get a scholarship to Morehouse. Then I'll come to Georgia and visit you and we'll—"

"Shut up," he says.

Usually Elias doesn't live on the edge of his mind like me, so right about now I don't know what to think.

"Don't you know 'bout Medgar?" he asks.

"What's that?"

"Medgar Evers got shot. Down in Jackson. Late last night. Someone killed . . ." His voice stretches and tightens. Then he swipes the side of his hand under his nose. That's what he does when he gets close to tears. Usually it stops them from sliding down.

Here one guy I never heard of gets shot dead, and now my brother's all ripped up and I'm just about crazy. "He a friend?" I ask.

"No."

"He owe you money?"

"No!" Elias rolls his eyes.

"Well, if he ain't a friend and he don't owe you money, what's a matter?"

"Don't you know anything?" he asks.

I turn away. Elias knows I know something. Otherwise, why did I get the highest score on the geography quiz in the whole sixth grade? Okay, sure there are only four kids in the sixth grade at Acorn Elementary, but still, a ninety-six is a ninety-six. I want to remind Elias of this but my throat squeezes shut. I swipe my hand under my nose but my tears get out anyway.

My brother puts his hands on my shoulders, tries to turn me round. "Sorry," he says. "Sometimes I forget you're a little kid."

"Seventh grade's not little," I tell him. Then I blink a lot to get the tears to stay inside. "Now come on. Tell me! Who's this Edgar Mevers?"

"His name is Medgar Evers," Elias says. "He's from the movement."

I nod so my brother will think I know what he's talking about. But I wonder why he can't answer my questions plain and simple. If he's so smart, why doesn't he tell me this: Why do they call it the movement? How can he swipe under his nose and stop crying? And why did Medgar Evers's mama give him such a silly name?

"Well, someone killed him," Elias says, and looks away again. "Left three young children without a daddy."

I reckon Elias probably knows how those poor children feel.

Our daddy died of pneumonia when Elias was four. Mama still says, "Your daddy went to Heaven proud of his little boy." Whenever she says that, Elias grins, but truth be told, I get this hollow feeling in my chest because it's not fair. I was nothing but a lump in Mama's tummy when Daddy met his Maker. He never got the chance to be proud of me. He never watched me jump double Dutch. He never tasted my honey cake. He never saw my ninety-six on the geography quiz. Daddy missed my whole life because he went and died of pneumonia a couple months before I was born.

Bad as I feel thinking about Daddy, I know Elias feels worse. So here I am, trying to think of a way to help him feel better, but I can't. Still, Elias rubs his hand over my head like I'm his good-luck charm, and I get the notion he likes knowing I'm here.

I follow my brother across the pumpkin patch into the forest on Mr. Mudge's land. We don't say a word. All we hear are blackbirds chirping in the trees. We cross the thick woods to the parking lot of Mr. Mudge's Corner Store. Then we head out of the lot and turn down the road to the Very Fine Fabric Shop.

At the Very Fine Fabric Shop, Elias doesn't take but two seconds to get caught up chatting with my best friend Delilah's second cousin Bessie. Bessie's in tenth grade. She cleans all the shops on the white side of town. And I can't deny it: Bessie's fetching. She's got green eyes and all kinds of curves. I reckon I shouldn't be too surprised that the whole while I'm picking out the dye—and I could use some help deciding the color—Elias is yapping with Bessie about that Medgar guy. So without a hint of advice, I choose yellow and pay. And even though it's getting dark, Elias won't leave the store, not till Bessie sprays the counters and sweeps the floors.

The sky's between hawk and buzzard when at long last Elias and me set off home. I know Mama won't be happy with us. But that doesn't seem to bother my brother.

The whole way back, Flapjack weaves round my calves while Elias talks about that Medgar guy and the movement to get us our rights. I reckon my brother thinks he's the reverend and he's got to convert me to the fighting side.

"Now everybody's got some fire, some rage," he says. "It's how you use your fire that counts."

While we cross the tracks, I tell him to stop preaching.

"I'm just trying to help," Elias says. Then he shakes his head like he's thirty years older than me, not just five.

❦

By the time we get home, the sun's under the earth. Elias and me slog into the kitchen where Mama's sitting at the table with Uncle Bump. As expected, she's in a dither. There's no sweet smell of hen wafting through the house. Worse, her usual I-been-working-hard-and-I'm-glad-I'm-home smile is gone.

"Where you been?" she snaps.

My bottom lip shakes. I hate how that happens. Then everyone can tell I've got the fidgets. I wonder why I've got to have a giveaway lip.

"Sorry," I tell her. I pull out a chair and sit. And I don't know how I think so fast under pressure but I do. I cross my fingers under the kitchen table so God won't hold anything against me. "What actually happened is . . . ," I say. I'm about to tell Mama and Uncle Bump how a big mean dog came and chased Flapjack up a tree right outside the Very Fine Fabric Shop. I'm about to tell them that no matter how much I whistled and clicked, Flapjack wouldn't come on down. I'm about to tell them that if I left Flapjack there, that dog would've eaten my poor cat for supper, but before I do, Mama cuts her eyes at me real mean and says, "If there's one thing I can't stand, it's a fibber!"

And I just put my lips back together right there.

Mama turns to Elias.

"I've been worried sick! You know how I feel 'bout you being out late! 'Specially when you got your sister with you. She's just a little girl, Elias."

"Sorry, Mama," Elias says.

"I'm not little!" I say.

Uncle Bump tries to change the subject. He bows his

head. "Thank you, Lord, for the food you placed before us," he says.

There's a bowl of gray boiled potatoes in the center of the table. And one thing's clear: they sure aren't hen. Mama probably fixed up the hen so good that the Tate family ate it all and there wasn't any left to bring home.

"This looks delicious," Elias says. He spears a potato with his fork.

But Mama, she yanks that forkful of potato right out of my brother's hand. "I don't want to see no one eating till I get an explanation." The fork trembles in Mama's hand because she's so worried and mad. Being worried and mad is like biscuits and gravy for Mama. The two just go together.

"We were picking out dye for Addie Ann, when we run into someone to talk to," Elias says. "It was real important."

But Mama doesn't see it that way. Not at all. She points her potato fork at my brother, then at me. "When I send my kids over to the white side, I don't expect them to come through that door after the sun has set." Mama's so angry she doesn't even ask what color dye I have in my sack. "Now who's so important to talk to when it's already getting dark?"

"It was just Bessie," Elias says. "She was working at the shop. We got to talking 'bout Medgar Evers and . . ."

It seems Mama's heard the news too. She sets down her potato fork, closes her weary eyes, and starts praying for the dead man's soul.

But her prayer sounds more like complaining. "Dear Lord," she says, "that Medgar didn't deserve to die. He been stirring up trouble, trying to get them schools mixed up, colored and white, as they should. And he been helping sign up Negro voters, Lord, 'cause don't every person supposed to have a voice in these United States?"

What's so special about the vote? Mama always carries on about it, but what difference could one of her votes make anyway? Well, one thing's clear: she thinks Medgar Evers's work to help Negroes vote is more important than eating dinner while it's hot.

Now Mama shakes her head like she just can't believe this Medgar guy's dead and gone. "Lord, you listen to me," she says. "You bless Medgar's hardworking, full-of-courage soul."

After that, how am I supposed to eat? Hen or no hen, my stomach's knotted up knowing someone can get killed for doing heaps of good.

CHAPTER 2

❧

June 16, 1963

Old Man Adams, our boss, comes from a long line of white folk. He used to own the five-hundred-acre cotton plantation that separates Kuckachoo from Franklindale, but he sold that off. The only land he kept was his garden that's right here in his backyard.

Sometimes the old man's garden is full of tomatoes, purple hull peas, and a whole lot of squash, and other times it's covered with watermelon, collards, and string beans. That's because he's always changing his mind about which crops are best, though one thing's clear: at six acres, Old Man Adams's garden is the largest in town. Why, I reckon the whole Negro side of Kuckachoo could fit right inside it!

I was five when I started working his garden. It was only last year, when I turned eleven, that Uncle Bump decided I knew enough cooking to help Elmira in the kitchen. Now instead of hunching over to pick squash, I stand up straight and fill gleaming vases with daffodils that have already been picked by someone else. And instead of cutting my fingers when I dig up sweet potatoes, I turn the silvery handles on the kitchen faucet till the sparkly water flows out.

My favorite thing to do here in the big house is a secret. Sometimes I watch television in Old Man Adams's living room. So long as the other servants aren't around, Uncle Bump lets me. I flip through the three channels on the black-and-white set till I decide which show is best. After that, I settle onto the sofa and press my bare calves against the cool leather. One time, Uncle Bump even made lemonade and plunked down next to me. Then we watched the old film *Poor Little Rich Girl* from start to finish.

Today, even though I'm working beside Elmira in Old Man Adams's kitchen, everything's different than usual. I look over my shoulder into the dining room, where Uncle Bump gives the old man some slippery elm to help clear his airway. The old man, just a shadow, sits in his rocking chair beside the oak table, while the chandelier above the table lights up each of his chalky wrinkles.

The mayor, the sheriff, the white preacher, and seven other white men join Uncle Bump hovering by the old man's side. That's because everyone knows how much is at stake once the stale air blows out his nostrils for the last time. You see, Old Man Adams has no siblings, was never married, and has no other relatives to speak of, so the white folk are sure when he passes, he'll leave his property to one of them.

While the white folk feast, Uncle Bump steps into the kitchen to see how me and Elmira are getting on. And that's when Elmira tells him the dreaded news. "I seen many a man close to death, and right now our dear Adams is too."

Me? I've never seen a dead man before.

But now Elmira says, "It's time to take the pillow from behind his head, Bump. When you're ready for home, all the everlasting tea in China can't keep you on earth."

So Uncle Bump sighs and returns to the dining room to do as Elmira says. But I won't let my uncle be there alone. I follow him, and to make like I'm busy, I take a shiny pitcher from the cabinet and polish it some more.

After Uncle Bump removes the pillow from behind his head, Old Man Adams wheezes one last time. Then his face falls gently onto the table beside a vanilla cake.

While the white preacher lifts his hands above Old Man Adams and murmurs a prayer, I drag myself back to the kitchen. I remember how Old Man Adams's ivory corpse was filled with life, how a year ago he welcomed me to the big house and showed me where he hid his chocolate under the fruit in the refrigerator. "Here's for when you need somethin' sweet," he told me with a wink. Of course, I never dared take a piece. I didn't want to give Elmira a reason to send me back to the fields.

When the men from the funeral parlor arrive, they heave Old Man Adams's body onto a stretcher. They drape a sheet over him and haul him out the front door. But the click of the closing door, it has nowhere to settle. And with the old man gone, there's too much echo left in the dining room and no reason for the white folks to stick around. They file outside, heads low, voices lower, all of them praying Old Man Adams left them the property in his will.

Now Uncle Bump lumbers into the kitchen, where I'm waiting to give him a hug. But he steps right past me, out the servants' door.

Unlike Uncle Bump, Elmira's grief erupts out each pore. "No better man," she cries. She leans her elbows on the sink, hangs her head between them. "No better man." Elmira dries her eyes on the corner of her apron, then leaves the big house too.

While I follow her out the servants' door, I try not to think of all the good laughs we had in the kitchen. I try not to think it's the last time I'll ever be in Old Man Adams's place.

Outside, Elmira and me can't find Uncle Bump anywhere. Then a ghostlike note dances through the air. We trail the sound through the backyard. And wouldn't you know it, there's my uncle, his back against the garden gate, blowing grief out his harmonica.

CHAPTER 3

June 22, 1963

They went and buried Old Man Adams a couple days back, but none of us Negro hands were allowed to attend. Of course, ever since he went and died, I've got no work. And sure I'm sad he's gone, but I'm not going to mope. At least now I've got time to jump double Dutch. Trouble is I can't find anyone to jump with me. My best friend Delilah's sewing at the tailor shop across town. And besides, now that she's passed fifth grade, she says she's not interested in jumping ever again. My next-best friend Lovetta's chopping grass on the cotton plantation sunup to sundown, so she isn't around either.

Without any work and without anyone to jump with, I

reckon now's the time to dye my dress a brilliant yellow and get it ready for my first day of junior high school, even though it's still months away.

So here I am, standing on the porch, hunched over the washbasin, minding my business, when I spot a white man I've never seen before hobbling toward me. First thing I notice: his prickly white beard runs over his dimpled cheeks. Second thing: he was picked before he was ripe. He's no taller than me.

"This the Pickett home?" he asks when he gets close.

Here I am, my sopping school dress in my hands. "Yes, sir," I tell him. "I'm Addie Ann Pickett."

I can't imagine what this little man wants. I notice he's got a paper in his hands, and his hands, they're shaking. Well, maybe it's the heat. Or maybe it's the shacks we live in. Sure he probably heard the Negroes are dirt-dog-poor—maybe he even drove past our houses—but I reckon seeing close-up that a whole family lives in a home the size of his garden shed can be a bit of a surprise.

"Lawyer for Mr. Adams," he says.

A lawyer? I'm not sure exactly what that is, but I know it's got something to do with the law, and from everything I've heard, that's not good.

While the lawyer looks at his paper, I squeeze my wet dress in my fists, afraid there might be trouble. But then the most amazing thing happens! The little lawyer looks at me and says, "Addie Ann Pickett, you and your uncle, Charles 'Bump' Dawson, are requested at the estate at four p.m. for the reading of the will. Mr. Adams left you each a gift."

And wouldn't you know it, my heart flies up and clogs

my throat. There's no way for words to get out. Never in ten billion years did I think Old Man Adams would go and leave presents for Uncle Bump and me!

The lawyer makes me promise to tell my uncle the news right away. Then he asks, "Now where would I find the cook, Mrs. Grady?"

It's the best I can do to point round the bend. Even if I could speak right now, I wouldn't tell him Elmira hates when folks call her Mrs. Grady, because it makes her feel old as the stars.

As soon as the little man struts away, I drop my school dress on the edge of the basin and run round back, where Mama's pinning clothes on the line. I tell her what the lawyer man said.

"Don't that take the whole biscuit!" Mama says, and grins. Together, the two of us dash across the yard to bang on the door of Uncle Bump's shed.

As soon as he opens it, I tell him, "Old Man Adams left us presents!"

Then Mama explains about the will.

"My, oh my!" Uncle Bump grins.

"Now then, I've gotta get this girl ready," Mama says to Uncle Bump. "You gonna tidy up too?" she asks, and rubs her chin.

"Oh, sure," Uncle Bump says. He touches his beard. "Sure."

Mama and me shuffle back across the yard and into our kitchen. Mama sits on a chair and I plop down on the floor-boards between her legs. Well, all I can say is Mama's fingers work real good under pressure. Lickety-split, she braids up my hair in a hundred little rows. Then I slip into the white dress I usually save for church.

An hour later, I'm standing in the yard between our house and Uncle Bump's shed, wondering whether Old Man Adams left me all the chocolate he hid under the fruit in the refrigerator. "Come on," I call through the window of Uncle Bump's shed. "We can't be late for *this*!"

Uncle Bump steps out the door. He's trimmed his beard real short and nice. Together, we take it down the lane. While we walk, the keys to Old Man Adams's place jangle from his belt loop. But those keys have been hanging there so many years that now the sound of them seems no louder than the sound of his breathing.

After we turn the bend, we stop to get Elmira, who's equally round on her bosom and bottom, which is lucky for her, because it keeps her upright while she waddles back and forth across town.

The three of us set off down the lane and across the railroad tracks, to Magnolia Row, which runs alongside Old Man Adams's field at the edge of town. Today white magnolia petals litter the path. Springtime fills up my lungs. I see one blossom still on the branch. Through that flower, Old Man Adams sends me a message: life keeps blooming, things keep on.

After we get to the big house, we walk up the side steps, only to find the servants' door already unlocked. That's when I get a bad ache in my chest. For as long as I can remember, Uncle Bump has unlocked these doors, raised the curtains, and given servants their orders, but now a little lawyer's taken charge, and I can't help but feel my uncle's been thrown out like trash.

Inside the big house, there's no smell of roast beef or sweet potato pie. The air is empty and stale. Elmira clings to the kitchen sink. But Uncle Bump steps into the dining room. I'm about to follow him in there, when I spot the sheriff and the mayor sitting at the oak table. The sheriff's arms are folded across his giant body, but his head is small, so it looks like God mixed up the parts. As for the mayor, he wears a stiff smile on his face, so it looks like his lips are curtains tied up at the corners with ribbons. No doubt both the sheriff and the mayor have been tossing in their night-clothes, because rumors are flying that Old Man Adams left his house and land to one of them. And everyone knows that whoever it is, he'll be a very rich man.

Now I plant myself in the doorway between the kitchen and the dining room. I watch the little lawyer strut into the dining room from the hallway. He sets his black suitcase on the table. Then he unlatches the suitcase, takes out a pile of paper, and reads aloud like he's mumbling in-structions for how to build a scrubboard, like nothing could possibly be duller.

But you can bet my ears, they perk right up when he reads out Uncle Bump's gift: " 'I bequeath my gold pocket watch to my head servant, Bump Dawson.' "

The lawyer removes a small felt bag from his suitcase.

As Uncle Bump crosses the room to pick up the pocket watch, the sheriff mutters, "What kind of name is 'Bump'?"

The mayor guffaws.

My cheeks burn. To hear them poke fun at a man kind and patient as Uncle Bump makes me want to hurl them into a bucket of dirty mop water. If they knew Uncle Bump's friends named him for the bumpy muscles in his arms, they'd both hush up quicker than a dog can lick a dish.

But Uncle Bump walks to the lawyer as if he's heard nothing and slips the sack into his pant's pocket.

Then the little lawyer reads, " 'To Elmira Grady, my cook, I leave my Dutch oven.' "

Elmira throws her hands over her mouth and waddles from the sink to the Dutch oven to examine her new prize. Not that she's got more food to cook in it, but still, she releases a sob of joy.

Then the lawyer reads, " 'To Miss Addie Ann Pickett, my cook's assistant . . .' " I reckon that little man said my name. He's talking about me! I don't think I've ever heard a white person say my whole name before. " 'I leave my television set.' "

It's too much to believe! I'm going to be the only person on the Negro side with a working set. I can see all the movies starring Shirley Temple. There's no doubt about it: I'll be the *most* popular girl in school. Cool Breeze Huddleston will *pray* I invite him over to watch! One day I'll be on television myself. I'm going to be a television geography teacher! Not an ordinary geography teacher. A *television* geography teacher like Miss Shirley Smith. I read all about her in *Ebony* magazine, the one I got from the church lending library. Miss Smith teaches children about all the countries in the world. Her program comes on in Ohio. Mine will come on in Mississippi! Why, my family will watch me on this very set!

But wouldn't you know it, the happiest moment in my

whole entire life is chopped off like the branch of a dead hickory tree.

The mayor snickers, "There ain't no . . ."

And the sheriff howls, "No electricity . . ."

"On Kuckachoo Lane!" snuffles the mayor.

And there you have it. *No electricity?* I was so excited I didn't stop to think. But it's true. Ever since the tornado last month, the power lines have been down on our lane. No matter how many times Uncle Bump complains, no one comes to put them back up.

While the sheriff and the mayor yuk it up good, Uncle Bump rests his bulky arm round my shoulders and draws me toward him. Tears burn under my lids. But I'll tell you one thing: I'm not going to let them see me cry. I'm not! I'll save that television set for sometime soon. Sometime soon when we get our electricity back.

"I've got to get going, so listen up," the lawyer says. The sheriff and the mayor swallow their chuckles.

The lawyer picks up the papers. Then he clears his throat and reads, " 'I hereby bequeath my furniture, my books, and the remaining contents of my home to my alma mater, Ole Miss.' "

The lawyer reads on: " 'The house itself will be used as a gathering spot for the people of Kuckachoo. I expect the annual Christmas party to carry on without me.' "

The sheriff and the mayor are whomper-jawed! The old man didn't leave the house to either one of them! Now they're desperate to know which of them will get the land.

But the next thing we know, the lawyer reads this: " 'Most importantly, I leave my land to all the people of my community. Together whites and Negroes shall plant a garden.' "

The instant the words leave the lawyer's mouth, a train of gasps ricochets from the sheriff to Elmira to the mayor to Uncle Bump to me.

Then Elmira throws up her arms and cries, "Hallelujah!"

None of us can believe Old Man Adams left 417 beautiful rows for us to sow together, plus his huge house for *all* Kuckachookians! And those rows are smack in the middle of town. Sure we knew Old Man Adams was freehearted, but this is another breed!

All of a sudden, my stomach gurgles. I can smell the delicious food that will come from that land: corn chowder, pumpkin pie, and best of all, warm button squash with cane syrup dripping down the sides! I'll bet we can sell the vegetables we grow at the farmers' market. Then we'll take our money and buy batches of Mr. Mudge's famous chocolate chip cookies! I'll bet those will keep our tummies full all night long.

The lawyer fumbles with his papers till they're all buckled inside his suitcase. "I'll keep the will in my office," he says to us all. Then he looks at the sheriff and the mayor and says, "As leaders of Kuckachoo, you two are responsible for seeing that the home and the land are used according to the will."

The sheriff stands and strokes the holster of his shotgun like it's a puppy. And by the way that little lawyer hustles to the front door, I reckon he can't leave the big house fast enough.

As soon as the lawyer's gone, the mayor smacks his

palms flat against the dining room table, cranes his torso across it, and shouts, "You heard what that man said!"

"We're in charge!" bellows the two-ton sheriff. Then he turns to Uncle Bump and shouts, "Give us the keys!"

There's the key to the big house, the key to the garden gate, and the key to the garden cabin. But Uncle Bump doesn't hand any of them over. Instead, he reaches down to his belt loop and clenches those keys tight in his fist.

So the sheriff picks up his shotgun and cocks it with a loud *clackity-clack*.

Nothing about the scene stays put: the bulging veins in the sheriff's neck, the bald circle on the mayor's scalp, the rocking chair beside the dining room table. Everything shimmers like it isn't real, like I'm not real, like this isn't happening.

I want to yell what I know is true: *This land, it's ours too!* But the words are stuck inside me. I'm afraid we're all going to die. And I wonder if it's worth it, for the land.

Then the sheriff points his gun at the ceiling and blasts who's who and what's what sharply into focus, just in case we didn't already know who was boss here. The chandelier crashes down on the dining room table, and a thousand glass beads thunder onto the wooden floor.

I dart into the kitchen where Elmira's crouching behind the refrigerator. I turn myself into a shadow under the drying rack. A shadow's shadow. From my hiding place, I peer out at Uncle Bump. He's in the doorway between the kitchen and the dining room, still as a boulder.

"Hand 'em over!" the sheriff roars at Uncle Bump.

Elmira shrieks, picks up her oven, and rushes outside. I

want to bolt into the yard behind her. But I can't leave Uncle Bump. I can't leave him here alone.

"Please!" I beg him.

And wouldn't you know it, without a moment's hesitation, Uncle Bump unhooks the keys from his belt loop. But he doesn't hand them to the sheriff. He gives them to the mayor. Then he pulls me out from under the drying rack, lifts my television set, and together we rush out of the chaos. Out of the mess.

While we scramble across the big house yard, my heart aches. While we trudge down Magnolia Row, my tears sting. And while we cross the railroad, I imagine the tracks turn upright like jailhouse bars to lock us on the Negro side of town.

Later, after we set down our gifts and wipe away our tears, me, Elmira, and Uncle Bump head over to First Baptist Church. We slip into the front-row pew while Reverend Walker stands at the pulpit, asking all kinds of questions.

"Who has the will now?"

"The lawyer in Jackson," Uncle Bump says.

"What's the lawyer's name?"

The three of us rack our brains up, down, and sideways, but not one of us can remember.

Then the reverend shrugs. "I reckon it doesn't much matter," he says. "Even if we could track him down, a white city lawyer won't care what we've got to say."

When I get back home, I wait and wait for Elias. I've got to tell him all that's going on. He'll find a way to make the sheriff stop bullying us. He'll hatch a plan to get the mayor to share the garden.

But now that both Uncle Bump and me have lost our jobs, Elias is working extra hours to try to help us get by. And tonight, by the time he comes through the door, the sky's dark as eggplant.

He mutters hello to Mama and me. Then he grabs a hunk of hoop cheese and stumbles into the bedroom. I follow him there, while Mama lights the stove to heat up his supper.

Elias lies down on his bed.

I know soon as I tell him what happened today at the big house, he'll get real quiet. Then he'll get real mad. Then he'll turn into a preacher before my very eyes and start yammering on about things like mercy and justice.

"Get this!" I say. I sit on the edge of my bed while, step by step, I describe just what happened today.

My brother doesn't say anything at all.

"Ain't you mad?" I ask.

"I am," he says. But Elias sounds more tired than anything.

So I wait a while longer but he doesn't start preaching. Instead, he lets out a snore that scares me half to death. My poor brother! I walk over to his bed, pull his sneakers off his feet, and set them on the floor. Then I go back to the kitchen and tell Mama to put away his supper and save it for tomorrow.

CHAPTER 4

July 1, 1963, Morning

Ever since we got chased out the big house, I've been jumping rope triple time, Uncle Bump's been holed up in his shed playing the most dreary tunes on his harmonica, Elmira's been burning sage to clear out our bad luck, and the reverend's been thinking how we can get our share of the garden back. Needless to say, with everyone so glum, it sure came as a relief to have something to laugh about this morning.

Now get this: Elias and me were sound asleep when we heard someone shouting bloody murder. We both scrambled bleary-eyed to look out our bedroom window. And there she was, Delilah's mama, our next-door neighbor,

25

storming across the yard, a dripping piece of plastic wrap in her hand. "Delilah Montgomery!" she screamed. "Lord help you!" Elias and me both split a rib.

A few days back, Delilah told me she was going to teach her mother to get a sense of humor. "You can't teach someone that," I told her.

"Why, sure you can!" she said. "Just watch."

But from the look of things, covering the outhouse toilet seat with plastic wrap didn't get Mrs. Montgomery any closer to a laugh. In fact, she was stinking mad!

"Now Mrs. Montgomery will never let Delilah go to the meeting tonight," I told Elias. Then again, I almost didn't get to go to tonight's civil rights meeting either. That's because I didn't want to go. But a few days ago, when Mama said I couldn't go, something inside me switched and I needed to go real bad. So I got Elias on my side. He told Mama the meeting would be all singing and praying, nothing I couldn't handle, so at long last Mama agreed.

But before that meeting, I've got loads to do.

As soon as I get dressed, Mama and me grab some biscuits and step outside, where the air is soft and breezy. I *tweet, click, click* for Flapjack. Together we cross the tracks to Honeysuckle Trail, where I'm starting work at the Tates' house with Mama.

Once we get there, I tell Flapjack, "It's just like when I used to work at Old Man Adams's big house. Remember how you used to wait for me there? Now see if you can find some mice or birds to play with." Flapjack looks at me with glassy green eyes. "We'll be done before you know it," I say. Then I kiss his head and follow Mama through the Tates' back door and into the kitchen.

The second Mrs. Tate sees me she says, "My you're all grown up. Well, I'm sure glad you're here, Addie Ann. What with Ralphie one year and crawling, he's getting into everything now." And just then, as if to prove what his mama says is true, the wide-eyed boy on the floor reaches up and shoves over the trash can. Orange rinds and coffee grounds scatter across the tile.

Ralphie giggles.

Mama grabs the broom and dustpan and sets about sweeping up the mess.

"It's impossible for your mama to help me with Ralphie and do all the cooking and cleaning too. And since I'm running the Kuckachoo Garden Club now, I'm out of breath thinking of all I've got to do," Mrs. Tate says, and sighs. "Just wait till he's walking! Then how will we ever keep up?" But Mrs. Tate doesn't wait for an answer. Instead, she disappears up the stairs.

All morning long, Mama teaches me new tasks, like how to change Ralphie's diaper, give him a bath, and buckle him into his high chair. Then she shows me round the Tates' house, and I've got to admit, I'm a tad disappointed. The Tates' house is eight times smaller than Old Man Adams's place. They don't have a marble floor or even a winding staircase. But one thing they do have, which we sure could use, is electricity! And of course, being on the white side, they've got their outhouse inside. It's got plenty of running water.

In the afternoon, I read Ralphie a couple stories. His

books are beautiful. It seems the pages have only been turned a few times. After the stories, I pick him up and stroke his black hair like he's my cat. I don't much want to set him down for a nap, because he's warm and soft here in my arms, but that boy's already sleeping.

Back in the kitchen, I tell Mama I sure could use a teeny tiny catnap myself, maybe out back under the dogwood tree, but she just laughs and pushes the laundry hamper full of Ralphie's dirty clothes into my arms.

It seems all too soon that I'm carrying Ralphie's wet clothes out back. I *tweet, click, click* a couple times, but wouldn't you know it, that cat of mine is nowhere to be found. One thing's clear: Flapjack needs to practice following directions a whole lot better.

I'm pinning Ralphie's little pants and shirts on the line when I hear that boy cry through his open bedroom window. I run back upstairs.

"Hi, Ralphie," I say.

He coos at me through the crib bars.

I lift him out and change his dirty diaper. But I can do a heck of a lot more than change a dirty diaper. I'm going to teach Ralphie to walk today. Why, just this morning didn't his mama say she couldn't wait for her son to take his first step?

I get straight to work. I pick a blue rattle out of the toy chest and set little Ralphie on the floor beside his crib. Then I kneel down next to the crib and shake the rattle.

Ralphie crawls over to me and grabs it, but when I try to take it out of his hand, he turns red and bawls. "It's okay," I tell him. "Here, you can have it," I say, and hand the rattle back. But Ralphie just throws it on the floor and cries harder. Well, thank goodness Mama's here. I pick Ralphie up and run downstairs to see if she's got any ideas for how to tame a wild beast.

Mama tells me to set him on the kitchen floor. Then she takes the pots and pans out of the cupboard and hands Ralphie a wooden spoon. The louder he bangs, the bigger his six-tooth grin. While he plays the drums, I set the table and Mama fries up vegetable croquettes for the Tates' dinner. After Mama's done, she says, "We'd best be on our way. I don't want to be late for the meeting."

I'm putting the pots and pans back in the cupboard, and Mama's threading her purse strap over her shoulder, when Mrs. Tate waltzes into the kitchen.

"Before you leave, Maisy, I just want to ask you something," she says.

"Yes, ma'am," Mama says.

"Well," Mrs. Tate says. She pulls an emery board out of her purse, sits at the kitchen table, and files a nail. "Are you Negroes . . . angry?" she asks.

"Angry, ma'am?"

"Well"—Mrs. Tate looks up at Mama—"my husband says you people don't think you're treated right. He says you're holding some sort of meeting tonight so you can fuss 'bout the voter-registration rules."

I stick my head deep inside the cupboard.

"That's just outside agitators using our church for their meeting, ma'am. Them folks aren't from here. Negroes in Kuckachoo are perfectly happy," Mama says.

No matter how much Mama hates a fib, I reckon fibbing to white folks is an altogether different matter.

"Well, that's good," Mrs. Tate says. "I'm glad to hear it."

I pull my head out of the cupboard and shut the door. And soon as I do, Ralphie knocks over the trash can again.

Mrs. Tate holds her son in her lap while Mama and me clean up the mess lickety-split.

Then we say good evening to Mrs. Tate, and weary as we are, we skedaddle out the back door, down Magnolia Row, and across the tracks to First Baptist.

CHAPTER 5

July 1, 1963, Dusk

As soon as we get to church, I spot Mrs. Jacks in the last row. I suck in my breath and hold it. Her big curls fall round her face, and her mahogany walking stick rests in the aisle by her side. Mrs. Jacks lives all the way in Weaver. She's going to be my teacher at West Thunder Creek Junior High School. Elias had her in seventh grade too, and that's how come I know taking her class will be rougher than swallowing uncooked grits.

But I can't dwell on my future too long before Mama pulls me by the hand to the fourth row, where Elias, Uncle Bump, and Elmira saved us seats. Elias said he wasn't going to miss this meeting for anything, not even working late for Mr. Mudge and making extra money.

Mama kisses him, then scoots past my brother and Uncle Bump to settle down next to Elmira. I sit on the end of the pew beside my brother.

"See that man?" Elias asks. He looks toward the pulpit.

Up front I see Reverend Walker talking to a man in a dark blue suit and tie. The man has deep lines running from his nose to his chin.

"Whoever he is, he looks like a walrus," I tell my brother.

Elias laughs. "Well, he's very important in the Mississippi movement. He's our speaker."

"Oh," I say, and nod.

Soon enough, all the pews are full. Lovetta and Marcus Johnson, along with their parents and six other siblings, file inside and lean against the brick wall on the other side of the church. We all wave and smile. Then the next thing I know, someone squeezes into the seat beside me.

Delilah Montgomery can do that. She's long and slinky like her name, except for her chest that just popped out this year. Why Delilah has enough breasts to fill a bra and I only have daffodil buds seems like God made a big mistake. After all, she's four months younger than me and a whole year behind me in school. But even with her chest, Delilah can fit almost anywhere. Needless to say, I'm shocked to see her out and about.

"We thought your mama would keep you locked in your room till you was old and gray," Elias tells her.

"Nope! She thinks this meeting's too important,"

Delilah says. "My mama says I can be grounded tomorrow instead. Of course, she'll still let me work at the tailor shop. I'm just not allowed to go outside after that. Not officially, anyway." Then Delilah looks at me and winks. And we both smile, because we both know that unofficially, we can sneak outside whenever we want.

In no time Delilah spots Cool Breeze Huddleston standing beside the window. "He's so fine!" she says. She rolls her eyes up in her head all dreamy. And I can't disagree. Cool Breeze Huddleston is all that and then some—inside and out. He's got sparkly brown eyes and he talks with a wink in his voice, like there's no one more special than you, even if he only says "hi."

Don't get me wrong. Cool Breeze hasn't always been cool. In third grade, he spent recess memorizing times tables. In fourth grade, he shortened his name from Curtis Bertrand to Curt Bert and collected rocks. In fifth grade, Delilah told him, "You know, you could be cool if you wasn't such a windbug." So wouldn't you know it, Curt Bert took that as a sign of hope. The next week, he changed his name to Cool Breeze and started talking about the boxer Cassius Clay. Then last year, in sixth grade, he started to look like Cassius Clay. He grew biceps and triceps and flashed a smile bright as milkweed.

No doubt Delilah's eyes will be stuck on him the rest of the night while she figures out what new muscles are bulging up inside his shirt. But mine wander to the pink and blue dusk. Framed by the window, the evening looks like one of the beautiful paintings hanging in Old Man Adams's living room.

After the church door clangs shut behind us, Reverend

Walker yells, "Praise the Lord!" and I turn my attention back to him.

The reverend stands at the pulpit, leans on his elbows, and looks out at us all. "Word has gone out," he says. "And not just in Kuckachoo, but along the length and breadth of our county. Now anyone here from Weaver?"

Mrs. Jacks and the whole back row yell, "Yes, sir!"

"How 'bout Bramble?"

"Here! Here!" call a couple men leaning against the wall.

Once folks from Titus and Jigsaw are accounted for too, Reverend Walker says, "We've got Thunder Creek County covered!" Everyone hushes. "Tonight we'll find out the latest about the struggle to get us our rights. But first, let us join hands and pray."

I hold hands with Delilah and Elias. Then I bow my head while the reverend asks the Lord to guide us through the fields to the waters and help us find our way. And it feels like a regular Sunday morning to me till Delilah starts tickling the inside of my hand.

I laugh, and of course whenever I laugh, I always let out a snort or two. And that sends Delilah into a wild fit of giggles.

"Hush up!" my brother snaps.

So I fix my eyes on the back of Brother Babcock's fuzzy gray head, and one by one, I stuff my snorts and giggles back in my throat.

As soon as the prayer is through, the reverend gives the pulpit over to Tyrone Tubbs, the happy-looking walrus man with wide eyes, round glasses, and skin dark as elm bark. "I'm proud to be with you tonight," Mr. Tubbs says. "Our struggles together go way, way back."

Whenever I hear words like "way back," I feel like I'm stuck in a history book, and sleep crawls all over me. But soon enough, Mr. Tubbs says, "Medgar Evers was a friend of mine," and the sleep, it flies away. There's something about that Medgar guy and his funny name and his sad story and the way Mama and Elias are so upset he died that wakes me up.

"Last month, after an assassin shot him, do you know what Medgar said?" Mr. Tubbs asks.

Folks are quiet.

" 'Turn me loose.' Those were Medgar's very last words. But how can we turn Medgar loose to God without finishing the business he fought and died for?" Mr. Tubbs asks. Then he smiles a quick smile, crosses his arms, and steps away from the pulpit, his head hung low.

When he comes back, his smile's gone, his eyes flash with anger. "You know Medgar went to war for the United States of America? He risked his life in the Second World War. And you know what else? When he got back to this country, he was still just a black man from Mississippi, a black man who couldn't get a drink of water at a regular fountain, who couldn't stay at a regular motel, who couldn't sit down and get a burger at a regular counter. No sir!"

And I can't quite believe what Mr. Tubbs is telling me: that a Negro can serve his country—maybe even die for his country—and if he's lucky enough to survive, he'll come back to this. Hearing it makes my blood churn, and I can't believe that before now I didn't think about how unfair things are. I mean, I thought of it, sure, but I didn't really dwell on it, because up till now I thought that's just the way life is. There's nothing I could possibly do to change it.

But then Mr. Tubbs tells us that when Medgar Evers got back from fighting a war, he decided to fight for his rights here in Mississippi. He worked for the National Association for the Advancement of Colored People, a group trying to change the laws to help us get treated like first-class folks.

"Medgar fought to integrate the schools. He wanted his three children, Darrell, Reena, and James, to go to the same schools as white children instead of going to older, smaller, crowded schools with torn books and beat-up desks," Mr. Tubbs says. "And Medgar worked to register voters. One day he wanted his children to vote for their leaders without being humiliated and turned away from the polls."

As I sit here in this pew between Elias and Delilah, all of a sudden it occurs to me that a movement is just what it sounds like. It's like when the wind blows hard and all the milkweed sways in one direction. Or when a bird in the sky changes course and hundreds of birds in the flock behind make the same shift. That man, Mr. Tubbs, he's like the wind or lead bird.

"Now things don't have to be the way they're looking to be. Even President Kennedy agrees," Mr. Tubbs says. "A couple hours before some racist shot Medgar, our president went on television. Any y'all catch that speech?"

Elias raises his hand.

"You did not!" I whisper.

My brother turns to me. "Did too!" he whispers back.

"Where'd you see television?"

"Didn't say I seen it. I heard the speech. On the radio

36

Bessie listens to in the Very Fine Fabric Shop." A faint smile creeps across his lips before he turns back to stare at Mr. Tubbs.

Of course, I could start wondering about what my brother was doing listening to the radio with Bessie on the white side, but I don't because I'm too busy burning up about the fact that we still don't have our electricity back. If we get our electricity back, then the next time the President speaks, all the Negroes in Kuckachoo can watch him on my television set. Of course, after the electricity comes back on, we'll still have another problem: we're going to need a TV antenna to get the picture clear. But Uncle Bump says he's thinking on a way to get us one of those.

A breeze blows through the open church window. The night air chills me.

"Well, for those of you who missed it," Mr. Tubbs says, "let me read you the words of President Kennedy." Then he pulls a piece of paper out of his pants pocket and reads real slow so we can take in the shocking news: " 'The Negro baby born in America today, regardless of the section of the nation in which he is born, has about *one-half* as much chance of completing high school as a white baby born in the same place on the same day, *one-third* as much chance of completing college, *one-third* as much chance of becoming a professional man, *twice* as much chance of becoming unemployed, about *one-seventh* as much chance of earning ten thousand dollars a year, a life expectancy which is seven years shorter, and the prospects of earning only *half* as much.' "

Well, I know my fractions. And hearing all those halves, thirds, and sevenths, I know right now it's true: white folks really do think a Negro is less than one whole person. And I can't even believe Mama considered keeping me home from this meeting when we're talking about what kind of school I'll go to, what kind of job I'll have, and how long I'm going to live.

Mr. Tubbs folds up the sheet of paper and tucks it back in his pocket. "It seems to me that the coward who killed Medgar delivered a message with his bullet: 'You want integration? You want to vote at the polls? Never, Evers!'

"When Medgar was shot dead, he was standing in the driveway of his home holding a stack of shirts, and on those shirts were printed the words 'Jim Crow Must Go.' All these laws that make us less than equal, these Jim Crow laws, they might get reversed, struck down, if Congress votes for President Kennedy's civil rights bill. So I ask you, do you want Jim Crow to go?"

I feel hot all over.

"Jim Crow must go!" we all shout.

Mr. Tubbs points to the heavens. "Tell it to Medgar up there!"

"Jim Crow must go!" we all roar.

All except Mama. When I lean forward to look over at her, she's sitting squinty eyed, still sizing up our guest speaker.

But whether Mama likes it or not, Mr. Tubbs isn't through. "If Jim Crow must go, then we've got to tell our government we're not gonna take it anymore," he says. He paces in front of the pulpit. "If Jim Crow must go, we've gotta go down to Washington, D.C., and tell our Congress! Now how many y'all reverends here?"

Reverend Walker and four other men raise their hands. I reckon they're preachers from nearby towns.

"I'll tell you what," Mr. Tubbs says. "I'm going to pay you reverends to come on board my bus. We'll march together on the nation's capital." Mr. Tubbs turns to Reverend Walker. "What're you doing August twenty-eighth?"

Reverend Walker's mouth falls open but no words come out. I reckon it's the first time he's ever run out of things to say. And one thing's clear: our reverend never planned to take a bus across the country to tell our nation's leaders that Jim Crow must go, that they'd better pass this civil rights bill right now.

"Compassion without action is no compassion at all," Mr. Tubbs says.

Reverend Walker stands there, still saying nothing, and it occurs to me that while the reverend always tells us Kuckachookians about our civil rights, so far as I can see, he's never really done anything to help us get them.

But here's his chance.

So with all eyes on him, at long last Reverend Walker says, "Why, yes! Yes, Mr. Tubbs! I'll go, sir."

We all applaud.

"That's why I came all the way to Thunder Creek County—to get your reverends on board! Any questions for me before I head over to Laknahatchie County?" Mr. Tubbs asks.

And before the words leave my lips, Mrs. Montgomery yells out, "The garden!"

And Mrs. Jacks asks, "What garden?"

And Mrs. Montgomery shouts, "Old Man Adams's. He

39

left six acres. Left it for the Negroes in Kuckachoo to share with the whites."

"The whites is making like it's all theirs," Brother Babcock calls out.

Up front, Mr. Tubbs turns to Reverend Walker. "Well, well," he says, "seems you've got your own civil rights battle right here in Kuckachoo."

"Reckon we do," Reverend Walker says. He steps back to the pulpit. "We're gonna have to talk this over," he says.

But Brother Babcock shouts out, "When? When we gonna talk it over?"

"Now's not the time," Reverend Walker says.

"If you don't mind me saying," Mr. Tubbs says to all of us, "when it's your time, you'll know."

"Uh-huh!" my brother says.

"You won't be able to sit on your rumps and watch," Mr. Tubbs says.

"Oh, yeah!" my brother calls out.

"You'll feel it in your bones," Mr. Tubbs says.

"Yes, sir!" Elias punches his fist in the air.

"You won't have a choice but to get up and—"

Suddenly Delilah shrieks. A wretched howl of a shriek. It pierces my eardrums. The chapel falls silent. At first I think she's pointing to Cool Breeze. But then I see I'm wrong. She's pointing out the window.

There, against the black of night, is a warning. A warning to us. A giant burning cross. Burning fire. Burning death. I'm struck to the bone.

Elias throws his arms round my shoulders, pulls me close. I grab Delilah's hand and look at the reverend. He's shaky. And why not? Everyone's heard of a church-burning or two.

"Those Klanners are cowards," my brother whispers.

But I know those cowards are capable of cold-blooded murder. Cool Breeze told me all about how they used to hang Negroes from trees and invite their children to picnic and watch.

Well, one thing's clear: we need to get out of here. Fast! But it seems everyone's got the same idea. Folks clamber for the window or the back door. And poor Delilah, skinny as a reed, she's shoved so hard her feet lift right off the floor.

Everything throbs: the crowd. The screams. The lights. The church. Nothing makes sense anymore.

"Take the fight home," I hear Mr. Tubbs call.

But we're trapped, desperate to get out, not knowing if this building will burst into flames first.

Then a raspy voice sings out. It's calm and low. It soothes the screams. *"We shall overcome."*

My face is pressed to the side. I can't turn my neck. But I can see right where that voice comes from: Mrs. Jacks. She's still. Still there. There in her seat in the last row. Her eyes are closed. Her head sways. Elias joins in her song.

"We shall overcome."

Soon the song fills our one-room church like a prayer.

Everyone lets out a breath.

Delilah's feet land back on the floor.

And one by one, we're turned loose into the black night. The panic, it's still there inside us. But it'll have to wait. For now, we walk steady and strong. The burning cross lights our way home.

CHAPTER 6

July 12, 1963, Late Afternoon

Ever since that cross burned, I've been hoping my best friend would come up with another good prank to cheer us all up. But these days, I reckon no one feels like laughing, not even Delilah. So I'ma try to make folks happy myself. Today being Friday, Mrs. Tate takes Ralphie to visit his grandmama in Bramble. I've got the afternoon off. And I've got it in my head to bake something special for Mama.

I stand in our kitchen, measure the flour, and think about her. What I love about Mama is she never gives up trying to make our little house a home. She sewed yellow pillows to brighten the living room, and since she couldn't spare money to buy real doors for the bedrooms, she embroidered old sheets with suns and stars and hung them from the door frames. Then she strung fishing line from one end of our bedroom to the other so Elias and me could have a closet for hanging up our church clothes. And if that wasn't enough to turn our house into a palace, she also stuffed ticking with corn shucks so each of us could have our very own mattress.

When Mama isn't cooking, cleaning, and sewing for the Tate family, she's cooking, cleaning, and sewing for us. But no matter how she scours the counters or sweeps the dirt from the floor, our home still looks exhausted. In the kitchen, where the floorboards split beside the oven, you can even see the ground. The two bedrooms tilt, and when it rains in summer, our house smells of mildew.

Pretty soon, though, it'll smell nothing but sweet.

Don't it just figure, I already mixed up the brown sugar and flour for the world's best honey cake when I find out there isn't any honey in the cupboard. Sure Mama's taught me how to bake butterscotch cookies without baking soda and a pumpkin pie without butter, but how to make a honey cake without honey? I've got no idea, so I get cracking over to the Montgomerys' place, but they don't have any honey either.

So I whistle and click for Flapjack. *Tweet, click, click. Tweet, click, click.* Together we cross the tracks to find Elias, who's knee-deep in parsley on Mr. Mudge's farm. By the time he locks the last sack in the shed, the sun's starting to set. I ask him to take me to the Corner Store.

At a time like this, all I can say is it's a real good thing Mr. Mudge built his Corner Store just across the railroad tracks on the edge of the white side, because ever since that civil rights meeting, I don't feel like going any deeper into white Kuckachoo than I have to.

While we cut through the forest, I ask my brother if Mr. Mudge knows the garden belongs to us all. "The mayor came by and chatted with him a good long while, but he never mentioned the will or any of us," Elias tells me. "Then the mayor handed Mr. Mudge the keys to Old Man Adams's place."

All of a sudden, I'm madder than September frost. I can't stand the thought of them passing round those keys that belong to my uncle.

When we get to the Corner Store, I'm so angry I can barely talk. Still, I tell Elias, "Hurry on up!" because I'm not about to risk getting home after dark. Not with Mama so tense these days, and not when I'm working so hard to bake her favorite cake.

Flapjack and me stand on the grassy patch between the bayou and the parking lot and wait. We've got to wait outside, because Mr. Mudge won't let cats in his shop.

I watch Mrs. Montgomery come out of the pay telephone booth behind the store. Mrs. Montgomery's always saving her nickels and dimes to call her brother, who lives in New Orleans and actually has a telephone right in his house. Now Mrs. Montgomery waves to me. Then she crosses by the front of the shop and walks out the parking lot to Main Street.

As usual, there's a white girl sitting on the shop steps. Her name's Honey Worth. Her blond hair falls like a bale of hay across her forehead. She's wearing cutoff denim shorts and she's hugging her fat cat, Sugar, in her arms.

44

I don't let Honey see I'm watching her because Mama always tells me not to look at white folk too close. Some of them are members of the Ku Klux Klan. And Lord knows I don't want trouble from cross-burning haters, so I got in the habit of fixing my eyes to the ground while I wait for Elias to come on out of the store.

Adding all the times I've waited on the grass beside the Corner Store parking lot, I bet I've seen hundreds—maybe even thousands—of feet go by. Black patent leather shoes with frilly white socks. Brown penny loafers oiled to shine in the sun. Saddle shoes scuffed on the black and white leather alike. And bare feet that never wear shoes, except maybe to church on Sunday.

Today, though, it doesn't take but a few minutes till I notice a pair of feet different from any I've ever seen: two plump sausages strapped in six-inch high heels teetering along the gravel edge of the parking lot. And this time I can't help it. I've got to see the southern lady who can actually walk in such things!

My eyes climb the green heels to the red-and-white-checkered dress, to the bright red lips, to the hat on the lady's head. And there they are—a bunch of plastic strawberries stuck right on the brim.

Before I know it, my eyes get ahead of my brain and hang a second too long on the far-out sight.

"Just who do you think you are?" the lady snaps, and soon as she does, I see she's got enough freckles to fill a pepper mill. Her face is the spitting image of Honey's. I reckon she's Honey's mama, Mrs. Worth. "A stare like that can get a girl like you in big trouble!" she says.

When Mrs. Worth talks, the strawberries on her hat jiggle, and something about the moving strawberries makes the laughter bubble up inside me like cola shook up in a bottle. Thank goodness she disappears inside the store, because even though I cup one hand over my mouth, a giggle gets out anyway. And then a snort. I stare at the hole in my sneaker and try to stop, but the more scared I am, the more giggles I get, till an ugly voice splits the sky.

"Ain't you got manners, dirtbag?"

I look up, only to see Buck Fowler skulking toward me, Jimmy Worth steps behind him.

There's no mistaking what kind of trouble these two bring. And I'll tell you one thing: if I knew they were here at the store, I would've waited for my brother round the bend.

But now it's too late. Buck hovers above me. "Nobody laughs at Jimmy's mama," he says. "Nobody."

My bottom lip quivers worse than ever.

I pick up Flapjack, glance across the parking lot to the shop steps, and wonder what's taking Elias so long. No doubt there's plenty of white folks to ring up first. Well, soon as my brother does come on out of the shop, he'll know what to do. He'll make Buck and Jimmy leave me alone. In my head, I beg for Elias to open that shop door, while my breath, it flames inside my chest.

I take a step toward the store.

Buck whips out an elbow to block my path. "Gimme the cat," he says.

I hug Flapjack tight, but Buck clenches the scruff of Flapjack's neck and tears him from me.

Flapjack moans.

I jump up to save him but snatch twilight instead.

Honey's voice scrapes across the lot. "Leave the cat alone!"

"Stay out of it, pudgeball!" Buck yells.

I turn to see Honey slink back down on the store steps. I open my mouth and gulp the sky like it's water. But it's hard to get enough. I look round real quick. For Delilah. For Cool Breeze. But who am I kidding? They're not dumb enough to be stuck out here when the sun's starting to set.

Soon it hits me: even though Buck and Jimmy play for the white high school's football team, I've got no choice but to fight them off myself. So I ram my shoulder into Buck's stomach. Then Buck throws me to the ground with his free hand—the one that isn't wrapped round Flapjack's neck. The pavement rips open the skin on both my knees, and through the blur of my tears, I see Flapjack's paws scrape the blue-gray sky.

"Reckon coloreds don't learn manners at school," Buck says, cackling. "Think we ought to teach this one a lesson?" he asks Jimmy.

Jimmy is Honey's big brother. He's got butter white hair and looks like he tumbled into a bucket of freckles.

"Go out for the pass!" Buck yells. He shakes Flapjack up and down while my liver slams into my spleen or whatever's in there next to it.

"The pass?" Jimmy asks. Jimmy's the star quarterback, so all the white folk are counting on him to take the Kickers to the state championships come December. But anyone can see Jimmy Worth, three bricks shy of a load, has been tackled one time too many.

"Yeah, Jimmy, the pass," Buck says.

Jimmy sprints across the parking lot toward the bayou, arms open like he expects to catch a ball.

Buck hoists Flapjack back in his right arm. Even from here, I can see Flapjack's green eyes bulge under the streetlight while Buck hurls my cat halfway across the lot.

Standing at the bank of the bayou, Jimmy catches Flapjack round the ribs. And Buck is so excited he jumps up and down. "Drop-kick!" he shouts, and laughs.

Jimmy stretches out his arms and holds Flapjack between them. Then slow, real slow, Jimmy swings back his leg to take the kick.

I squeeze my eyes shut, prepare for the worst.

But what I expect to hear—the crack of Jimmy's boot against Flapjack's skull—is not what I hear at all. Instead, I hear glass crash against pavement.

When I open my eyes, I see Flapjack scamper free across the lot and Jimmy's body strewn across the rocky ledge of the bayou, looking dead as they come. A shattered honey jar rests by his side. And there on the Corner Store steps stands my brother, looking mighty pleased his pitching practice paid off.

From the look of things, that brother of mine threw the honey jar and knocked Jimmy down the stony drop to the bayou. And I reckon Jimmy must've caught his foot on the root of a cypress tree, because now he's passed out cold.

After Buck takes a second to figure out Jimmy's not getting up, he bolts after my brother.

As soon as he does, Elias hops the railing of the Corner Store steps. He sprints across the lot to the bayou, and when he gets to the water's edge, my brother turns to me and shouts, "Run!"

Usually I do what my brother says, but when I try to stand, my legs buckle.

So I sit here on the pavement and watch my brother jump into the bayou. Buck Fowler splashes in after him. Then my brother and Buck vanish behind the cypress trees.

I can't feel my bloody knees. I can't feel anything. So I take in the scene like I'm watching television in Old Man Adams's living room: Here's Honey rushing to her brother Jimmy's side. And there's Mrs. Worth running out the shop, dropping her ham hocks on the steps, holding her hands over her mouth. Customers are swarming out the store to see what's what. And, oh look, there's Jimmy groaning about his leg while he's loaded onto the back of a flatbed truck. Then Mrs. Worth and Honey slip into the seat beside the driver. They're off to find a doctor. And that's the end of the show.

CHAPTER 7

July 12, 1963, Night

When at long last I peel myself off the parking lot pavement, I race across the tracks to the Negro side of Kuckachoo, where there aren't any streetlamps to light up the dirt roads and news travels faster than shooting stars.

By the time I stumble through the front door, the blood on my knees has dried, my head pounds, and the fact that this is real and not some made-up television program boils inside me like water in a steaming kettle.

Mama blinks at me, backs herself against the wall, and whispers, "My baby, my baby." Then she wails. And one thing's clear: she's already heard about Elias.

I wet a rag in the kitchen, lie on my bed, and rest the

cool cloth across my forehead, but as long as Mama keeps screaming, there isn't a thing I can do to make my head stop thumping. So I start to play a game. I light the lantern and stare at the paper map of the United States hanging on the wall. Each time Mama lets out a howl, I move my eyes to a different state and try to name its capital.

Lots of nights Elias quizzed me, but now I've got to quiz myself. "Alabama . . . Montgomery," I whisper. My eyes roam across the southern states. "Tennessee . . . Nashville," I say. My gaze gets stuck on Georgia. What's the capital? I can't remember, so I get out of bed to check the small print.

Whenever times get rough, Reverend Walker finds men with guns to stand guard by the railroad track and surround the home of anyone threatened. Folks call it the Reverend's Brigade. But tonight one of their own is missing, so now the brigade has a different job: find Elias before the sheriff. It doesn't take a genius to figure out the sheriff wants my brother dead after what he's done to Jimmy Worth.

But playing the geography game reminds me how smart Elias is. Why, he's going on to college after he finishes his last year of high school. How many folks can say that? And remembering how smart my brother is makes me feel a whole lot better, because I know he'll survive whatever trouble chases him down.

My eyes settle on my television set that rests in the corner just beneath the map. Well, I'll tell you one thing: if I was teaching geography on television right now, I'd stop the program to make an emergency announcement. "If you find my brother, Elias Pickett, hide him! I'll give you a big reward." I think of what the reward would be. Something

51

that would make everyone want to help. "If you keep my brother safe, I'll give you my very own television." But then I reckon folks watching my program already have a television, so I'd add, "And I can guarantee my television is bigger than yours!"

I take the cloth off my forehead and leave it on my bed. I want to go into the living room and hold Mama till she's calm, but hugging Mama when she's out of her mind with fright would be downright strange.

So instead, I climb onto my brother's bed that's against the window. Then I lift the screen and stretch my leg down to the overturned bucket. I set my weight gently onto it and stumble onto the pine needles that cover the yard. That's how I get outside without getting in Mama's way.

Even before I whistle and click, Flapjack meows and rubs against my ankles, so I pick him up and carry him to the swing that hangs from the oak tree. My tears fall onto the scruff of his neck. "You were stolen," I tell him. And that's the honest-to-goodness truth. He needs to know I'd never give him to those bullies, Buck Fowler and Jimmy Worth.

I brush my cheek against Flapjack's fur and feel how it's smooth in one direction but prickles in the other. Together we swing in silence, back and forth to the rhythm of Mama's wails, while neighbors carry trays of food into the house.

And it seems like forever till Delilah comes on outside. She strings her skinny body onto the swing to sit beside Flapjack and me.

Most times being with Delilah makes me feel more

alive, because I never know what she'll do next. She might wear a rope bracelet round her ankle or walk on the white side with her head held high. But tonight, even though I sit beside her for hours, I feel nothing but dead inside.

Later, after most of our neighbors have gone home to bed, Delilah whispers, "Tomorrow we can jump double Dutch," and I know things must be even worse than I thought, because like I said, after she finished fifth grade, Delilah swore off jumping for good.

After we say good night, I tiptoe up the steps into the front room where Mama's on the couch, eyes puffed out worse than ever. I try to give her some comfort. "Elias is smart," I tell her. "Strong too."

Then Uncle Bump lumbers in from the kitchen and sits on the bench across from the couch. "You go on to sleep," he tells me.

So I lug myself into the bedroom. All of a sudden, that nook I share with my brother seems bigger than the United States of America. And of course, I'm not going to sleep. How can I?

Instead, I stand behind the sheet that hangs across my bedroom doorway and listen. For years, Elias and me practiced eavesdropping through this sheet. Between us, we could make sense of the softest whispers.

But without him, it's hard to understand it all.

I only hear these words from Mama: "He goin' home."

Those are enough words for me! I can't stand how she talks like my brother's never coming back. I've got to stop myself from bursting into the living room to set her straight. But I know that what's going on, it's more than any of us can handle. And I don't want to yell at Mama and upset her worse than she already is.

Then—I don't know why—I get into Elias's bed instead of my own. Under the sheet, I close my eyes and breathe that too-much-baseball smell mixed up with the smell of sage from the farm. My belly rises and falls. I hear my own breath. Then I feel a river in my chest. And even though my eyes, they're shut, I see sunlight. Glittery bits. Yellow and orange. Everything round me sparkles.

"You here?" I whisper.

My brother tells me he is.

CHAPTER 8

July 12, 1963, Night

It's the middle of the night when someone rushes through the side door into the kitchen. I bolt awake in bed. I hear a tapping sound. Through the sheet, I hear Mama say, "Rub it on the bottom of your sneakers!" and Uncle Bump say, "Take this!" Then the side door bangs shut and there's a splash.

I jump out of bed and fly into the kitchen. My eyes sting. Real bad. And there's Mama cutting an onion, sobbing too. Why Mama's chopping vegetables at a time like this, I'm fresh out of ideas.

"Get in your room!" she shrieks.

Uncle Bump stands by the side door, his hand on the

knob. He doesn't say a word till Mama heaves out another sob. Then he tells me, "Do as she says."

I've got no choice. I run back to my room and flop down on my brother's bed. In the moonlight, I see the map on the wall. I imagine Elias outsmarting the sheriff and all his deputies. I'm lost in this vision till it lures me to sleep in a better world, a dream world, where my brother darts down hidden paths and dashes across farms and little-known brooks.

That's where I stay till a bark from a dog tears through me.

My heart, it freezes like the icebox.

I run to the front door. Uncle Bump's already there. A minute passes. Then a hound dog leads the sheriff up our front steps.

"Step aside," the sheriff tells us.

"He ain't here," Uncle Bump says.

"Oh, he's here all right," the sheriff says. "This hound don't lie." The sheriff pets the dog's head.

Then I see Buck Fowler creep up the steps behind the sheriff. Buck's drenched. His teeth chatter.

I run to my room, collapse on my bed, bury my face in my pillow. Seconds later, the hound's leash clangs against my bedroom floor. I look up. There's Buck Fowler standing in my room, pulling the sheet across my doorway, so I can't see Mama and Uncle Bump anymore. He's hiding something behind his back.

"This your brother's bed?" the sheriff asks.

I don't answer. I glance across the room. The sheriff pushes Elias's bedsheet against the dog's snout while Buck stands behind him, holding up a flashlight. And I wonder, who made Buck the sheriff's special helper?

Through the sheet that hangs across the door frame, I hear Uncle Bump and Mama whispering real frantic.

Now the sheriff bends down on the floorboards to search under both beds. Then he stands up and shrugs. And I reckon he doesn't see anything worth seeing in my room except my unplugged television set in the corner. He saunters over to it.

I know what's about to happen, so I cross my arms over my stomach, as if I can soften the blow.

The sheriff kicks my television. Hard. The glass screen shatters to bits, and the sheriff and Buck bust their sides laughing.

"You all right?" Mama calls. Her voice cracks.

I want to tell Mama I'm okay, but looking at my set, I can't.

"Hush up!" the sheriff snaps.

I swallow.

Then the sheriff turns to Buck and says, "I'll check out the rest of this dump. Why don't you show this colored girl what you've got?"

The sheriff yanks his hound back to the living room, pulling the sheet on the door frame closed behind him.

Buck stays here in the bedroom with me. With one hand, he holds the flashlight under his chin. His face lights up like a ghost's. Then he pulls his other hand out from behind his back.

I hear myself scream.

57

He's got my brother's sneaker! If he's got the sneaker, he could have Elias too! I want to strangle Buck Fowler with my bare hands, but he stomps out my room before I get the chance.

Mama and Uncle Bump come racing in.

Uncle Bump touches my hair. Mama sits down next to me on the bed and hugs me tight. We all shiver with fear while the sheriff and Buck rummage through the rest of the house.

Then the front door bangs shut and the dog's leash clangs down the steps. We hear the sheriff and Buck circle the house again and again. While they do, Mama sweeps up the broken glass and Uncle Bump whispers, "I'ma find a way to fix that screen, and soon as I do, I'ma get a TV antenna for the—"

"Shhh!" Mama says.

The sheriff and Buck are stopped just outside my window. "Hound's not picking up any tracks leading from the shack," the sheriff says.

"Well, the tracks the hound picked up from the bayou to the shack must be old," says Buck. "And if these tracks are old, he probably did get caught on the bottom of the bayou. As you know, coloreds can't swim."

I watch the blue vein on Uncle Bump's forehead bulge out his head. Soon the bark of the hound and the mumble of voices fade, but the racket of my heart in my ears is louder than before.

A couple minutes pass till Mrs. Montgomery shouts through my bedroom window screen. "I been watching. They's gone!"

Mama gets off my bed and drags herself to the front door, where she tells Mrs. Montgomery the latest. And at long last, I've got Uncle Bump to myself.

Hard as it is, I spit out the words to say what Buck held in his hand. Lord knows I could never tell Mama. She'd likely die on the spot.

"Hmm," Uncle Bump says after I tell him. He rubs his finger over his beard. "Your brother's smart."

I can't imagine what he's talking about. Buck Fowler's got Elias's sneaker, probably found it on the bottom of the bayou. Like Buck said, Elias could be on the bottom of the bayou too.

Uncle Bump sits on the edge of my bed. "You're not a little girl no more," he says. "But your mama? She don't see it that way. You'll always be her baby. And Elias too. Always, forever, no matter what."

"I know," I say and lean my back against the wall.

"I'm thinking you're old enough to keep a secret," Uncle Bump says. Then he tells me this: Just before the sheriff barged into our house, Elias stopped home to say goodbye. When he did, Mama rubbed onion on the soles of my brother's sneakers and poured whiskey over his head to throw off the sheriff's hound. "Then I gave your brother the gold pocket watch, so he can sell it for cash if he needs to," Uncle Bump explains.

The whole while he talks, my heart plunges real slow into my belly.

When Uncle Bump's through, he reads right into my mind. "You know your brother had to run bookity-book. That hound was after him. But before he left, he told me just one thing: to say a special goodbye to you." He pushes aside my hair and kisses my forehead. "Now try to get some rest," he says. "There's still a couple hours 'fore mornin'."

But something about the way my bottom lip trembles seems to make Uncle Bump talk some more.

"My opinion 'bout it? Your brother planted his sneaker there in the bayou. Must've wanted the sheriff to think he drowned."

By the time Uncle Bump leaves my room, he sounds real confident about his theory. Me? I get out of bed to check on the television. But soon as I see it, I feel sick all over.

My sleep, it's short and fitful.

It's the crack of dawn when I wake to a tangle of voices. I pull on my dress and step outside to the porch. The neighborhood men are too busy listening to the reverend read from the *Delta Daily* to notice me.

The reverend holds the newspaper open in his hands. " 'The Negro assailant, Elias Pickett, seventeen, ran out of the Corner Store and, without provocation, attacked Kuckachoo High School's star quarterback, Jimmy Worth, also seventeen. When the assailant attempted to flee into the bayou, receiver Buck Fowler, eighteen, who also plays defensive tackle, led the search for . . .' "

All I can say is it's a good thing Mama isn't on the porch, because soon as the reverend finishes, Uncle Bump strings together a bunch of curse words.

"Now surely you remember Emmett Till?" the reverend asks.

"Uh-huh," I say. And that's when Uncle Bump notices I'm here. He puts an arm round me while I remember what happened to that fourteen-year-old boy. I was only four years old when two white brothers murdered him. It happened in the town called Money. Some folks say Emmett Till whistled at the white lady who worked in the shop. Others say he called her "baby." Either way, he was out of line. But he wasn't from Mississippi. He was from the city of Chicago, in the state of Illinois, way up North. Emmett didn't know how things are down here. And those boys, his friends, they dared him to do it. They hardly expected it would get him killed.

"As you know," the reverend says, "they tied Emmett's body to a cotton gin fan. Then they threw him into the river to swim home to the Lord who gone and made him a Negro in the first place."

Every time I hear about Emmett, I can't help but wonder, *How could grown men murder a teenage boy?* I asked Mama this a couple times, but wouldn't you know it, each and every time she changed the subject. And when I asked Uncle Bump, he just said, "There's some questions that ain't got answers."

Now Reverend Walker looks to the sky. "Listen, Lord," he says. "You can't take Elias the way you took Emmett."

I want to tell the reverend to hush up. I want to tell the reverend that sure Buck chased Elias into the bayou, but my skinny brother's strong as a hailstorm. I want to tell the reverend Elias can outrun anyone, white or Negro don't matter.

But there's so many sobs coming out my throat, I can't say a word.

Uncle Bump pulls me closer to his side. "Shhh . . . ," he says.

I feel dizzy. Things look fuzzy. And I can't quite believe my brother, he's gone.

Most of the men here are members of the Reverend's Brigade. They've been up all night, searching for my brother without luck. Now they rub their red eyes and set off for the day's work.

Uncle Bump stays on the porch with the reverend, while I lug myself back inside the house.

If there's anyone dead, it's Mama. She's lying on her bed, heavy as a sack of unshelled beans. Stale tears cling to her cheeks. I climb onto the mattress, lie down beside her, and fix one of her limp arms round my waist. Then I curl my body into the nook she makes when she rests on her side. "Don't fret," I tell her. "He's still with us."

But Mama? She doesn't find comfort in my words. She turns over and hugs the pillow, not me, in her arms.

CHAPTER 9

July 17, 1963, Night

Tonight at dinner, after we worry ourselves sick talking about Elias, we dish all about the Garden Club. Ever since Old Man Adams went and died last month, the Garden Club has held a bunch of meetings to figure out what to plant on his land. But Mama, Uncle Bump, and me agree: their meetings are nothing but a bunch of hooey.

"This garden belongs to all Kuckachookians, Negro and white," I say, and swallow my last bite of beans.

"No matter how much they quibble 'bout what to plant, you can bet they agree on one thing," Mama says.

"What's that?" Uncle Bump asks. He wipes his face with an old piece of towel.

"Us Negroes won't never share the land," she says, and sips her water.

Uncle Bump laughs, not because what Mama says is funny, but because it's true.

"Why don't they know Old Man Adams left the land for *all* of us?" I ask. I walk over to the stove and scrape one last spoonful of beans off the bottom of the pot.

" 'Cause the mayor and the sheriff lied, Addie Ann. They told folks Old Man Adams wrote in his will the land is just for whites," Uncle Bump says.

"Course, there's a couple rumors starting to spread, but you know white folk," Mama says. "They believe whatever's most easy."

"Well, we should tell 'em. . . ," I say, and sit back down.

And that's when Mama gives me one of her ain't-you-got-no-manners, suck-in-her-breath expressions. I reckon it's because I'm talking with my mouth full of beans. I can't say I see what the big deal is. If you've got to chew and talk, why not do both at the same time? But I don't feel like picking a crow with Mama, so I swallow.

"That's better," she says. "Anyway, the reverend says the truth is gonna make itself known."

"Well, when?" I ask Mama. "When's it gonna make itself known?"

"Whenever it's supposed to," she tells me, as if that clears everything right up.

Uncle Bump pulls his harmonica out of his pocket, says good night, and leaves out the side door. Of course, while Mama and me clean up from supper, we go straight back to fretting about my brother.

64

Five days gone since Elias ran off, and we can't go three minutes without thinking about him.

❦

The next morning, soon as Mama and me get to the Tates' house, she goes on upstairs, while I pour some milk into the tin bowl to set out back for Flapjack. I'm trying to teach my cat to wait for me till I'm ready to go home. A couple days ago, I showed Mrs. Tate the bowl I'd brought and asked her if she'd mind. "Training a cat!" she said, and laughed. "Now there's a good idea! Most folks think you can only do that with dogs! Sure, I'll donate milk to the cause."

This morning, after I place the bowl outside, I step back into the Tates' kitchen.

Mama shuffles down the stairs and plops Ralphie into my arms. "I've gotta dust this house floorboards to ceiling before the Garden Club meeting. You've gotta take him on your own," she says.

At once I feel a rush of excitement, because I'm going to prove I'm more than capable.

Mama tells me after I give Ralphie walking lessons, lunch, stories, and a nap, I'd better give him a bath. "Don't forget to check his bottom," she says.

Later, while the bathwater runs, I take a good look at myself in the Tates' washroom mirror. The last time I saw myself in a big mirror was more than a month ago in Old Man Adams's place. I gather the cloth of my dress tight behind me and see what Mama's been telling me, it's true! My hip bones decided to spread apart from each other like butter. Mama says it means I'm starting to get a figure. And I figure a figure is a good thing, because Delilah's already got one even though she's only going into sixth grade, and all the boys think she's the cat's meow.

I'm still noticing my new figure, and I forget all about Ralphie till I feel his little hands press against my legs. Wouldn't you know it, when I look down, I see that boy took three rolls of toilet paper out of the washroom cabinet. Now he's got himself wrapped up like an Egyptian mummy. And he's trying to wrap me too. "Stop that!" I say, and try not to laugh. But Ralphie just looks at me with a goofy grin.

I turn off the bathwater and gather up the toilet paper. It's so soft! Truth be told, I'm tempted to fold it up and take it home, because ever since Uncle Bump stopped working, all we've got to use in the outhouse are the free department store catalogs that come in the mail. But I've got no bag to save the toilet paper in, so I stuff it into the trash can seconds before Mrs. Tate wanders into the washroom looking for her lipstick.

"I can't imagine what you and your poor mother are going through with your brother gone," she says as she rummages through the washroom drawer. "Well, I suppose working hard is the only way to get by."

"Yes, ma'am," I say. And she's right about it too. After Mrs. Tate finds her lipstick, she leaves. But the whole time I'm bathing Ralphie, pinning on his diaper, and dressing him in the sailor outfit, I can't stop thinking about my brother.

Not till I inhale.

Usually after a bath that boy smells sweet as a lace cookie. But today Ralphie doesn't smell anything but rotten, so I carry him back to the changing table and clean him up.

Then I take him down to the kitchen and set him in the high chair. "Woof! Woof!" I say, and hold up the new stuffed dog that Mrs. Tate bought him. A few days ago, I heard Mr. Tate yell at his wife for spending too much money all the time, but if you ask me, buying this dog was worth it. Ralphie loves it!

Now he grabs it out of my hands and hugs it tight, just as Mrs. Tate comes into the kitchen. She's all dressed up. Special for the Garden Club meeting, she wears a straw hat with a giant white bow. Her black hair shines flat down her back like the highway after a rain.

When the doorbell rings, I turn my kitchen chair and peek into the Tates' living room. And there's Honey and Jimmy's mama, Mrs. Worth, strolling through the front door. Laying eyes on Mrs. Worth, I feel a scratch in my throat. A scratch that burns. She's got on a yellow hat that matches her hair. Today there's nothing funny about her hat, but even if she had plastic frogs tied to the brim, you could bet I wouldn't smirk.

Next Miss Springer arrives. She's got a newspaper rolled up under her arm, and instead of a hat, she wears a yellow pencil tucked behind her ear. Mama says Mrs. Tate would never be friends with a single lady like Miss Springer if Miss Springer didn't do so much good. But each year Miss Springer decorates the float for the Thanksgiving Day parade. What's more, she's raising money to build a library here in Kuckachoo.

Mama tiptoes into the living room, sets down a plate of gingersnaps for the prim and proper members of the Garden Club, who act like they're planning a charitable event—not a cold-blooded crime. Then she hurries back into the kitchen.

Soon Mr. Mudge comes through the front door. Mama and me, we're surprised to see him here. He's a very busy man. When it comes to doing business in Kuckachoo, everyone knows he wears the britches. He not only owns a farm the size of two football fields but also the Corner Store. With Old Man Adams dead and buried, Mr. Mudge is now the richest man alive. At least in Kuckachoo he is. What with the Corner Store being the only grocery shop in town, he's got what you might call a regular monopoly. And if that's not enough to put pennies in his pockets, he's preparing for the grand opening of another shop in Muscadine County.

Now Mrs. Worth sits on the sofa and asks him all about it.

"Ain't Muscadine County an awful far drive?"

"Ninety miles straight down the highway," Mr. Mudge says. "But I'd drive a hundred ninety to open my shop there."

"Why's that?" Mrs. Worth asks, and reaches for a gingersnap.

"All kinds of show business folks are moving to Muscadine County. In a couple years that place will be the new Hollywood. Now's the time to invest."

I reckon that given all his business experience, Mr.

Mudge is going to tell folks exactly what to plant on Old Man Adams's land. But get this: when at long last the meeting starts, he tells the seven ladies and the mayor something else entirely. "Gardens? Who needs gardens?" he says. "Why, if you need a garden, plant one in your own yard."

Well, that's easy for Mr. Mudge to say. The dirt round his house isn't dry and crumbly like the dirt round ours. Plus, his front yard takes up half the town. He's got plenty of room to plant a whole variety. And he's got enough vegetables to eat *and* to sell. Now the rest of the Kuckachookians want the chance to do the same. Folks don't just want to eat the vegetables they grow. They want to sell them at the farmers' market in Franklindale. But I reckon Mr. Mudge doesn't care a hoot about that.

"Picture this," he tells the Garden Club members. "That land could be the perfect spot for our new *pri-iiii-vate* high school. You know the Supreme Court is coming down rather hard in the area of integration," he says. "I don't have to tell you it's a dog-eat-dog kind of world." Then Mr. Mudge starts talking about how folks on my side of town are getting uppity.

All of a sudden, my breath turns light and stiff like an egg white beat too long. And I can't imagine how Mama's going to fill their glasses, because her hands tremble while she takes the pitcher of iced tea out of the refrigerator. But Mama takes a deep breath and walks back into the living room.

I mix up some dough for Ralphie to play with while I listen to the rest.

"They're gaining rights at our expense," Mrs. Worth

says, as if Mama and me aren't in the house. "If we give them a mixed education, next they'll want to swim in the same pool as our kids."

Well, of course I want to jump in that pool behind the white high school. One time, Delilah dragged me all the way over there to peek at it through the wire fence. The water looked so cool and blue.

But I know I've got as much chance of ever splashing in that pool as I do of kissing Cool Breeze Huddleston—just about none.

"If we use the land to build a new high school, a *pri-iiii-vate* sort of school, it'll protect our children if and when the white high school lets the coloreds in," Mr. Mudge says. "By then it'll be too late to tell the coloreds, 'Scram!' "

I have to say, I'm shocked to hear Mr. Mudge talk this way. And I reckon the mayor doesn't like what Mr. Mudge says either.

"With the greatest respect, sir," the mayor says, "but the Supreme Court passed a law that violates our state's right to educate the children of Mississippi as we see fit." The mayor takes a gingersnap off the serving plate. "Fortunately, I'm in charge of the schools in Kuckachoo, so I'm just not gonna follow that law. Integration here?" The mayor takes a bite. "That ain't nothin' but a thousand never evers!"

All of a sudden, Mrs. Worth shouts, "The tea! Watch it!"

My breath gets shorter and shorter till it's barely there.

I see Mama in the living room, crunched up small as a cricket, hands shaking while she tries to scrub the spilled tea out of the white carpet with her rag.

"Sorry, ma'am," Mama says.

Mrs. Tate looks at Mama but doesn't say a word.

But Mrs. Worth turns to Mrs. Tate and says, "That maid's too old. Just look at her. Time for a new one."

My eyes narrow to slits.

When Mrs. Worth turns away to grab another gingersnap, Mrs. Tate's other friend, Miss Springer, stares at Mama till Mama lifts her eyes from the carpet. Then Miss Springer waves her hand in front of her face. With that one gesture, she tells Mama the spill, it's fuss and feathers. No big deal.

While Mama runs past me in the kitchen to wet her rag, I see she's got a tear in her eye like she's wondering if she's too old for this work. But she's also got a smile on her lips, like she can't stop thinking about the wave from Miss Springer.

CHAPTER 10

July 18, 1963, Afternoon

At long last the world's most precious carpet is clean, so Mama runs upstairs to iron the linens.

I give Ralphie a ball of dough to play with. Then I sit down beside him and peek into the living room. I've got to pay real close attention so I can fill Mama in later.

The mayor picks up where he left off. "What we need is a garden—a garden that will provide free food for the community and extra cash for those who need it. Nobody can beat that!"

"Well, we can't plant a dang thing till next May anyhow," Mr. Mudge says.

That's when Miss Springer chimes in. Miss Springer has

the *Delta Daily* crossword puzzle open on her lap. She looks plainer than a wheat roll, but I can tell you one thing: there's nothing dull about what she has to say. "Wait till next year? Hogwash! Just 'cause most folks in the Delta are afraid of a cool-season garden doesn't mean we have to be. My grandpa always planted a fall garden. He always told me, 'Violet, thank your lucky stars we live up here in the northern part of the state. We're spared the worst of the Mississippi sun.' Why, we can go ahead and plant our garden next week."

"Next week!" Mrs. Tate gasps. She throws her hands over her mouth like she just won the Fourth of July cake-decorating contest.

The mayor stands. "Why, a fall-season garden is an excellent idea! We're Kuckachoo, after all, not Bramble or Weaver. We're not afraid to be on the leading edge."

But Mr. Mudge wants his advice followed and I can see why. That man has what you call farming experience. "If you're going to insist on a garden, then might I propose an altogether different sort," he says. "It's impossible to be an expert in everything now. Better to pick one crop and do it right, like Henry Ford did with the Model T. In my personal opinion, due to their nutrition value and all-around robust flavor, turnip greens is the only wise choice."

"Or garlic," Mrs. Worth says. "We could plant all garlic."

"Or butter beans!" Mrs. Tate says.

I can see by the way Mrs. Tate opens her blue eyes real wide, she's proud of her idea. "I read in the magazines that movie stars like Audrey Hepburn and all the ladies in New York City eat a steady diet of butter beans," she says.

"They make butter bean soup, butter bean sauce, and even butter bean pie!"

Mr. Mudge chuckles. "With all due respect, Mrs. Tate, you can't believe everything you read," he says. "Besides, Mr. Adams didn't leave any butter bean seeds in his shed. None at all."

That's when Miss Springer pushes her horn-rimmed glasses up farther on her nose. "Well, Mr. Mudge, since you've already taken stock of what seeds Mr. Adams left in his garden cabin, perhaps you might be so kind as to make a quick list of the inventory." With that, Miss Springer tears out the crossword-puzzle page from the *Delta Daily* and hands it to Mr. Mudge, along with the pencil that was resting behind her ear.

Mr. Mudge leans over the coffee table and scrawls the list of seeds onto the torn sheet of newspaper. When he's finished, he slams Miss Springer's pencil on top of it, folds his arms across his chest, and stares out the window.

Miss Springer examines the list written on the crossword-puzzle page. Then she says, "Mr. Mudge, Mr. Mayor, we ladies have a plan. According to this list, Mr. Adams left a wide variety of seed in his garden cabin. We can't plant tomatoes, though. Too tender in the August heat. And no watermelon. Wouldn't be ready before the frost." Miss Springer turns to Mrs. Worth and Mrs. Tate. "Sorry to say, girls, there aren't any garlic or butter bean seeds in his garden cabin either," she says.

And I reckon this is the start of a real hullabaloo.

"Regarding the rows," Miss Springer says, "there's only one way to figure it. We'll plant sixty-eight purple hull peas, nineteen string beans, twenty-three cabbage, forty-five crowder peas, fifty-three mustard greens, thirty-two crooked-neck squash, forty-nine collards, thirty-six kale, forty-seven black-eyed peas, forty-one button squash, and well, I reckon four turnip greens wouldn't hurt."

"And there you have it," Mrs. Worth says, as if she knew it all along.

Mrs. Tate nods.

One thing's clear: both Mrs. Worth and Mrs. Tate will gladly give up rows of garlic and butter beans to have a garden planned by a lady. And it seems Mr. Mudge and the mayor don't have the nerve to disagree.

I want to stand and cheer for Miss Springer, she's got so much grit. But now Ralphie throws his stuffed doggie onto the floor, and it's near supper time, so I set the water to boil and drop some noodles in the pot.

"Well, of course I'd be more than happy to donate the labor to plant the garden," Mr. Mudge says, "but surely that's not enough to keep a garden growing. Who's going to pick the weeds? Who's going to fertilize? Water? Take it from me, you can't grow a garden without hiring field hands to tend it for months after the planting."

"Can't, couldn't, shouldn't! That's all we hear from you, Mr. Mudge!" Miss Springer shakes her head. "We are Kuckachookians. We can do anything we set our minds to."

"Well, of course," Mr. Mudge says. "I don't mean to imply we can't, but . . ."

Ralphie squirms. I know I should read him a story but I can't stand to miss a word. So I pick up his doggie, wet its nose in the tap, and stick it in the sugar bowl. Then I hand it back. Just as I hoped, Ralphie stuffs his sweet doggie's nose into his mouth and chews on it like a pacifier, while I wait to hear what Miss Springer will say next.

But the minutes pass and Miss Springer doesn't say "boo." It's so quiet I can hear the bubbles burst in the pot.

At long last the mayor asks, "Just what do you propose, Miss Springer?"

"Just this," she says. "We, the Garden Club, accept Mr. Mudge's most kind offer of hiring field hands to plant our garden."

Mr. Mudge snarls.

"After that," Miss Springer says, "we'll call on the bored, potbellied men this side of town. They'll meet up at the garden a couple evenings a week to pull weeds and water. They'll shed pounds and revitalize themselves by reuniting with the land. They'll form a weeding-and-watering committee."

Miss Springer stops and stares at Mrs. Tate and Mrs. Worth. "Your husbands will be the committee leaders," she says.

"Well, how on earth am I gonna get my husband to work our garden?" Mrs. Tate asks.

"You just tell him you see his waistline growing faster than his hothouse bulbs, and I guarantee you one hundred percent, he'll be weeding the acres by hand every night of the week.

"And as for your husband," Miss Springer says to Mrs. Worth, "ever since he switched from firefighting to lumber, he's lost that gleam in his eye. You get him to show up at the garden just once, and I promise, you'll find a changed man!"

Mrs. Tate and Mrs. Worth nod like Miss Springer could be on to something.

Then Miss Springer takes her pencil off the table and slides it back behind her ear. "So you see," she says to Mr. Mudge, "that's the way it's fixin' to be."

"You sure make a lot of noise for a librarian!" Mr. Mudge says.

Miss Springer huffs out such a strong breath it knocks the curl dangling in front of her forehead off to the side of her face.

"Oh, I'm just joking," he says. "But there is one problem you've overlooked."

Miss Springer raises her eyebrows.

"Weedin' and waterin' is Negro work!" he says.

Now Miss Springer's fuming! "I'll have you know," she says, "my daddy and his daddy before him did that work. So did your daddy. If he hadn't, you wouldn't be where you are today."

And that's when I hear the sizzling sound. I run to the stove. Each noodle's the size of a live oak trunk. I've got just enough time to feed Ralphie supper before the Garden Club meeting finishes and it's time for Mama and me to head back home.

Later, when me and Mama get outside, I see the milk in Flapjack's dish is almost finished. Mama waits while I clean out the bowl with the Tates' hose. Then I *tweet, click, click,* and wouldn't you know it, Flapjack leaps over the neighbor's fence into the Tates' yard. The milk worked! I kiss his furry head and together, we all walk home.

CHAPTER 11

August 3, 1963

Mama, me, and Uncle Bump meet up with Bessie in Kuckachoo Lane. What with Elias still missing and us going to plant this garden that should be ours, no one's got to say a word for all of us to understand things couldn't be worse.

Last week, the week after the Garden Club meeting, Bessie carried us a message from Mr. Mudge. She sat at our kitchen table and took out a receipt from the Corner Store. Then she turned it over to show us what he wrote on the back:

Keep the faith. You're all invited to help plant Saturday.
Good wages. Tell Bessie if you'll work.

"Mr. Mudge is reaching into his own pocket to pay us, 'cause he wants to hire help he knows is good," Bessie told us. "Plus, he knows y'all could use the cash. And he said I could come too."

Mama's eyes brimmed with tears. "Mr. Mudge's actions sure speak louder than his words," she said. "No matter what he says about Negroes, you can't deny that man's looking out for our family."

That's when Bessie spread out her long, light fingers and rested them gentle on Mama's arm. Then Mama wiped her eyes with the corner of her apron and smiled at Bessie like she was real grateful for her kindness. And I wondered why I didn't think of that. Why didn't I rest my fingers real gentle on Mama's arm? I reckon it's because folks who are fetching, like Bessie, know when to do things like that, the same way folks who are plain, like me, know just when to hiccup or sneeze.

Sometimes Mama and me work Saturday mornings for Mrs. Tate, so Mama had to talk over Mr. Mudge's offer with her first. But Mrs. Tate said, "Why, of course y'all should plant the garden! Mr. Mudge wouldn't be hiring beyond his own field hands if he didn't think we needed the help." And Mama was glad to hear her say that, because by planting the garden we're guaranteed a whole day of Saturday work, not just half.

Now I *tweet, click, click,* and Flapjack scampers down the trunk of the giant oak. Then Mama, Uncle Bump, Bessie, and me set off for Old Man Adams's place.

"I reckon Mr. Mudge went and changed his mind about the garden," I say as we cross the tracks.

"And from what I can tell, Mr. Mudge doesn't know a thing about what Mr. Adams wrote in his will," Bessie says.

"Well, aren't we gonna tell him the garden's ours too?" I ask.

Mama glares at me. "With Elias gone, don't you think we've got enough to worry 'bout!" she says. Then she tugs Uncle Bump's arm and the two of them hurry on ahead of Bessie and me.

When we turn down Magnolia Row, Bessie picks up a stick and runs it across the tall fence that lines Old Man Adams's garden. "You ready for seventh grade?" she asks.

"Ready or not, here I come," I say.

"At first, Mrs. Jacks seems scary." Bessie's stick clicks along the fence. "But she's not that bad once you learn how to survive."

"Oh." I gulp.

"There's not much to it, really," she says. "Just bake her a pan of corn bread each morning."

Corn bread each morning, I say to myself, fixing the words in my mind.

"Always do double the math problems she assigns."

Double.

"And stay after school at least once a week to rub her feet."

Rub feet.

My lip quivers. I knew I should've flunked sixth grade!

Then Bessie busts out laughing. "Just jokin'," she says.

So I laugh out loud too, and while we cross through the yard of the big house, I add a couple snorts just to make sure Bessie doesn't think I was taking her serious.

Soon Bessie, me, Mama, and Uncle Bump meet up with the other twelve hands at the garden gate. Besides little Lydia Cook, who's here with her mama, all these folks are Mr. Mudge's regular help.

As the lot of us look through the iron bars into the garden, one thing's clear: someone got a head start on this planting. Why, there's already a couple rows of something growing up right against the gate. "Looks like corn," Uncle Bump says. "But them stalks is too close together."

After being head servant here so many years, my uncle sure knows his vegetables.

When I spot Mr. Mudge riding toward us, all I can say is I'm sure glad that man's on his tractor, because that means he can lay most of the seed himself. Why, with the help of his new machine, he could plant over the garden with something simple like crowder peas in just a couple hours. Of course, from what I heard Mrs. Tate say, this planting's going to be a lot more complicated. We've got a whole variety of seed to lay. But still, that tractor will help.

After Mr. Mudge steps down from it, he unlocks the garden gate with the keys that used to belong to Uncle Bump. And I reckon it hurts my uncle just to look at those keys, which is how come he's staring at his work boots.

"Y'all meet me at the garden cabin," Mr. Mudge tells us. Then he hoists himself back on the tractor and chug-a-lugs off.

While us field hands march across the farm, we can see Mr. Mudge already smoothed over the land with his chopper, heaped up the dirt so it's ready for planting, and numbered all the rows with orange flags.

When we all get to the garden cabin, Mr. Mudge says, "As you know, I'm donating the cost of your labor. There's a pitcher of water round the other side of the porch. Feel free. And Bump, I'll need you to set the attachments on my tractor."

Uncle Bump nods.

Mr. Mudge points to the trays of baby cabbage, kale, and collards napping in the shade on the cabin porch, and he assigns the rows. Then we get started.

It's hot as blue blazes out here! When I crouch down to hole the land, I squeeze the warm earth in my fists—the warm earth that's supposed to belong to me. By the time I've got only two rows left to hole, the sun's been up a few hours and my shirt's soaked through. I head over to the cabin porch, where rickety Mr. Washington huddles by the pitcher, drinking water.

Mr. Washington runs Mr. Mudge's stable of cows and pigs. He wipes his sweat with a handkerchief. "It's hot enough to melt cheese," he tells me.

"Sure is!" I say.

"You're lucky you're young," he says.

"Reckon so," I say, and help myself to two cups of water.

As soon as I finish drinking, I fill up two more cups for Mama. But on my way across the rows, I pass Lydia Cook. Lydia's in the first grade, and just from the look of her, one thing's clear: when it comes to sweat, young or old don't matter. Little Lydia's covered with even more sweat than Mr. Washington. Looking at her, I remember how hard it was to work in this garden as a little girl, before I moved into the big house. I can still remember how my stomach growled with hunger, how the minutes went on for hours and the hours for days.

"You're real good at this, Lydia!" I tell her.

She looks up from under her straw hat and gives me a weary grin, so I give her one of the cups of water in my hand.

When I get to Mama, she sucks down the other cup of water. She hasn't worked the land since she was a little girl. Lucky for her, Old Man Adams liked his privacy, so he built a tall fence around his farm so no one could see inside it. Now Mama rests in the thick stripe of shade at the edge of the garden.

While I walk back to my rows, I glance across the field and see Mr. Mudge unlocking the garden gate for Mrs. Tate and her friends. Truth be told, I've had quite enough of Mrs. Tate. All week at work, Mama and me listened to her talk about the details of the planting. She was so excited you would've thought she was seventeen years old planning her wedding again.

Just the other day I was washing out the pots in the sink. Mrs. Tate was sitting at the kitchen table with her husband, who was wearing a cowboy hat and spitting watermelon seeds into a bowl. "Oh, it's going to be fabulous!" she said.

I made like I didn't hear a thing while Mr. Tate hid under that big old cowboy hat of his and slurped up the juice left in his watermelon rind.

"Ralph, didn't you hear me?" Mrs. Tate asked. "We won't have to pay through the roof for food. No one will. This is gonna help a lot of folks, Ralph."

"The only reason I said I'd work the garden is because I need to get in shape if I'm gonna coach the Kickers football team next year," he said. "To tell you the truth, I'm sick of hearing 'bout the stupid garden!"

Mrs. Tate set down her fork. "Oh," she said.

I could hear by the way she said that one little "Oh," something inside her broke. I could also hear Mr. Tate didn't understand his wife at all. And I was afraid he was going to get even meaner, so I grabbed a rag and ran upstairs to dust the sitting room. And all I could think is it's too bad sweet Ralphie has to share a name with his mean old daddy.

After that, Mrs. Tate didn't stop talking about the garden—she just stopped talking about it with her husband. When she couldn't find Miss Springer or Mrs. Worth, she talked about it with Mama and me.

Every so often, in between talking about what she would wear to the planting and what food she would bring, she'd say how sorry she was about Elias. Just the other day she said, "I'll bet he's only run off with some girl. Soon as it sours, he'll be back."

And even though Mrs. Tate meant it to be kind, there was glass over Mama's eyes the second she said it.

Now I watch Mrs. Tate, Miss Springer, and Mrs. Worth climb onto the porch of Old Man Adams's garden cabin. Once they settle into their chairs, they unpack their feast from a picnic basket, while Mrs. Tate carries on about how wonderful Mr. Mudge is. "See, I told you he'd come around," she says, and pours herself a drink from a thermos. "A couple days after our garden meeting, he was already out here on his tractor planting us a border of Indian corn. He says the cornstalks will protect our baby crops from high winds, so they'll grow up big and strong."

But I pretend I don't see these ladies, and I make like I don't hear them, while I finish holing the land. Then I slog on over to the porch to pick up a tray of cabbage seedlings. When I get there, I see Mrs. Tate pouring Mama's fresh peach juice and sharing Mama's homemade blueberry muffins with her friends like this is a regular celebration, while here I am sweating so much a rash erupted over my thighs.

I carry a tray of seedlings to the far end of my row. By the time I work myself back near the cabin porch, Mrs. Tate and her friends have been out there for hours, and I reckon they've forgotten I'm here.

"Well, at least that colored boy got what he deserved," Mrs. Worth says.

My fingers turn to sticks in the ground.

"I have to admit, much as I like my own help, the Negro problem's getting out of hand," Mrs. Tate says. "They just make everything so . . . complicated."

"That dead boy broke Jimmy's leg!" Mrs. Worth says. "What's so complicated 'bout that?"

Dead boy. I turn the words over in my mind.

But Mrs. Worth goes on. "Now we don't have a prayer of winning the state championship. And Jimmy might lose out on a scholarship to college!"

I'm so mad I see raspberries! Right about now, I hate Mrs. Worth more than I've ever hated anyone in my whole entire life, Buck Fowler included. And I can't believe Mrs.

Tate would let Mrs. Worth call Elias a "dead boy," when just the other day she told Mama and me not to worry, that of course he's fine, of course he'll be back.

"Where are your priorities?" Miss Springer asks.

"Oh, come on!" Mrs. Worth shouts. "Don't tell me you feel bad for an uppity colored who messed with my son!"

Mrs. Tate sniffles and I'm glad. But all too soon the roar of Mr. Mudge's tractor drowns out the sound of her tears, so I transplant the last of the cabbage and go to help Mama. Of course, I'm not about to tell her what I heard, because I know she couldn't bear it.

Mama smiles when she sees me come her way. Her cheeks are rosy. Together we broadcast button squash seed across the fresh-turned soil. And I'll tell you one thing: I wish I could get myself a life supply, because if you ask me, there's nothing better than hot button squash with cool cane syrup running down the sides.

By the time we finish planting, Mrs. Tate and her friends are long gone. I *tweet, click, click,* and Flapjack comes running. But when I lean over to pet him, every muscle in me aches, the knuckles in my fingers throb, and my body hurts so bad that for a minute or two, I forget what's going on in my life—till I traipse over to the cabin where Mr. Mudge brings it back up.

"And let us pray," he says.

All of us field hands sink down our heads in the dusky light.

"Let us pray Elias Pickett comes home safe and sound," he says.

We all say, "Amen."

Then Mr. Mudge says there's a sale on for bacon. "Whole pack for a dime. Can't beat that!" He tells us we've done outstanding work and pays Uncle Bump twelve dollars and fifty cents: five for him, five for Mama, and since I'm not a grown-up yet, two dollars and fifty cents for me.

When Uncle Bump takes those bills and sticks them in his pocket, I feel good for the first time since Elias disappeared. But as I follow Lydia Cook and her mama across the rows toward the garden gate, I see a thousand mounds of dirt that will burst with collards, cabbage, and button squash come fall. And I see those bills in my uncle's pocket, they don't amount to a bucket of spit.

CHAPTER 12

August 8, 1963

This afternoon when I get to the Tates' house, I find Mama circling the kitchen table, a rag flying up and down in each hand. Just yesterday, Uncle Bump brought home super news: he got work at the General Merchandise Store in Franklindale handing out the government commodity and sweeping up the floors. Sure it's only part-time, but still, any bit of money will help. Of course, last night Mama was all hugs and smiles. But now here she is, the very next day, already a regular wreck.

"I can't believe I forgot to put these things in her car," Mama says. "She told me twice and I said I'd do it. Right away. Well, I meant to do it but I plum forgot. Now how they gonna play bingo without bingo boards?"

"Slow down," I tell her.

Upstairs Ralphie cries, waking from his nap.

"See these here things," Mama says. She's got a pile of bingo boards and a box full of cardboard bingo numbers in her arms. "Mrs. Tate needs these. She just left but five minutes ago. She said she was going to the courthouse first to pick up a friend of hers for the game. You'd best grab Ralphie and get these supplies to her right away."

So I run upstairs, give Ralphie a quick kiss on the cheek, scoop him out of the crib, change his diaper lickety-split, and tell him about our important mission. Then I carry him downstairs, grab his bottle, and set him in the baby carriage.

Mrs. Tate keeps saying she's going to get Ralphie a big-boy stroller, one he can sit up in, but after Mr. Tate yelled at her for buying the stuffed dog, I can't help but wonder if she's afraid to spend the money.

Now Mama rests Ralphie on his back in the carriage and sets the bingo supplies beside him. "Go round the side entrance. That's where Mrs. Tate's friend works. If you get a move on, you should catch Mrs. Tate at the courthouse," Mama says.

Out of nowhere, Ralphie starts to cry. I bend down and rub his head.

"He's fine," Mama says. "Just cranky. Nothing a little fresh air won't cure."

I hate to leave with Ralphie upset, but off we go, down

the driveway. The sun's beating something fierce, and I've got to wipe my brow on the sleeve of my dress more than once. I pull down the shade on the carriage so Ralphie won't get overheated. But by the time we reach the end of Honeysuckle Trail, he's wailing.

So I walk round to the front of the carriage. "What's wrong?" I ask. And that's when—if I'm lying, I'll be a beggar's wife—that little boy parts his lips and says, "Doggie!"

For a minute, I'm not sure if the heat's toying with my mind.

But again, Ralphie says through his tears, "Doggie!"

"Ralphie!" I scream. "You talked!"

And now I'm stretched like taffy between Mama, who doesn't want Mrs. Tate to get mad about the bingo boards, and Ralphie, who needs his stuffed doggie that we've left home. In my panic, I *tweet, click, click,* and here comes Flapjack, scampering toward us. I pick him up.

"Cat," I say. "This is a cat."

But Ralphie just says, "Doggie!" Then he laughs and laughs like he told the funniest joke that ever was.

Well, problem solved. Ralphie's stopped crying, so now we can continue our important mission. I thank my doggie-cat and set him on the ground beside me.

And I reckon Ralphie likes being pushed fast through the hot air, because he starts to purr like a kitty. By the time we arrive, I'm out of breath.

Flapjack scampers under a bush while I push the carriage through the side door of the courthouse. There's a sign on the wall that says Voter Registration. A few folks are inside, and wouldn't you know it, Delilah's granddaddy's one of them. He holds his cane and leans against the wall.

"Hotter than an oven," he tells me.

"Sure is," I say.

I push the carriage over to Mrs. Tate, who sits on a red vinyl chair.

"Oh, goodness!" she says. "I was just gonna head back home to get these. Well, I'm glad your mother remembered." She scoops the bingo supplies out of the carriage and sets them on the ground beside her.

Ralphie cries for his bottle, so I lift him up and hold him while he drinks it.

"Oh, have a seat," Mrs. Tate tells me, and pats the empty chair beside her.

But the instant I sit down, a sandpaper voice calls out, "That seat's reserved."

"Oh," says Mrs. Tate. "For who?"

"Whites," the voice says.

That's when I see that Mrs. Tate's friend who works at the courthouse is none other than Mrs. Worth. I leap up out of that chair so hard I almost break both my kneecaps.

"Well," Mrs. Tate mumbles, "why don't you lean yourself against that wall over there."

And I reckon I'll have to wait till later to tell Mrs. Tate that her son just spoke his first word.

I lean against the wall like Mrs. Tate suggests, but being so close to Mrs. Worth makes me quake all over. And I'll tell you one thing: I can't wait till Ralphie finishes his bottle so we can get on out of here!

While Ralphie's drinking, Mrs. Tate chats with Mrs.

Worth. "Of course, I want to be surprised, but then I just couldn't help peeking through the garden gate on my way over here this afternoon. Let me just say, everything looks splendid. And you know what else? The red and black ears of Indian corn are gonna be just perfect for our Thanksgiving decorations."

"Wish I had time for such pleasantries," Mrs. Worth says, "but I'm stuck here. Say, Penelope, did you hear 'bout the colored man in Laknahatchie County?"

"What colored man in Laknahatchie County?" Mrs. Tate asks.

"Happened just yesterday," Mrs. Worth says. "Somehow this colored man managed to pass the voter-registration test only to get a .45-caliber bullet through his window."

I reckon this voting business is dangerous stuff.

"Next . . . ," Mrs. Worth calls.

A Negro man wearing church clothes walks to her desk.

"In order to register, you must first pass a test. Now then, how many steps on the Thunder Creek County Courthouse?" Mrs. Worth asks.

And I wonder what kind of horse-brained question that is. Here I've been living in Kuckachoo all my life and I've never had reason to climb those courthouse steps. Even if I had, why would I bother to count them?

"Six?" he guesses.

"I'm sorry, the answer is seven. Under the state law of Mississippi, you are not eligible to vote at this time," she says. "Check back when you have a better understanding of what it takes to be a citizen of our country. Good day!"

After the man leaves the office, Mrs. Worth comes out

from behind her desk. Thank goodness, Ralphie finishes up his bottle right then. He lets out a big burp and I set him back in the carriage.

"Thank you for the bingo boards," Mrs. Tate whispers to me. "And thank you too, pumpkin pie," she says to Ralphie, and kisses his cheek.

Then Mrs. Worth turns out the office lights, even though Delilah's granddaddy's still waiting on her. "You'll have to come back tomorrow," she tells him.

One thing's clear: Mrs. Worth's used to breaking hearts. It's her job.

CHAPTER 13

August 15, 1963

Last week Ralphie spoke his first word, but he still hasn't said it for his mama who's desperate to hear it. Lord knows working with Ralphie on his talking and walking's the only thing that gets me up each morning, because if I had to sit home all day with nothing to do but think about my brother, I'd go cock-a-doodle mad.

Tonight I can't stand how Mama talks at dinner, so I leave my plate full of rice and beans and run to my bedroom. I lie on my mattress and listen through the sheet as she continues to fear the worst.

"I can't help it, Bump. If he was out there, he'd a sent word."

"Now how he send word without risking somebody find out?" Uncle Bump asks.

"He's smart. He'd a found a way."

Dishes clang in the sink while Mama and Uncle Bump talk on.

Right about now I wish I could run away, but I feel too heavy and sad to lift my head off the pillow let alone get up and run. So instead I stay in bed and imagine I'm running, till Mama comes right in without even knocking on the door frame.

I pull the sheet up over my head.

" 'Less there's an extra-large potato hiding under this sheet, I'd say it's my little girl under there."

Mama thinks cracking a joke will make me come out from under this sheet, but she's wrong.

Now she gets all demanding. "Come on out!" she snaps.

There's a sound in her voice that says I'd darned well better. So I roll the sheet down, but not so far she can see my bottom lip shake. "Why you acting like he's dead?" I whisper.

"I need the Lord," Mama says.

She sits on the edge of my bed and bows her head while she stumbles through the words. "Dear Lord," she says in a voice soft as fur. It's the voice Mama uses when she's praying with her whole soul. "I know you say you won't give me more than I can handle, but this time you gone done it. I need you to tell me somethin', Lord. Can you do that?"

She pauses, then nods, as if she hears the answer in her head. "I need you to tell me, where is my son?"

But I reckon the Lord doesn't answer that one, because

Mama wipes a tear with the corner of her apron. Then she gathers me up in her arms, pulls me to her bosom, and hugs me almost as tight as I hugged Flapjack at the Corner Store the night Buck Fowler snatched him.

Thirty-four days gone since Elias disappeared, and even though he hasn't sent word, I have a creeping feeling inside my chest he's still alive. Sometimes, I feel a flicker, and I'm certain. But Mama? She's losing faith.

Later, when Mama leaves me alone in my room, I go just about crazy. I get into my brother's bed and smell the baseball mixed up with sage from the farm. Then I close my eyes and wait. But I don't see any yellow or orange glitter the way I did the night I talked to my brother. I don't see any colors at all. "You really dead, Elias?" I hear myself whisper in the chilly dark. My breath's shallow, and I reckon there's no river in my chest, just my quickly beating heart. And there's no answer from my brother, only the silence of a night stretched far too long.

I roll on my side, but no matter which way I turn, how I curl, or how many stars I count, my head keeps throbbing from too many questions. They're sharp. They won't go away: Why is Uncle Bump always telling me to hush? Why is Mama so quiet? And why am I sure Elias can hear me if he's nowhere near, and some folks think he might even be dead and gone?

I can't stand the questions and I don't want to be alone, so I squat on the windowsill, push up the screen, and stretch my leg down to the overturned bucket. Then I *tweet, click, click* for Flapjack, and together we scuttle across the dirt, past the swing, to Delilah's house.

It's a good thing she's the onliest child, because Delilah's got her very own bedroom, and when I sneak out and knock on her window, I can wake her up and Mr. and Mrs. Montgomery don't hear a thing.

Delilah has a mischief inside. If I didn't know her, I don't think I'd ever fix my hair in all kinds of styles or sneak out to the bayou. I bet I'd look real funny and be real sad.

At night, Delilah thinks she owns Kuckachoo. Tonight, when at last she steals through the window, she grabs my wrist and, as usual, pulls me to the path.

A lot of times when we head to the bayou Delilah says, "After sixth grade, I'ma go to charm school. And after charm school, I'ma send my picture to *Ebony* magazine and they'll ask me to New York City to be a fashion model. After I get tired of New York, I'ma walk the runways in Paris."

One time Delilah was sitting in our kitchen talking about her future, when Mama said, "Honey, I hate to tell you this, but there just ain't no Negro fashion models." Delilah threw her head back and laughed. "Mrs. Pickett, please don't tell me you've never heard of Helen Williams or Dorothea Towles!" One thing was clear: Delilah studies the old *Ebony* magazines she borrows from the church lending library just as hard as I study my vocabulary words. Of course, Mama had never heard of those model ladies in all her life, but I could tell she was impressed that Delilah was preparing for the future, because to Mama, preparing for the future is what life's all about.

Whenever Delilah talks about being a model in New York City, I imagine how I'll visit her there. We'll walk with our arms linked through each other's. We'll go to fancy restaurants, eat butter beans, and tell everyone we're sisters. But whenever I picture that part, I get stopped by reality. How's anyone going to believe we're sisters? After all, Delilah's light brown skin's always dewy like a petal, while mine's muddy like the bottom of the bayou. And Delilah's eyebrows? They arch real graceful, like dancers leaping, while there's no doubt about it, mine scraggle like hawks crashing down for a landing. In fact, never since I can remember has a Sunday in church passed without someone telling Delilah she looks pretty as a speckled pup. And never has a Sunday passed with anyone telling me I look cute like a pup, speckled, striped, or just plain.

Whenever Delilah talks about New York City, I can taste jealousy in the back of my throat. To make it go away, I tell her more stories about Old Man Adams's big house, even though I don't work there anymore. "You wouldn't believe them deep red carpets and frilly white curtains!" I say. "When the sun came in, dust speckles—blue, yellow, red—danced in the air till I wiped down the banisters." But whenever I talk about the big house, Delilah scrunches her lips to one side like she still hasn't decided if it's true.

Tonight, though, as we head off Kuckachoo Lane onto the darkest path, we don't say a word. There's only moss and pebbles under our feet to guide us to the clearing and Flapjack winding round my ankles. And soon as we enter the bank of the bayou, there's the bright white of the moon skipping on top of the water. As usual, I toss aside the pebbles and spread the corner of my nightgown so Delilah can sit on top of it. That way she doesn't have to get dirty.

Then we stay real quiet till I say, "Night's always telling me what to think."

"Like what?" she asks.

"Like everyone says Elias isn't coming back. That he really did get stuck under the bayou." Flapjack curls into a ball on my lap. "But it's in my head he's alive," I say.

"How so?"

"Last night . . ." I stop to check her face but she can read right into my mind.

"I won't laugh," she says. "Swear."

Most always Delilah's good on her word, so I rub my hand over Flapjack's head, take a breath for courage, and close my eyes. Then I play my dream from last night all over again in my mind. While I watch the pictures, I tell her what I see. "Elias, he runs faster than any of them. When they chase him, he dives into the deepest part and slips between the tree trunks."

Nothing in Kuckachoo's as magic as the cypress trees wading in the bayou. They spring from the middle of the water. Each tree's winding roots twist above the surface, forming a maze the size of our kitchen table.

"You know how dark he is?" I go on. "Well, he blends with the night, clings to the cypress trunk. Them fools, they can't see him for nothing." My breath is shallow. "And thank goodness, the moon isn't too bright," I say. "There's no reflection of his face. Them murderers, they can't find him anywhere. As soon as they leave, he swims across the bayou, escapes in the cotton."

My eyes are still shut—I'm watching Elias cross the

99

cotton—when Delilah wraps her arm around my shoulders. When I open my eyes, they're all runny, so I wipe them with the back of my hand. Then I stare straight ahead. The silver sky collides with the water's surface, creating a mirror. In it, I see Elias, his long limbs wrapped round the roots of that tree.

I reckon Delilah's worried up my mind is haunted, because she says, "Look, Addie Ann, dead or alive, you'll feel better once you know for sure."

"I do know!" I tell her. "He's alive and on the run. We've got a soul connection." And now Flapjack wonders if I'm losing my mind too, because he stands in my lap, arches his back, and prances away.

"You can't keep living like this, not knowing, always wondering," Delilah says.

And I reckon she's right. It's the not knowing that's driving me mad. "How we gonna find out?" I ask. My bottom lip trembles.

But Delilah doesn't answer. Instead, she takes my hand and pulls me away from the bayou, along the muddy path. Soon enough, I catch sight of our destination: the graveyard. I peer through the gate. In the moonlight, cement crosses lean this way and that. And I can't imagine what she's got in store.

I've got the heebie-jeebies so bad my voice comes out like a shiver. "We can't go in at night," I whisper. "We'll get in trouble."

"Who's gonna get us in trouble?"

I look round. There's no one in sight and I've got to admit, Delilah's right.

She pushes open the gate, leads me through.

My insides get tight. Most graves, long forgotten, are covered with nothing but dirt. I kneel down beside Daddy's.

"Sittin' on your daddy's dirt is a right fine place to get our ceremony under way," Delilah says. She sits across from me. Her back rests on Daddy's stone. "We're gonna contact Heaven. Ask if your brother's ghost is there."

I knew Delilah was mysterious but I didn't know she had secret powers.

"How do you know how to contact Heaven?" I ask.

"Bessie," she says. "That's how I learned to call on Granny's ghost in the first place."

Well, I can't say I'm surprised. Delilah learns just about everything she knows from Bessie. "Now you can't start talking to ghosts with your eyes open," she says, as if I should know.

And even though part of me doesn't believe a word Delilah says about ghosts, my breath, it's barely there.

Delilah closes her eyes, looks like she's concentrating real hard. So I shut mine too. She presses her pointer fingers on my temples and rubs in tight little circles.

"Light as a feather, stiff as a board," she murmurs. "Light as a feather, stiff as a board."

I don't know what I've got myself into. But I reckon Delilah's right about one thing: if my brother's dead and gone, it's best to face up to the truth here and now.

"Say it with me," Delilah says.

"Light as a feather, stiff as a board," we chant a couple times.

Then Delilah claps.

My breath, it's gone.

"Ghost of Elias Pickett, we summon you to this here graveyard. If you're dead, come show your face," she says.

What if it's true? What if my brother drowned? And now he'll show up a tall, swirly white light.

"Look!" she shouts.

My eyes fling open.

Delilah points at the sky.

A hawk crosses in front of the moon.

"He's comin'!" she shouts.

At least I thought it was a hawk.

"Soon he'll show his ghost face," she says.

Then we wait and wait for my brother to come.

Something jostles the bush beside us. We both gulp.

"It's him!" Delilah whispers.

But then Flapjack scampers out from under a bush and prances into the cemetery.

"Oh, no it ain't," Delilah says, and sighs.

We wait and wait. Before I know it, Delilah's snoozing, sitting up, back against Daddy's stone. Here I am, teeth chattering in the dark, hugging my knees to my chest, praying my brother's ghost won't show. The cemetary's a grainy black-and-white photograph stuck between morning and night, when at long last the first rooster crows.

"He didn't come!" I tell Deliliah. "He's still alive."

My groggy-faced friend rubs the sleep from her eyes. "You know what?" she says, and yawns. "You're right! He must be alive 'cause this ghost ceremony works every time."

Well, all I can say is this was the best ghost ceremony

that ever was! It filled me with new power, just what I need to race back home and climb through my window into bed, all before Mama finds me up and gone. I give Daddy's stone a quick rub and I'm off running. Flapjack follows close behind.

CHAPTER 14

August 24, 1963

Ralphie has three words now: doggie, cat, and pickle. Every time Mrs. Tate hears him say something, she can't help but run and hug her boy, she's so proud. And since his talking's coming along so good, Ralphie's concentrating on walking. Today he wraps his little hands round the legs of the changing table, pulls himself up to stand.

"Let go, Ralphie! Walk!" I say.

Just then Mama pokes her head into the room, and Ralphie topples onto the floor in a heap. "Change the baby for the party," she says.

"He's not a baby," I tell her.

"Well, just change that big boy and bring him down fast."

I'm glad to see Mrs. Tate's set out a respectable outfit for her son: a red cap, a white button-down shirt, and red knickerbockers. I dress him, pick him up, and shuffle down the stairs. The smell of roasting pork makes my stomach rumble. And I pray I'll get a bite.

When Ralphie's father hears me coming, he calls, "Addie Ann, bring me my little boy," so I carry Ralphie into the living room, where the guests poke their toothpicks into the fruit salad Mama set on the table.

"How old's the baby?" one of the men asks.

Ralphie's not a baby! I want to tell him. *He can talk and he can almost walk!* But I keep quiet and hand Ralphie to Mr. Tate.

"Fourteen months," Mrs. Tate answers.

"Oh, he's darlin'!" coos a lady. Her beehive hairdo's so high on her head, she'll likely need a harness to keep it perched up there for the rest of the night.

I slip into the kitchen. Mama fusses about the pork roast and I cook up the green beans, while we listen to the lady with the beehive hairdo ask Mrs. Tate how the garden's coming along.

"It's only been a few weeks since the planting," Mrs. Tate says, "but Mr. Mudge called the other day and told me to hurry on over. It was the perfect time in his busy schedule to give me a tour. And I have to say everything looked marvelous till the sky split and we was stuck out there in the thunder and lightning without an umbrella. Mr. Mudge said, 'You can never know the weather in advance,' but I tell you, that's the last time I get caught out in the middle of a garden like a soaked squirrel!"

"Golly!" says the lady.

"I still can't get the mud stains off my shoes!" Mrs. Tate says.

"I reckon it's safer to check on things from the garden gate," says the lady.

"You're probably right," Mrs. Tate agrees.

Then the lady with the beehive hairdo tells Mrs. Tate how to get the mud stains off her shoes with carbonated water.

I'm moving the collards into the serving dish when all of a sudden I hear Mrs. Tate yell, "Careful!" I look into the living room, and there's Mr. Tate tossing Ralphie into the air high above his head. "You'll make a great linebacker, little man," he tells his son.

Poor Ralphie!

A few minutes later, I'm taking the rice off the stove when I hear Ralphie cough.

"Spit-up!" I murmur, and grab the cloth.

But when I get to the living room, everyone's faded, pale. Everyone except Ralphie. He's red. Bright red!

Mrs. Tate, she's frozen, hands over her mouth, eyes round as stones. The lady with the beehive hairdo yells, "Get it out!"

Mr. Tate, he reaches his finger into Ralphie's mouth. Ralphie gags.

"I can't get it!" Mr. Tate yells.

Then Ralphie stops gagging.

"He's turning blue!" a man says.

And it's true. Ralphie's blue round the lips. He's not breathing.

Neither am I.

Before I know it, I grab that boy from his father, dash to the kitchen, sit down, turn him over on my lap. Ralphie's little hands and feet flail in the air. I whack him on the back between his shoulder blades. Hard! Nothing happens. *Just one breath, Lord!*

I hit him again with the heel of my hand, the way Mama showed me back when I started here, just in case. And this time Ralphie coughs. A mashed-up grape dribbles out his mouth onto the floor. Then Ralphie starts screaming, quick and high. I've never heard him so frightened. It sounds like he can't breathe even though I know he can.

Mrs. Tate stands in the kitchen doorway crying, "Thank God! Thank God!"

"Ralphie!" I say, and pull him to my chest. And now that it's over, I feel all trembling inside like I've walked miles in the heat without drinking water. A warm rush flows through me. And I know how much I love this little boy.

And I reckon Mama feels how much she loves me, because she whispers, "You done good, Addie Ann Pickett." Then she plants a squishy kiss on top of my head.

Mrs. Tate sits down at the kitchen table, but she's too upset to take Ralphie in her arms, so she rubs her finger across his hairline while I hold him and sing, *"Hush, little Ralphie, don't say a word. Mama's gonna buy you a mockingbird."*

At long last Ralphie's breath calms.

Now Mr. Tate's in the doorway. "Can't you see he's fine? Come on!" he whispers to his wife so the company in the living room won't hear.

"You can't throw him in the air when he's got food in his mouth!" Mrs. Tate whispers back. She picks the purple grape off the floor and holds it up for her husband to see.

"It was just one grape," he says.

Mrs. Tate glares.

"Is little Ralphie all right?" a man calls into the kitchen from the living room.

"Everything's fine, thank you," Mrs. Tate answers through her tears. She throws the grape in the trash and washes her hands in the sink.

Mama gives Mrs. Tate a handkerchief, and she pats under her eyes. "Is everything ready?" Mrs. Tate asks.

"Yes, ma'am," Mama says.

I've still got Ralphie in my arms, but Mrs. Tate walks over to us, holds her son's pudgy cheeks in her hands, and plants a long kiss on his forehead. Then she struts back into the living room.

I can only see the back of her hat, but from the song in her voice, I imagine Mrs. Tate must be smiling a southern-lady smile when she tells her guests, "Thank you kindly for your concern. The baby's fine. And dinner will be served in the dining room."

Mama pours the sauce over the roast. In no time, the guests are chewing up their pork. They just can't get over how delicious it is! And I know sure as sugar there won't be a bite left for Mama and me.

Later I'm up in Ralphie's bedroom, changing him into his nightclothes, when Mrs. Tate comes in. I can still hear the company downstairs and I wonder what Mrs. Tate's doing.

"How'd you know how to do that?" she asks.

For a second I get real scared. Is she angry I saved her son? Was I supposed to let her do the saving?

I'm thinking what to say, when she says, "Well . . . ?"

"Mama showed me, ma'am," I whisper. "When I first came to work here. You know, just in case."

Mrs. Tate's quiet. I pull the nightshirt over Ralphie's head.

"Bless your heart!" she says. "Bless your heart!"

I breathe a sigh of relief. Then I pick up Ralphie from the changing table. But I feel real odd here holding Mrs. Tate's boy while she watches me.

"You know, Addie Ann, you remind me of Messy Melvinia," she says.

I must be looking at Mrs. Tate crooked, because she sets out to explain.

"Well, her name wasn't really Messy Melvinia, it was just Melvinia, but I took to calling her that 'cause she was my maid when I was growing up, and she knew just what to do with me, the way you know how with Ralphie."

"Why'd you call her *Messy* Melvinia?" I ask, and hand

Ralphie to her, so she can hold him close like I know she needs to.

Mrs. Tate holds Ralphie over her shoulder. "Messy Melvinia was always complainin' 'bout the mess I made wherever I would go. We was like friends, me and Messy Melvinia," she says, and laughs. "Papa was off fighting the war, so Mama took a job ringing the cash register at the Corner Store, back when it was owned by Mr. Mudge's late daddy. Each morning, after Mama left for work, Messy Melvinia and me cleaned the house together. I mopped the floor and dried the dishes, but I wasn't much good at any of it. Messy Melvinia put a chocolate drop in the middle of my lunch sandwich every day."

Mrs. Tate touches Ralphie's hair. "But after I went off to first grade and left Messy Melvinia alone in the house all day and played with my new friends after school, it never was the same between us." Her eyes fill up. "I reckon what my mama says is true."

"What's that, ma'am?" I ask.

"Negroes are good at loving other people's children."

I have to stop myself from shouting right out at her: *It's not because I'm Negro I know how to love your son. It's a deep-in-the-heart connection between Ralphie and me. Got nothing to do with anything else! And Ralphie loves me right back. He doesn't care what color I am.*

One thing's clear: Mrs. Tate only sees what happens on the outside—me bathing Ralphie, changing him, making him laugh—and maybe anyone can do that, but it's what's going on inside me that's important. I'm loving her son with all I can. Even though Elias takes up the back of my mind, I'm giving the whole front part to Ralphie. Mrs. Tate can't imagine how hard it is to do that. She's got no idea how I struggle inside to smile for her boy each day. Course, I can't tell her how I feel, so I look at the carpet and say nothing at all.

"You don't even have a baby of your own but you know just what to do with him," she says. Then she kisses Ralphie's forehead and hands him back to me. "Well, I'd best get back to the company," she says, and leaves.

I hug that boy tight, the way Mama hugs me after she's been good and worried. Then I set him in the crib and turn out the light.

When I get back home, my stomach rumbles. All Mama and me had for dinner were some collards and rice, since the guests licked the pork bones clean. But I know how to get by. I drink down one and a half glasses of water, just enough to fill my belly, but not so much that I'll have to go to the outhouse in the middle of the night.

CHAPTER 15

September 2, 1963

A couple days after the Tates' dinner party, Ralphie took his first step without holding on to the side of the changing table. Then he took his second. A few days later, he wobbled all the way across the kitchen floor. I thought Mrs. Tate would jump for joy watching her son walk. For a second, I thought she might give me a raise. But instead, she just turned to Mama with a forehead full of wrinkles and said, "Oh, my! They do grow up fast!"

Well, I'm sure glad Ralphie's coming along, because starting tomorrow I'll need to cut back on my time with him. That's because tomorrow I'm starting seventh grade. Even though school lets out at noon this month on account of the heat, I'll have to come straight home to do home-work before I head across town to see about Ralphie. Up till now, I was nothing but excited about seventh grade. But come to think on it, maybe I shouldn't be. After all, this is junior high school and I've got Mrs. Jacks for a teacher, so I'ma have to study round the clock.

Still, Mama's keen on celebrating the big event. She even cooked up a new dish for supper. "Crawfish stew!" she announces, and sets the creature in my bowl.

My stomach lurches.

After Mama serves Uncle Bump, she carries her own bowl to the table, and the three of us sit together in the lantern light.

"I'm so proud of my little girl I could just burst!" Mama says.

"I'm not little," I say.

"Well, I'm catching the jitterbug thinking 'bout you going to seventh grade at County Colored tomorrow!" she says.

"How many times do I have to tell you?"

"Forgive me! What I most certainly meant was"— Mama clears her throat like she's going to make a special an-nouncement—"West Thunder Creek Junior High School."

But I reckon I shouldn't get mad, because Mama doesn't know much about schools at all. She grew up on a cotton plantation and went to the plantation school. Now get this: the plantation school was only open six months— November, December, March, April, and then July and August. The rest of the time, all the children were planting, chopping, and picking cotton.

Mama's father, my granddaddy, was a sharecropper. He had a house on the plantation and a couple acres. Instead of paying money to the boss man who owned the plantation, he paid a share of his crop. When Mama got to the fourth grade, Granddaddy needed her to work his land all the time, so Mama dropped out. Because of all that, Mama can only read baby books and she can barely write, so she keeps the grocery list in her head.

But my daddy grew up in the city. And when he married Mama, he made her promise their children would get a high school education like he did. "That's the only way for them to live free," he said. He told Mama that no matter how much money they'd lose by sending us to school instead of work, it would pay off in the end. So hard as it was for her to do, Mama raised us the way Daddy wanted.

"Nervous?" Mama asks.

A sharp pain jabs my belly. "I'm not nervous," I tell her. "No reason to be." I poke the crawfish in my bowl.

"Why's that?" Uncle Bump asks.

Something inside me snaps. "'Cause I'm not going."

It's the first time since Elias disappeared that Mama laughs the way she used to, straight from the gut.

I fix my eyes on the spindly sea creature in my bowl. Life's hard enough without my brother. What's the point of making it harder by going to junior high school without Delilah? Besides, Delilah won't ever be coming to junior high school with me, because next year, after she finishes sixth grade, she'll go to charm school. She says she's almost got her parents convinced to let her.

But seeing as I'm not a charm-school candidate, tomorrow morning I'ma have to walk three miles to Weaver with Cool Breeze Huddleston. Three whole miles! For all the times I dreamed about holding his hand, now the thought of walking beside him makes me queasy. If the white folks would let me into their junior high school, I could just mosey across the tracks, because their school's right here on the edge of town. Then I wouldn't have to walk miles with Cool Breeze, and I wouldn't have to think of what we could talk about while we walk.

Mama clears my dish. Then she smiles at me and winks.

My stomach growls but there's nothing else to eat except rice and beans, and I have the fidgets so bad, I've just got to jump.

I take my rope outside to the dirt patch next to the swing. But instead of saying something dumb while I jump, like "Miss Mary Mack, Mack, Mack," I say a list of all the things me and Cool Breeze can talk about in case I decide to go to school after all.

As soon as the roosters crow, my gut somersaults, and I don't even think about not going to school. How am I going to teach geography on television if I don't go to junior high school to learn it? I pull my new yellow dress over my head, but it doesn't slip on as easy as it did back when it was the color of flour. After all, I've done a heck of a lot of growing this summer, though not in the most important place. But at long last this dress fits. And just in time! No doubt Mama had it all figured out when she bought it for me way too big back in fourth grade. Now I tighten the ends of my braids and run into the kitchen.

"Don't she look beautiful!" Uncle Bump says, his mouth full of biscuit.

"Sure do," Mama says, but her smile from last night is gone. She stands at the counter flattening dough with her palms. "Remember what I told you. No crossing to no place you don't—"

There's a knock at the door. Mama hustles to get it. No one's got to tell me she's still hoping it's someone with word of Elias.

But it's only Cool Breeze.

"She'll be out in a minute," Mama tells him and returns to the counter to pound out the dough.

I put on my blue sneakers. I just got them last year. "This girl's growing like a weed," Mama told the salesman at the dry goods shop. "We'll need 'em big enough to last a good long while." As soon as I got them, I stuffed the toes with cotton so they'd stay on my feet.

Now I tie up the laces and step outside. I exhale summer and inhale fall. Deep in my nostrils a chill warns me times have changed.

I hang the straps of my canvas sack over my shoulder and, like it's no big deal, stroll to the swing where the only other seventh grader from this side of Kuckachoo stands ready to start a new life.

"Hi!" I say.

"Let's go," he says back.

Even if Cool Breeze does notice my new yellow dress, he sure doesn't get to admire it too long before Delilah steps into the yard. *What's she doing here?* I ask myself. *She's not coming to Weaver with us. She's sure not going to West Thunder Creek Junior High School.*

"Your clothes gotta match the day," Delilah always tells me, so I wonder why she's wearing her red dress, the one for when love is in the air. I notice how the part round her chest fits real tight. Besides this one and her church dress, she's got two others: a polka-dot dress for good luck and an orange one with a yellow iris down the back for courage. How a dress can bring you love, luck, or courage, I've got no idea. But I reckon it works, because it was right after Delilah got the polka-dot one from Bessie that she grew enough breasts for a bra.

"You look nice," Delilah tells me.

Then she punches Cool Breeze in the arm. "You're not so bad either," she tells him.

Sometimes I can't believe how stupid Delilah is. I'd like to tell her that. Instead I just *tweet, click, click.* I only get to call for Flapjack once before Delilah says, "Don't tell me you're taking your cat to junior high school!"

"Course not," I say. "Can't a girl whistle a tune?" Then I turn to Cool Breeze and say, "Let's go." But he doesn't budge, so I've got no choice. I head off for school myself.

I'm all the way at the end of the lane when I hear his footsteps on the dirt road beside me. Together, we turn onto the highway. On both sides of the paved road, fields stretch into the horizon, exploding with fluffs of cotton. I hear awkward shouts and nervous laughs of kids from Titus and Bramble before I see them in their starched dresses and fresh-pressed collars. Almost all of them wear shoes.

Excited as I am, a part of me's stuck down low, because my brother's supposed to be here. He's supposed to start his senior year of high school today. And even though the high school for Negroes is four miles south on the highway, while the junior high school for Negroes is three miles north, I just know Elias would've walked me all the way to the front door of my new school. But now, instead of having my big brother lead me, knowing exactly how to go, I've got Cool Breeze Huddleston ramming right into me.

I take an extra step to the side. The truth is there probably isn't a seventh-grade student in the county moving on steady legs this morning.

"Scared?" I ask him.

At Acorn Elementary School our teacher always told us there's no such thing as a dumb question, but I reckon that was a lie, because Cool Breeze is looking at me like I asked the stupidest question that ever was asked in the history of the universe going all the way back to the dinosaur times.

I swallow. Well, at least I know exactly what to say next. "I've got a map of the United States in my bedroom."

"That right?"

"Uh-huh."

I think he might ask to see it, but he doesn't. I think he might ask where I got it, but he doesn't do that either. He just keeps walking crooked, his eyes fixed on the highway, his broad shoulders stretching out the white cloth of his shirt. I take in how his long fingers wrap firm round the handles of his canvas book bag. And I reckon maybe he doesn't like maps. Maybe just little kids like maps. Maybe he thinks I'm dumb for talking about maps at all.

The slow grind of a motor sneaks up behind us. A tractor waddles by and I think of what Uncle Bump told me about my daddy. "Your father used to get in his jalopy, put down the top, take off his city hat, and go eighty on that two-lane road, waiting for another speeder to pass in the other direction so his car would spring off the ground. Up, up, away and sideways. That's how your father took life," Uncle Bump said, laughing. "He'd drive forever to catch freedom in his hair."

Whenever I think about my daddy, I picture a handsome man in a fedora hat with twinkling eyes and a breezy smile.

I know one day Cool Breeze and me will walk to school and I'll tell him all the stories about my father. That's when he'll hold my hand. But that'll have to come later, after we talk about other, less important stuff. So I move to the third and final topic I've got planned. "You think Cassius Clay will be the greatest boxer in history?" I ask.

"Already is!" he says.

"Better than Joe Louis?"

He nods.

"What about Jack Johnson and Sugar Ray Robinson?"

"Cassius Clay is better," he says.

"Yeah, I know," I say. And that's the end of our conversation.

I look out at the plantation shacks that dot the cotton field. I wish Lovetta and Marcus could be walking with us today. But Lovetta and Marcus have to repeat sixth grade because they missed so many days last year. Even though the plantation boss man got a cotton-picking machine, the crop was wet and high last year, so it didn't work too good. Every time it rained, Lovetta and Marcus had to stay home from school to trail the machine and pick everything clear.

Well, I'll tell you one thing: if Lovetta and Marcus and Elias and Flapjack were here with me, then everything would be hunky-dory instead of the way it is now, me walking miles with Cool Breeze without anything to speak of at all.

It seems hours pass till at long last the children walking a piece in front of us turn off the highway to Weaver. Once I saw a postcard with a photograph of a sign that said LAS VEGAS in pink neon lights. I'll bet there's going to be a lit-up sign that says Weaver. I'm pretty sure folks there rush in every direction, carrying heavy books under their arms, pencils tucked in their hair.

The more I think about Weaver, the less I think about Cool Breeze and the faster my legs move till—I can't help it—I'm in a full sprint.

"What's with you?" I hear Cool Breeze yell. "It's still school, you know."

I suck in my breath and close my eyes like I'm making a wish on a birthday cake. Then I open them and turn right into Weaver, into a brand-new world.

CHAPTER 16

September 3, 1963

Never mind signs with pink neon lights. The only signs I see here are the green street signs that crisscross on top of the yellow pole. The Main Street sign dips on a diagonal like nothing can hold it up anymore. I glance around for the sign in lights, the girls with pencils in their hair, but I only see a shop with a plastic Coca-Cola sign on the door. Wooden boards are nailed over the windows but the store's open.

An old white man with rippled skin and a rim of silver hair sits on a bench in front of the shop, his back curved like a crescent moon. I look at the ground like I'm supposed to, but when Cool Breeze catches up to me, I can tell he's staring at the man.

"Don't!" I whisper. I feel that worm stuck in my lip.

It seems Cool Breeze can't help himself.

But I can't help myself either. I've got enough troubles back in Kuckachoo. Lord knows I don't need more, so I grab Cool Breeze and yank him away.

As soon as we get down the road, he pulls a hand-drawn map out of his pocket. Me? I raise my eyebrows but keep my mouth shut.

"Left on Park Avenue. Cross the tracks. Then head north," he says.

And one thing's clear: Cool Breeze isn't too cool for maps after all.

When we get to the brick building, we see the school principal outside the door. He's dressed up special in a yellow and blue striped bow tie. "Welcome to West Thunder Creek Junior High School," he says.

When I hear those words, my chest opens up like a daisy.

I follow Cool Breeze through the crowded hallway to room 7, where I stand beside him in the doorway and take in the sight of our new teacher. The instant I see her, a rush of pictures fill my mind: The burning cross. The panic. The crowd. And Mrs. Jacks in the last row singing "We Shall Overcome."

Today she looks magical. She sits at a desk on a platform in front of the classroom. She wears a plaid dress and a string of beads—each one has a letter of the alphabet on it—and her carved mahogany walking stick rests at her side. But Mrs. Jacks isn't the most out-of-sight thing in the room. No sir! Get this: there's enough desks for every student in the class!

Well, Cool Breeze finds his courage somewhere. He juts his chin forward and saunters to an empty desk in the back of the classroom beside a girl wearing a pink skirt. When he gets there, he slinks down in his chair and sticks one leg out in the aisle.

Next it's my turn. I take a hint from him and thrust my chin forward. Then I claim an empty seat in the first row in front of a boy who's got horn-rimmed glasses. I choose that seat for two reasons: First, I can get there with the least number of steps. Second, I can't have Cool Breeze thinking I want to sit next to him.

Once all the seats fill, Mrs. Jacks clears her throat and leans across her desk. A hush grows as she looks up and down each row, inspecting one student at a time. When she sets her eyes on me, I feel her drink in the details of my life. A faint smile crosses her lips. I can't help but wonder, does she see the bald spot in the middle of my left eyebrow? Does she think I'm not ready for seventh grade? By the time she raises her head to examine the boy behind me, all I can say is it's a miracle I'm still alive.

The minutes drag on. There's no talking, only the sounds of kids setting pencils on their desks, fidgeting with their lunch bags, smoothing wrinkles in their clothes.

At long last our teacher smiles wide enough for all of us to see her thirty-two teeth, including the gold ones on the bottom.

Then *thwack!*

Before I can smile back, Mrs. Jacks slams her walking stick flat against her desk.

I cover my lip with my hand.

"That's it for the nice stuff," she says. "Listen up and listen up good. Y'all talking to the only teacher in the school who'll get within eleven feet of twelve-year-olds by choice. Y'all probably noticed that once you reach that special birthday, most teachers run from you like you've contracted the bubonic plague. Now I'm sure y'all understand to the utmost that other teachers here would rather be buried alive than take up such a despicable, unrewarding task as teaching the likes of you."

All I can say is when I'm a television teacher, I'm going to be nice. I'm not going to say things that make people twitch on the inside.

Mrs. Jacks lifts her walking stick over her head. "Y'all got one foot stuck in childhood, the other stuck in growing up. One hand plucking sun from daylight, the other picking moon from night. That's why I call y'all Midnights. And the thing is, you Midnights are losing your balance. That's where I come in. You need my help."

It's true. Sometimes I'm so mixed up I don't know what to think. And with Elias missing, and folks believing he's dead and gone, I could sure use someone to set me straight.

"We're all Negroes in this room?" she asks.

"Yes, ma'am," I answer along with everyone else.

"As Negroes, we've got to run faster, work harder, and think better than all the white folks combined, so that's what I'm going to expect y'all to do in the presence of a lady like me."

Again, Mrs. Jacks leans across her desk. Her eyes scuttle from student to student. "Well, at least y'all aren't dumb as a donkey's bottom like most grown-ups I know. They only believe what they see with their eyes," she says. She raises her eyebrows, her shoulders, her neck—almost her whole waddling body—without getting up from her seat.

Then she calls roll. When Mrs. Jacks gets to me, she says, "Miss Addie Ann Pickett, come over here."

While I push myself up from my seat, I hear kids from Darwiler, Titus, Bramble, and Weaver lean across their desks to gossip with their neighbors. "That gawky girl? Couldn't be *his* sister!"

Then *thwack!*

Silence.

As soon as I get to her desk, Mrs. Jacks whispers, "I'm awfully sorry about your brother." She takes my hand. "That boy was brilliant beyond brilliant. He was going places. College was just the start. He was going to join the movement, wake up this world. He was quite a speaker. Quite a leader. I know that wherever Elias is, he's thinking of you, wishing you well on your first day in seventh grade."

Well, I've already learned one thing in junior high school: Mrs. Jacks doesn't know how to whisper. Her raspy voice knits across the front row, tangling up one student after the next in its secret message.

If you're going to bawl, you should know why. But tonight, after my first day at West Thunder Creek Junior High School, I'm lying in bed, crying for no reason. I listen to the plinkity-plink of rain on the rooftop till nightfall before it occurs to me. Maybe there is a reason for my tummy turning inside

125

out. Maybe it's because at West Thunder Creek Junior High School nobody jumps rope at recess. Or maybe it's because I thought there might be a maid to clean out the classroom, but instead it's just like Acorn Elementary. We've got to scrub the classroom clean ourselves, so we can't start learning till the second week of school. Or maybe I'm a miserable wreck because I used to know Elias was okay even when Mama doubted it, but I don't have that feeling anymore.

I look at my brother's bed. A wreath rests on his pillow. The ladies from the church brought it with a basket of hush puppies. I lift the wreath off the pillow and place it against the window screen. Then I lie down on my brother's bed, and through the circle of the wreath, I watch the circle of the moon.

I know right now, when the moon is full, Mr. Mudge needs to harvest his crops. But who else besides my brother can pick four bushels of butter beans, three buckets of cucumbers, two bushels of peas, and seven bushels of sweet potatoes in a day? No one. That's why Mr. Mudge had to hire two people just to take my brother's place.

I remember the night Elias dragged himself into the kitchen last spring. "Picked my record!" he announced with a weary grin. "Y'all invited to free dinner at the Corner Store." Of course Elias was just joking. Everyone knows that even though we're free to buy what we want from the Corner Store, only white folks are allowed to sit at tables there.

Elias plunked a grocery bag onto our kitchen table. "But look at this," he said. He pulled out a sack of butter beans, four pork chops, and the four bottles of cola Mr. Mudge gave him for doing outstanding work.

By the time Mama and me cooked up the chops and beans, my brother was sound asleep. I pulled the sheet down from his face and said, "Time to eat!" But Elias snored on, so we celebrated without him. The chops were sensational! And Uncle Bump, Mama, and me ate those butter beans every which way: fried, mashed, and boiled.

That night, after I got in my bed, I belched louder than a tractor motor.

At long last Elias woke up. "Was it good?" he asked.

"The best!" I told him.

Elias grinned, but within a minute he was snoring again. Nothing could ruin his sweet dreams, not even me burping into the night.

Now rain thunders on the roof while I slip under my brother's sheet and smell baseball mixed up with sage. I shut my eyes. My breath slows till it sounds like the fall wind whistling through the trees. Then even the sound of my breath is gone.

There's a river in my chest. A river that runs clear and smooth over a hundred rocks in the way. I look down on the river from above. I feel the river from inside. Sunlight covers me. It is me. It's my skin. It's the sky. It's the edges of my mind. Gooseflesh runs over me like a wave. My skin prickles up high, waiting. And I know my brother's spirit is here—not his ghost but his spirit.

"What is it?" I ask.

I listen for his answer, but all I hear is rain hitting the roof.

"You don't need to say anything," I tell him. "I know you're proud."

CHAPTER 17

September 24, 1963

This afternoon I race home, plunk down at the kitchen table, and take out the short story called "Split Cherry Tree." It looks like Mrs. Jacks copied it on the mimeograph machine about five hundred years ago, so it's hard to make out all the words. The story was written by a man named Jesse Stuart. It takes place in the state of Kentucky, which in case you're wondering is two states north of here.

In the story, a boy goes on a field trip to a farm, where he chases a lizard up a cherry tree. Tough luck for the boy, the cherry tree breaks, so the boy's teacher makes him stay after school. For two hours! After school, the boy tells his teacher, "I'd rather you'd whip me with a switch and let me go home early. Pa will whip me anyway for getting home two hours late."

But the teacher in the story spares the rod and spoils the child. He won't whip the boy with the switch! I reckon that's why Mrs. Jacks likes this story, because tough as she is, she's just like that teacher. She doesn't believe in paddling our behinds to teach us our lessons either. So all told, I have to say "Split Cherry Tree" is real good.

The only bad part is I've got to copy the first three pages by tomorrow! Mrs. Jacks says copying stories is the best way for us to practice cursive writing and grammar. By the time I finish, my arm's asleep. But heck, I'd rather get my arm poked all over with pins and needles than get my behind whupped with a switch.

While I walk over to the Tates' house, I shake my arm to get the blood back in.

And wouldn't you know it, Ralphie picked today to fuss instead of sleep. As soon as I get him in the crib, I've got to use my tired old hand to run my finger back and forth across his forehead like Mama showed me. Back and forth. Back and forth. Till I'm almost dreaming myself.

But I'm not dreaming of good things. I'm dreaming a nightmare. Not a make-believe one but a real one, also known as my life.

It was nine days ago, and just when I thought things couldn't get any worse, they did. It was a Sunday, a couple hours after the morning service let out. The reverend sent word calling everyone back to First Baptist. Of course, after the cross burning, there was no way in the world Mama was going to let me go to church for anything other than the morning service, so I just stayed in the yard jumping rope, while everyone besides my family rushed back to church.

Only a few hours later, Mama, Uncle Bump, and me were finishing up supper, when someone rapped real hard on the side door. Mama opened it.

There stood Delilah, looking like she'd just come back from the underworld.

"Sit down, honey," Mama told her.

Even though it happened more than a week ago, I can see it clear like it's happening right now: Delilah standing in our doorway, Uncle Bump pulling out a kitchen chair, Mama taking Delilah by the elbow, leading her to the table.

"What's a matter?" I asked.

That was when Delilah spilled out the awful news. "There were four girls. They were at Sunday school. At the Negro church. In Birmingham. Birmingham, Alabama. They didn't do nothin' wrong. They didn't do nothin'."

Mama and me could only guess what horror was coming next, and I reckon we were content to let Delilah keep talking in circles so we wouldn't have to hear it.

But Uncle Bump went ahead and asked. "What happened, Delilah?"

"Someone bombed the church. Now they're dead. Dead!" Delilah buried her face in her hands and bawled, while questions fell all over me. *What did those girls ever do to deserve this? Were those girls just like Delilah and me? Will we get killed too?* I was sure I'd upchuck.

Mama's eyes filled. "That's terrible, just terrible," she said. Then she thought on it another second and said, "But

130

you know, girls, that was all the way over in Alabama."
Mama said it like Alabama was next to Japan, but I know
my map and that state's right next to Mississippi. Right
next to here! Mama stood, wiped her hands on her apron.
"Well, I'm gonna strike a match and bake some snicker-
doodles. You girls wanna help?"

Delilah and me both said no. Did Mama really think
baking cookies would make us forget what we just heard?
Delilah and me dragged ourselves outside to sit on the swing.

Ever since we heard the awful news, I try to play more
with Ralphie, because when I'm with him, I can almost forget about those four girls, and I can almost forget about my
brother a couple minutes in a row.

Now I look down at Ralphie. I'm still running my
weary finger across his brow, glad he doesn't hate me yet.
But I know one day his daddy will teach him to. So I try to
fix it in my mind how Ralphie is right now: how innocent,
how sweet. But the second I get a good look at him, I see his
cheeks, they're bright red!

I feel his forehead with the back of my hand. He's
warm. Then Ralphie moans. I'm not sure what to do. What
if he's caught a bug? What if he's got a fever? I couldn't
stand the sight of him sweating and groaning, so I run to
find Mama to ask if she thinks Ralphie's all right.

I rush through the sitting room into the Tates' bedroom, only to find Mrs. Tate at her desk, a pen in her hand,
a stack of envelopes at her side. She wipes her fingers under
her eyes.

"Sorry, ma'am," I say. "I thought it was Mama in here
changing the linens."

"She's out back hanging laundry," Mrs. Tate says, her voice scratchy. A tear rolls down her cheek.

"Ma'am?" I say. And I reckon it's best just to find Mama and ask her about Ralphie, because Mrs. Tate doesn't look like she needs trouble. I'm about to dash downstairs and out to the backyard, when I hear the sitting room door creak open.

"Where are you, Penelope?" Mr. Tate shouts.

And wouldn't you know it, here I am, stuck in the bedroom, frozen solid, while Mrs. Tate gasps. At first I think it's because she's surprised as I am to find that man home in the early afternoon when he's supposed to be on the road selling seeds. But that's not the half of it, because the next thing I know, Mrs. Tate hurries over to the bookshelf and pulls out a book.

But when she opens it up, I see it's not a book at all. It doesn't have any pages inside. It's an empty box. Mrs. Tate shoves her envelopes into the box, and she's sliding the box back onto the shelf when that good-for-nothing husband of hers stomps into the room. He slams his spitting glass down on the bedside table. Then he takes one look at me and shouts, "What's this dishrag doing in our bedroom?"

My heart pounds. I fix my eyes on the floor like I'm supposed to.

And that's when I see it: one of Mrs. Tate's secret envelopes. It's fallen smack in the middle of the carpet!

When Mr. Tate bends over to spit his chewing tobacco in the glass, he spots the secret envelope too. He reaches down to pick it up.

But I don't know what gets into me. I scoop it up first.

"Sorry, ma'am," I say. "Must've dropped your letter. I'll take it to the post office."

Then I hurry out the bedroom, through the sitting room, and down the hallway while my fingers, they dance all over that envelope, and my breath, it rattles around in my chest.

Somehow I get to Ralphie's room. I turn the envelope over in my hand and see it's addressed to J. D. Foster in New Orleans, Louisiana. Who on earth that is, I've got no idea. I'd sure like to find out, but seeing as reading this letter would get me fired or worse, I decide to check on Ralphie instead.

He's quiet. His forehead, it's dry and cool, and I reckon maybe he had a stomach upset is all. Well, I've sure got one too, because here I am holding this secret letter.

And now I hear footsteps.

Faster than a duck can dunk, I hide that letter under Ralphie's crib mattress.

"Sorry 'bout my husband," Mrs. Tate says, stepping into Ralphie's bedroom. "He doesn't mean anything by it."

"Yes, ma'am," I say.

"But I want you to know, Addie Ann, those letters . . . they're nothing."

"Yes, ma'am," I say.

Then that husband of hers yells from downstairs. "Tonight I want my dinner hot!"

Mrs. Tate sighs. And no one has to tell me she's sick and tired of that man. Why, he's meaner than a junkyard dog! Still, she rushes out the room to the top of the stairs and calls down, "Yes, dear."

After the front door slams shut, Mrs. Tate hurries back to her son's room. I can see by the squint in her eyes, she's wondering if I read her secret letter or not, so I dip my hand back under the crib mattress and fish around till my thumb bangs into a pointed corner of the envelope. Then I pull the letter out and hand it over.

Well, no use sticking around. I pick up the laundry basket. But just as I grab the doorknob, Mrs. Tate tells me to put the basket down.

"Have a seat," she says, "in the rocking chair."

She's got her letter back, so I can't imagine what else she wants. And it feels awful backward to have her standing in front of me while I'm sitting down like I'm on a throne.

"The thing is, Addie Ann," she whispers, her voice in a pinch, "those letters in the book . . ."

"What book, Mrs. Tate?" I ask. My mama didn't raise no stupid fool. I know when to keep my mouth shut.

"Well, I'm just writing my childhood friend J. D. Foster," she says.

"Okay, ma'am," I say.

But I must be looking at her funny because then she says, "Oh, I just hide the letters in the box 'cause my husband don't like J. D. Never did. So do me a favor, Addie Ann, and keep this our little secret. I wouldn't want it getting back to Mr. Tate."

All of a sudden, I've got to go to the bathroom. Real bad.

"I'll tell you what," she says.

I press my legs together. Then I pray Ralphie will wake up and give out a good scream so I can get on out of here.

But wouldn't you know it, he must feel a whole lot better, because his little tummy goes up and down in gentle waves.

"I been so lonely with my husband gone selling seeds dawn to dusk, and J. D. is the only one who would truly understand. The problem is J. D. moved to Louisiana last year and I ain't got the address. So I'm just saving all my letters inside the book box till I find out where J. D. is."

Mrs. Tate's crying, so I tell her, "Well, of course you keep your letters in the book box, ma'am. It's the right thing to do."

She sniffles.

"The right thing," I say, and hand her a cloth diaper so she can wipe her eyes.

At long last Mrs. Tate gets ahold of herself. "Now I know you're a good girl, so don't let me hear you've gone and told your mama or anyone else about this. I don't want trouble," she says.

"I don't want trouble neither, ma'am," I say.

By the time I get home and make it all the way through dinner, I can't think of anything else but Mrs. Tate's secret. I'm lying in bed and her secret's blowing up like a balloon inside my chest. I can't help but wonder what J. D. looks like. Does she wear a silly hat with plastic fruit on the brim or a pretty one with a white bow?

I dance into the kitchen where Mama's cleaning up.

"Why ain't you sleeping?" she asks me.

"Something juicy," I say.

"What's that?" Mama dries the lid of a pot.

"Oh, you'll want to sit down for this one," I say.

"All right."

I can tell Mama's trying not to act overinterested, but I know she is, because she dries the pot lid handle over and over again.

After I cross my fingers under the table, I say, "It's like this." Then I change the story just a drip-drop to fix the part about me busting into the Tates' bedroom without rapping on the door. "I knocked and Mrs. Tate told me to come on in. She was sitting at her desk writing a letter," I say.

"Yes," says Mama.

"Well, Mrs. Tate's envelope fell on the floor just as Mr. Tate stormed in. When he bent over to spit in his tobacco glass, Mrs. Tate pointed to the envelope on the floor like I should pick it up." Far be it from me to tell Mama I volunteered myself into this whole mess. "Then Mrs. Tate shooed me out the door, so I went to check on Ralphie."

"Don't sound unusual," Mama says. "That Mr. Tate's a mean skunk."

But then I tell Mama all about how Mrs. Tate let me sit in the rocking chair while she carried on about how lonely she is, and how J. D. is the only one in the whole world who truly understands her. No doubt she writes all about what she thinks of her husband in those letters to J. D.

Mama sits at the kitchen table and listens cotton-eyed while I describe the secret book box. By the time I'm through, Mama's got worried teardrops in her eyes, and I just know if those tears fall down her cheeks into her mouth, they'll taste bitter like horseradish. She cuts her eyes at me real mean. "Telling someone's secret is just like telling a lie," she says. "You told me. That's bad enough."

The balloon blowing up in my chest, it sinks.

"What?" I ask. I'm more than a little confused, because from all my experience, when someone keeps a secret, they're keeping the truth from getting out. So telling a secret's like spreading around the truth. What could be wrong with that?

But I reckon Mama doesn't see it my way because she says, "If you say one word of this to anyone—and that's Delilah included—I'ma send that cat of yours to live with Aunt Adelaide up in Baton Rouge!" She leans forward, reaches across the table, and lifts my chin with her finger. "I'll take that scoundrel there myself."

After I get in bed, I *tweet, click, click,* and Flapjack pounces through the open window. I snuggle up with him under the sheet, but I don't bother to scare him with what Mama said. He's got nothing to worry about. I'm not going to tell a soul.

CHAPTER 18

September 28, 1963

I've gone three and a half days without telling Mrs. Tate's secret to anyone else. I'm sitting on my swing, thinking about how much I've matured, when Uncle Bump moseys out of his shed and asks me to join him fishing down the bayou. It being Saturday, I tell Uncle Bump I can't see why not. I've already calculated twenty-two fractions, including improper ones, and I've already learned my Latin roots, like *vis*, which means "to see."

As soon as I change out my dress into my T-shirt and jeans, Uncle Bump and me set off for the river. He carries two poles and a jar of worms. Of course, I haven't been fishing in years, so I forget how disgusting the whole thing will be.

When we get to the bank, I get a sick feeling because I've seen some catfish and they're bigger than cats. I don't want to kill no catfish.

"We're just gonna catch them baby ones," Uncle Bump says.

But I don't want to kill no babies either.

Still, I can tell Uncle Bump's glad for the company. He's all about showing me the night crawlers. They're wiggling inside the glass jar. He pulls out one of the worms, stabs it with the metal hook, then ties the hook to the line, and casts the line into the water. Then he hands me the pole and fixes up his own.

Once Uncle Bump and me are standing on the bank holding our poles, there are no worms to look at and I like it better. We stare out at the river without a pull on our lines, while the fall wind sends ripples across the water, making it look rough and wild. And I reckon I get to thinking about things besides fish, because soon, I let out a sigh loud enough for Uncle Bump to hear.

"What's wrong?" he asks.

"Nothin'."

"That ain't a nothin' kind of sigh," he says. "Between you and me, I think your brother will be back."

The dandelion sun peeks out from behind the cottony clouds. To know Uncle Bump hasn't given up makes me weak all over.

Uncle Bump tells me whenever he goes to work at the General Merchandise Store in Franklindale, he stops to talk to my brother's friends who live nearby. He also sent another letter to Aunt Adelaide up in Baton Rouge and spent a pile of change at the pay telephone booth to see if any of the civil rights groups had word. "It's tough," Uncle Bump says. "But no one's heard a thing."

I stare out at the water two more minutes before I'm ready to talk. Truth be told, I tell Uncle Bump things most twelve-year-old girls won't tell their mamas. I can say anything, and I know he won't get worried or mad. Sure I got some hope from Delilah's ghost ceremony, but some days I can't help it, my faith dwindles to a drop. "It's hard to keep believing," I say.

Uncle Bump wraps an arm round my shoulders, pulls me close. And I'm more than grateful he's by my side.

Staring out at the water, I can't help but picture the bayou, Buck Fowler, my brother's sneaker. But I don't want to think about it anymore, so I do like Mama and switch the subject.

"When you were my age, did you ever like . . . you know?" I ask.

"Well, sure, sure I did!" Uncle Bump tugs on his pole and lowers the line.

"Who?" I ask.

"Who what?"

"Who'd you love?"

"Oh!" Uncle Bump says. "Hmmm . . . Loved my mama. Loved my papa. Loved my sister. Even loved that old man across the tracks."

"Not that way," I say.

"Ouch!" Uncle Bump tries to pick a splinter out of his thumb.

"Well, who'd you love?" I ask.

But he's silent like God cut off the supply of nouns, verbs, and adjectives in his throat.

"It's not a big deal," I tell him, even though it's a huge one. That's because everyone has the kind of love I want. Sure I'm only in seventh grade, but that kind of love is all stopped up in my heart. Maybe I don't know how to act with a boy. Maybe I don't know how to dress or what to say, which is bad enough, but what makes it eighty-five bushels worse is that Delilah always wears the perfect dress and says, "Thrills, chills, and charges!" at the exact right time, so any boy I love loves her instead.

"Seems something particular's on your mind," Uncle Bump says.

I nod but I won't look in his eyes. I don't want him to see all the pain whirling in mine. I fix my gaze on the swirling water.

"Cool Breeze?" he asks.

I swallow. I was going to tell him, but it would've taken hours to get there.

Uncle Bump nods. He knew it all along.

"He's everything," I say.

"Ain't that something! I never met a person who was everything."

"Well, I have!" I say. It's not just that Cool Breeze is the only other student from Kuckachoo going to seventh grade, but he can run a mile in four minutes fifty-nine seconds flat, not to mention he has the cutest dimples, and he can solve equations faster than Mrs. Jacks can write them on the board. "Thing is," I say, "he'll always like Delilah." Then I think about my Latin root and say, "To him I'm just in*vis*ible."

"Why's that?" Uncle Bump asks.

Tears sting the back of my throat. I swipe under my nose, but it doesn't work, because a couple of them fall right down my face. "Every boy likes Delilah. Nothing ever changes," I say.

"That's right," Uncle Bump says. "Nothing does change."

My breath is high in my chest, running. I can't believe he agrees. The future's stacking up in front of me, day after day, the same. Nothing changes. Me and Cool Breeze walking to school, back and forth from Kuckachoo to Weaver, three whole miles in each direction, the two of us together with nothing to say, Cool Breeze not even knowing I'm there.

" 'Cept for one thing," Uncle Bump says.

I wait for him to say what it is, the one thing. But wouldn't you know it, his fishing pole bends. He yanks hard to pull in the line.

Right now I don't care anything about catfish. I want to know what's the one thing that will change. "What is it?" I ask.

Uncle Bump doesn't hear me. He's too busy breaking out a smile bigger than the Magnolia State. That's because he's got a catfish huge as a dog on the line. When he gets it onto the bank, I can see it's got whiskers.

"What's the one thing?" I ask again. Then I turn away, my back to Uncle Bump and that fish, because I don't want to see the part that comes next. The part where the poor fish thrashes on the bank and Uncle Bump helps it to its death.

After he packs up the dead catfish and the live night crawlers, we walk back and Uncle Bump asks, "If you ain't got the belly to fish, then why do you eat it?" And I can't answer that question straight, because I like smoked Delta catfish with brown sugar much as anyone.

It's not till we get all the way home I ask him to tell me once and for all: What's the one thing that will change? What's the one thing that'll break me out of this dreadful existence?

"You," he says. Then he sets to work building a fire to smoke that catfish.

Later, after I swallow the last bite and lick the brown sugar off my fingers, I'm still wondering just what he means.

CHAPTER 19

October 13, 1963

Ever since Delilah gave up jumping double Dutch, she's taken up beauty. I don't mean just thinking about it and talking about it. I mean really working at it. Just this morning Delilah's cousin Bessie gave her some of Dr. Fred Palmer's Skin Whitener, so now Delilah has it in her mind I need a new look.

Here we are sitting on her front steps. She opens the jar of cream and dips her pinkie in. "It's gotta last me till I get to New York and make my own money," she says, and rubs one tiny drop into each of my cheeks. "Even this little bit should help."

Bessie also let Delilah borrow a plastic case with a rainbow of eye shadows inside it. Now Delilah holds the case up to my face to figure out which color matches my brown eyes best.

"You've got blue tones in your skin," she tells me.

"No, I'm brown," I say.

"You don't understand," she says, and laughs. "You've got cool blue tones and I've got warm red ones." She's still explaining the whole theory when out the corner of my cool eyeball, I catch sight of Reverend Walker harrumphing down the lane.

"Look!" I say, and point.

There's a large parcel of folks gathered round him and one thing's clear: something juicy's going down.

"You've gotta let me do it later," Delilah says. "It'll bring out your features."

"Only if you make me pretty as a speckled pup," I tell her.

"I'll try," she says.

Truth be told, I doubt any makeup can turn me into a speckled pup, but I still want Delilah to fix my eyes. I hate the way they look so plain like the rest of me, but I must admit, they're awful good for seeing.

Delilah and me join our neighbors in the lane. Since church let out just an hour ago, you'd think the reverend would be tired of talking. But that's not the way it's fixing to be. "Praise Jesus," he says. He holds a large cardboard poster in his hands. The second I see it, I know exactly what this ruckus is about.

A few days back, I was making Ralphie his favorite treat in the Tates' kitchen while Mrs. Tate and her friends were drawing up posters in the living room. I held Ralphie on my hip, as I stirred the pot of applesauce on the stove and listened to them talk.

"Between his new shop in Muscadine County and his poor mama in Florida, Mr. Mudge hasn't made it back to Kuckachoo for three weeks!" Mrs. Worth said. "He gave me the garden keys. He said with the grand opening scheduled for early November, there's no way he'll make it back to town for the picking."

"What a shame!" Miss Springer chirped.

She sure didn't sound sorry Mr. Mudge wouldn't make it to the picking.

"Well, at least the garden was laid by before he left," Miss Springer said. "After that, there's nothing to do but wait for everything to grow anyhow."

"Well, I stopped by the garden just yesterday," Mrs. Tate said. "The corn lining the gate is taller than me! I couldn't see a thing past it."

Then, out of nowhere, Miss Springer asked, "Have you heard the rumors?"

"What rumors?" Mrs. Tate asked.

"'Bout Mr. Adams's will," Miss Springer said.

I almost dropped poor Ralphie on the floor.

"Well, I was down at the Very Fine Fabric Shop the other day. Dorotha told me she overheard the girl who cleans the shop tell someone that in his will Old Man Adams left half his garden to the Negroes," Miss Springer said.

"You can't be serious!" Mrs. Worth said.

I pressed Ralphie close to me with one hand, stirred the pot round and round with the other.

"I am serious," Miss Springer replied. "And knowing how that man felt in his old age, I can believe it's true. This is a *community* garden. It seems Mr. Adams wanted the whole Kuckochoo *community* to participate."

Well, if that didn't send Mrs. Worth into a tizzy! "You don't know that and I don't know that. We'll never know what Mr. Adams intended. By the time he wrote up his will, that salty old buzzard was nothing but a colored-loving cuckoo," Mrs. Worth said.

Words fought inside my throat. They climbed all over each other trying to get out. *I know what the will said! He left us the land too!* I could hear the words inside me, screaming out, over and over. But who was I to interrupt a white ladies' conversation?

My hands got so shaky, though, I had to set Ralphie on the floor. And of course, he went running out the open back door into the yard. I turned the knob on the burner to low and chased after him, so I didn't get to hear another word those ladies said. But I can tell you one thing: they sure had a good fight, the three of them, before they finished drawing up their posters.

Now Reverend Walker holds one and shouts, "We need to be moving that movement—that movement that's brewing in Birmingham, that movement that's mixing life upside down in Jackson—we need to be moving it right here to Kuckachoo."

The reverend turns the sign round so we can see it. Then he reads it out loud:

*The Kuckachoo Garden Club
invites you to a picking party!
TUESDAY, SUNRISE
Free vegetables! Bring sacks!*

He points to the purple writing at the bottom of the sign and reads:

P.S. Negroes invited to pick at noon.

"This garden's supposed to be for everyone!" Mrs. Montgomery shouts.

"I hear you," says the reverend.

"What you sayin'?" Brother Babcock asks.

"I'm saying sure our empty bellies can go growling for another thousand years. We always got by on less than nothing. However"—the reverend raises a finger in the air—"we can't go hungering for our dignity one more day. We're not gonna pick at noon to gather no scraps!"

And it's clear that at long last the reverend's finished thinking about the garden. He actually does have a plan.

"We're going at the crack of dawn just like every other Kuckachookian," he says.

"Praise the Lord!" yells Delilah.

I reckon she belongs in the amen corner! And dog my cats, suddenly she's all about that picking. "I'll do your eyes later," she tells me.

Well, that's fine with me. I don't need any more color on my eyes. I've got all the color I need right in front of them. I'm seeing blue and red stars, I'm so angry about this garden.

148

"We need to do this for Emmett Till," the reverend shouts. "And for Medgar Evers. For the four young girls murdered last month in Birmingham—Denise McNair, Carole Robertson, Cynthia Wesley, and Addie Mae Collins. And for Elias Pickett, our very own son, wherever he may be."

I've thought of Emmett. I've thought of Medgar. I've thought about those four girls, one my age, one named Addie like me. And Lord knows I've thought about my brother. But to think of them all at the same time, Elias along with the dead, it's just too much. Too much to bear!

I stumble away from the crowd to the edge of the lane. But the reverend's words boom across the dirt straight to me: "There comes a time when a man's dignity's worth more than his life. Oh Lord, this is our time!"

I know the reverend's right. We can't just sit by and let them steal what's ours. They've taken our land, they've chased my brother away, they've taken too many lives. And even if I get beaten or put in jail, it doesn't matter. I'm ready to fight.

Reverend Walker charges down the lane. Most of the men follow. As usual, they're going to sort things out without us ladies and children, so Delilah and me hurry on over to my porch to sit beside our mamas. No doubt they're fretful as we are, and I reckon we could all lean on each other after what we've just heard. But soon as I settle on the step, I'm sorry I'm there. That's because Mama and Mrs. Montgomery, they're shaking their tails at each other about whether we should go to the picking or not.

Mama says, "There's no way for us to show up for the

picking at sunrise without infuriating the white folk. If we do that, we may as well shoot ourselfs 'cause that's what happens when you make white folk think twice before they even thunk once. If we go, we'll get ourselfs killed."

Mrs. Montgomery turns to me and says, "Looks like your mama's turned into Eartha Kitt."

I sure wish Mama looked like a beautiful actress, but right about now, her eyebrows are knitted together and the circles under her eyes look like mud puddles. I hate to say it, but Mama doesn't look like Eartha Kitt at all, so I'm not sure what Mrs. Montgomery's talking about.

But now Mrs. Montgomery says to Mama, "No need for the drama, Eartha. We should show up, but not till noon. That way, we're taking up good on the offer but not losing out on the food we need."

But Mama doesn't like Mrs. Montgomery's teasing. Her bottom lip quivers just like mine. "We're not going," she says. "We can't go. Not you. Not me. None of us. Sunrise? Noon? The hour don't matter."

Truth be told, sometimes Mrs. Montgomery takes things one step too far. Even though she and Mama, they're the best of friends, sometimes she hurts Mama real bad. "Since when can a Pickett afford to skip out on a free sack of beans?" Mrs. Montgomery asks.

I reckon that does it. Mama stands right up, hand on her hip. "Well, I don't see you bringing out the lamb chops on a regular basis neither," she says, and storms inside.

At dinner, Mama's still steaming. She yanks the maca-roni and cheese from the oven. "She ain't got no sense 'bout how to protect her family," she says, more to the food than to anyone. It seems Mama's cooked up an extra-special meal just to prove our family's got more than enough to eat.

"Mmm! Mmm!" Uncle Bump says.

I want to tell Mama that truth be told, I reckon Mrs. Montgomery's right. We should be at that picking. What's ours is ours. I want to tell her that Elias wouldn't like to see her all scared, that Elias would want her to fight for our rights. But right about now Mama's just a deer collapsing in the forest to lick her wounds. And nothing I say about the picking will do anything but hurt her more.

So I do what we Picketts do best: I change the subject. "Wow, Mama!" I say, and shovel in another spoonful of macaroni and cheese. "This sure is scrumptious!"

But what do you know? In the middle of my compliments, Mama goes and switches the subject right back. She stares at Uncle Bump. "You ain't going, I ain't going, and you, Addie Ann," she says, "you ain't going to that picking neither."

Seeing Mama so scared scares me. I reckon ever since Elias left, her age is speeding up faster than the days and the years. And one thing's clear: Mama isn't about to let any more danger destroy our family, no matter how much dignity it might cost.

" 'Scuse me," she says.

The instant she leaves the table, I get a twisty feeling in my belly. No one has to say my brother's name for us to know he's all she can think about. Yesterday Mama met with the reverend, and even he had to admit Elias might be in God's hands.

I don't know why the reverend thinks that the more days my brother's gone, the more evidence he's never coming back. But I reckon it's like Mrs. Jacks says: grown-ups only believe what they see in front of their eyes. If they don't see something, it isn't there. So even though the reverend's a spiritual man, he can't help it. He's still a grown-up.

CHAPTER 20

October 15, 1963, Dawn

From my seat on the swing, I see the sky's the soft blue it only turns fall mornings. A few stars still sparkle. And right about now, the world seems half-asleep, stuck in a place where everything's all right and everyone who should be in it is. Past the oak leaves, I watch folks stroll down the lane, wiping sleep from their eyes. Most every one of them is off to church, where they're going to meet up before the picking. They're following Reverend Walker's plan, showing up to pick at dawn, even though us Negroes weren't invited till noon.

No one seems to notice me out here on my swing. No

one except Delilah. She's wearing her dress for courage, the orange one with the yellow iris down the back.

"You coming?" she asks, and walks into the yard.

Course I'm more than dying to go to that picking and see what all the fuss is about. I want to see what Mrs. Tate's been planning for months. I want to know what stand the reverend will take, and if he'll get the white folks to give us any kind of respect. But if I go to that garden picking and Mama hears of it, I'll never see daylight again.

"Gotta go to school," I say.

But here's Delilah fixing her eyes on something bigger than her own appearance and getting all high-and-mighty about it too. "You should come," she says. "It's the right thing to do."

And I can't believe it: Delilah Montgomery telling me, Addie Ann Pickett, the right thing to do! I push my feet against the ground to set the swing in motion. "You're just jealous I get to walk all the way with Cool Breeze," I tell her.

"Thrills, chills, and charges!" she says, and throws back her shoulders. Her pecan eyes roast with determination. Then she turns round and folds into the wave of folk marching down the lane.

I want to jump off the swing and run after her, but Mama would boil up if she found out I even thought about going to the garden picking.

More neighbors shuffle by till at long last Cool Breeze saunters into the yard looking fine as ever.

"Well, come on!" he calls, and walks away.

I grab my schoolbag from beside the swing and race to

catch up. But when I reach him, Cool Breeze seems like he's concentrating on something real important. Together, we rush down Kuckachoo Lane. As usual, we don't toss a word between us.

But the second we turn onto the highway, Cool Breeze pushes the mulberry branches out of the way and steps into the bush. Before I know what's happening, his long fingers are digging into the crook of my arm. And here I am in the bush too, my face right near his. I smell ginger on his breath. I take in his long lashes. My arms and legs buzz. And all of a sudden, it's clear: the silence between us as we walk to school each day isn't empty silence. No sir. It's full. Full silence overflowing with yearning, desire, and love. Now I'm tingly all over.

Cool Breeze leans toward me.

I pucker up, and in the humid air, I relish the kiss to come.

My heart flutters like a sheet on a drying line. It all happens so fast. I think many thoughts at once, feel everything at the same time. Soon we'll kiss. Then we'll walk hand in hand. One day we'll get married.

But all of a sudden, his lips screech to a halt beside my ear.

"I'm going to the picking," he whispers.

My dream, it shatters like the honey jar in the Corner Store lot.

"You can't tell anyone at school where I'm at," he says.

I suffer my humiliation among the mulberry branches. Not only doesn't Cool Breeze kiss me, but now he's made me late. And being late for class at West Thunder Creek

Junior High School is nothing like being late at Acorn Elementary.

My chest tightens in a double panic.

"It'll be a sight!" he says, and smiles. "With the rumors floating, you know. I can't miss that." Then he says, "Why don't you come too?"

I pull my schoolbag over my shoulder. "I can't. My mama would find out."

"Now how's she gonna find out? So many folks will be there. They'll think it's odd if you're not there."

Well, I've got to admit, Cool Breeze Huddleston can sure think out a problem. He's got a point. If no one from my whole family goes to the picking, folks will wonder whether us Picketts are loyal to the cause. And right about now, we can't afford to have anyone thinking that.

I nod to myself, and Cool Breeze can see I'm coming along. But then I hit a rock in my thinking. A rock so big it's blocking the road and I can't see any way over it. "What about Mrs. Jacks?" I ask. "She's gonna rip you up, and me too, if we skip out." There's no explaining to Mrs. Jacks why you're late, or why your homework's only part finished, or why you slump down at your desk. I can hear her saying it right now: "I went to sixteen years of school—that's more years than any of you been singing to the Lord—and I never, I mean never, missed a day. Learning's too precious to give up even one minute for something silly like your stomach aching or goblins sneaking out your nose."

I push aside the branches and climb out the thicket.

Cool Breeze follows.

By the way he still tries to convince me, I reckon he

really does want me to go to the picking with him. And if I do, that kiss might land on my lips by the end of the day.

A school bus rushes down the highway. As usual, a few white students yell something nasty out the window. No matter how many times it happens, their taunting voices still make me want to scream.

"Do as you like," he says. "But trust me, even if Mrs. Jacks does find out, she'll be nothing but proud when we tell her we stood up for ourselves. Heck," he says, and laughs, "she's probably gonna make us give a report to the class so we can be examples to others."

It's true. Mrs. Jacks always says we need to dream bigger and fight harder than everyone else just because we're Negroes. Maybe Cool Breeze is right. Maybe she'll put us up in front of the class. Now wouldn't that be something! When Elias was in her class, Mrs. Jacks asked him to teach the other students how to give a persuasive speech. She said Elias could orate just like Frederick Douglass. Mama cried, she was so proud of him for that.

"We'll take the back path to church so your mama won't see," Cool Breeze says. Of course, he doesn't have to worry about his mama finding out, because he said she's gone down to Sunflower for the day to take care of her sick sister. And he sure doesn't need to worry about his daddy finding out, because he split when Cool Breeze was in first grade.

"You're already late for school anyhow!" he says. Then he takes off running down the path through the woods.

I haven't had time to make up my whole mind about it, but I figure, Cool Breeze, he's smarter than me. So I push the branches out of the way and tear down the path after him. My schoolbag thumps against my hip. By the time we turn off to First Baptist, I've got to hunch over, hands on my knees, to rest.

Cool Breeze huffs and puffs too, but he stands up straight like our sprint was nothing. "Here," he says. "Gimme your bag."

I hand over my schoolbag, and Cool Breeze sets it down beside his in a ditch. "Now no one will know we're supposed to be at school at all," he says.

I smile, thinking how smart he is, how he's seeing to all the details, how he's taking care of me.

Then the two of us go on inside the church and stand in back. If I didn't know better, I would've thought it was the Easter service. There's not an empty pew in the place. By the look of things, lots of kids from Acorn Elementary are missing class today. Why, they're sitting right with their parents.

Up front, the reverend bellows. Each word swells in his belly, then shimmies across his tongue. "This past spring, the young Negroes of Birmingham stood up when they marched for equality. Six, twelve, sixteen years old. Some were bitten by police dogs. Some were toppled by the force of fire hoses. But their actions helped desegregate Birmingham's downtown stores."

And I know "segregate" means "to separate," so "desegregate" must mean "to mix back together again." I whisper that word, "desegregate," and it tickles the roof of my mouth.

"In Jackson," the reverend says, "although it was

against the law, Negro college students stood up by trying to eat at a white lunch counter while white customers threw ketchup on them and beat them bloody. And even your little old reverend here stood up this summer, when he marched on the nation's capital and urged Congress to pass the president's civil rights bill."

And I still can't believe that our very own Reverend Walker went all the way to the nation's capital on a bus and told our country's president what he ought to do. One thing's clear: our reverend's come back a changed man. At long last his name fits him like a Sunday suit, because now Reverend Walker doesn't just talk the talk, he walks the walk! He wants to get up and fight! Of course, he won't fight with weapons—only wisdom and courage. It's what Martin Luther King Jr. calls nonviolent resistance.

"Kuckachoo may not be a big city and Dr. King may never stop at our door, but that doesn't mean we're gonna sit by and watch while white folks steal our dignity right out of our hands," the reverend says.

He shuts his eyes, rocks on his heels, and prays the Lord will watch over us. After all that, he picks up something from behind the pulpit and carries it down the center aisle. When he passes, I see he's got a long metal stick in his hand.

"What's that?" I ask Cool Breeze.

"A crowbar," he tells me.

The whole lot of us follow the reverend out the church door. Elmira hands us each a picking sack.

"Well, why's he need a crowbar?" I ask Cool Breeze.

"Beats me!" he says.

Then we all trek down Magnolia Row, and I wonder if

joining this garden picking will be the sorriest thing I've ever done in my life. But if I tell this to Cool Breeze, he'll think I'm nothing but a nervous Nelly. And I know Cool Breeze, he's impressed I'm here. So I walk on, my heart hammering in my chest, my soul praying the white folks won't fire on us.

When we get to the tall fence that borders Old Man Adams's farm, Reverend Walker sets the crowbar down on the grass. Then he weaves his fingers together and tells Cool Breeze to place a foot inside his clasped hands.

While Cool Breeze steps up and hoists himself over the fence, folks beside me hold hands and whisper. I hear only pieces. Pieces of whispers.

Dead.

The whispers get stuck in my hair.

Fight.

They wrap around my neck.

Ours.

The whispers cut off my breath and the grass moves and the reverend fades and the people fall and I can't breathe and the whispers and my breath are short and fast and I'm alone. Here alone. And I won't call Flapjack. This is my mess. Not his. Then there's sunlight. Sunlight bouncing off the silver crowbar back in the reverend's hand.

"Heads up!" the reverend shouts, and throws the crowbar over the fence.

The sunlight on the crowbar flying over the fence covers me in an arc. An arc of glitter. Yellow and orange glitter. I close my eyes. But I'm not under the sheet. I'm not in bed. *Breathe!* I tell myself. *Breathe!* The long strand of whispers breaks off my neck, breaks apart, into a thousand tiny butterflies. The butterflies fly. Fly away. Over the fence. Into the garden. *Breathe!*

My belly gets full. Full of sunlight. Full of breath. I'm not here. Not beside the fence. Not going to the picking. I'm above myself. Looking down at that river. That river flowing. That river rushing over rocks. Rushing fast. A force without beginning or end. A force that can't be broken. I'm above the river, looking down on it, watching sunlight sparkle on the water's surface. Gooseflesh washes over me. I hear him. I don't see him. I hear him. "Stand up," my brother says. "Stand up."

By the time I open my eyes again, I don't hear whispers at all. It's quiet. And I don't hear my breath alone. I hear everyone breathing hard together. Even though I'm terrified to be here at this picking, for one whole minute I'm sure I'm doing the right thing. I know Elias, he's proud. And now that Cool Breeze has followed the reverend's instructions—taken out the nails and removed a section of the fence—we all crawl through before the whole lot of us get too chicken and run back home.

We march single file down the edge of the field, between a wall of sky-high corn and the tall wooden fence, dragging our empty sacks, singing "We Shall Overcome." From the wavery sound of our voices, I can tell that everyone's frightened as me.

When we get to the garden gate, we spread ourselves across the iron bars, another wall of corn at our backs. I see faces on the other side of the garden gate. The mayor's red cheeks, the sheriff's bulging neck, and Mrs. Tate's wide-open mouth. And that's when the truth of the matter sends a chill right through me: We're inside the garden. The white folks, they're left out!

Before Mrs. Tate can spot me, I take a step back and hide in the cornstalks. Although I can't see the reverend, I hear his voice rumble as he shouts out to the white folks, "We don't want your leftovers!"

When I hear the reverend's words, I feel shimmery, like sunlight on steaming hot pavement. Here's the reverend yelling to white folks about what's on our minds and we all could die because of it! I reckon I never did think this picking thing through, because till about an hour ago, I was going to school like a good girl.

And for all the reverend's fighting talk, the mayor just chuckles like the sight of us inside the garden's nothing but a ridiculous joke. "We're happy to welcome y'all at noon," the mayor says.

"When nothing's left but rotten cabbage!" the reverend shouts.

All of a sudden, I see it plain and clear: Mama's smarter than all us fools put together. And now I'm cracking mad I was dumb enough to skip school and get caught up in this dangerous mess.

I glimpse out from my hiding spot in the stalks. Mrs. Worth uses the keys to unlock the garden gate. Then the sheriff pulls his pistol from its holster with one hand and pushes open the garden gate with the other to let the white pickers through.

Mrs. Worth crosses into the garden first. As soon as she does, she crinkles up her nose and shouts to us

Negroes, "Didn't you read the sign? You're not invited to pick till noon!" When she yells, the daisies on top of her sun hat shake, but not half as much as I do. Then Mrs. Worth turns to the sheriff and says, "Oh, my! I plumb forgot. Coloreds can't read!"

After the white folks push aside the cornstalks and stomp into the garden, the reverend blazes his own path into the rows. Cool Breeze grabs my wrist and draws me in behind our reverend. Then all of us stand at the garden's edge and watch the white pickers spread across the rows.

It doesn't take but a minute before we hear the white children laugh awful loud. They're delighted to pick those collards and squash that should belong to us all. And I can't believe how unfair this is, that they're squealing with joy while we stand here and watch them steal what's ours.

But soon the laughter fades. A scary silence surrounds us.

That's when I look real close at the ground. And all of a sudden, I realize why their giggles are gone. No one's ever seen such a field of horrors! Vines run everywhere, crisscrossing the rows, moving under and over the other plants, choking out the sun and the air, stealing the nourishment the garden crops need to survive. Cucumber beetles and spider mites creep everywhere. And everything's mixed up crazy. Brown button squash litter the dirt like dead mice.

"Check it out!" Cool Breeze says. He holds up a cabbage the size of a plum.

Mrs. Tate's at least ten rows away from us, but she screams so loud we can't help but hear. "Land sakes!" she yells. "The garden! It's ruined!"

One after the next, white pickers gasp with shock.

The reverend points to Magnolia Row. But no one needs to tell us Negroes that sticking around the garden is a bad idea. We know that whenever there's trouble for the white folks, there's trouble for us. So we all run out the garden through the missing piece of fence.

Wouldn't you know it, on our way back to First Baptist, Delilah manages to catch up to Cool Breeze and me. As soon as the three of us squeeze into a pew, she nestles her head into his shoulder and tells him all about how scared she is. I want to be sick. I'm scared too, but I don't go sticking my head into other people's shoulders because of it.

CHAPTER 21

October 15, 1963, Late Morning

Inside First Baptist, folks buzz, fuss, and share their theories of what will happen next. In no time, everyone agrees that someone planted over the garden with weed seed, though no one can say who did it or why.

Then Reverend Walker steps up to the pulpit and tells us to bow our heads. While everyone else prays, I toss things over. At first, I'm burning up because the reverend spoke his mind and near about got us slaughtered. But the longer I sit in my pew, the more tickled I am that our reverend doesn't just think his ideas, he speaks them. And he doesn't just speak his ideas, he lives them, even when he's scared inside.

When the silent prayer is over, the reverend calls on the

Lord to see us through. We pray and chant and sing together so long, I reckon it's hours by the time the reverend announces he's going to hold a meeting to prepare for any trouble that might come our way. "Members of my brigade, stay here," he says. "Everyone else can go on home."

Of course, there's one little problem with that. I can't go on home, because Uncle Bump's there. Sure Uncle Bump found work at the General Merchandise Store in Franklindale. It's his job to mop the floors and hand out the government commodity—rice, beans, and of course, cheese, cheese, cheese. But Uncle Bump only works three days a week, and today he's got off. If he sees me home early, he'll know I skipped out on school to go to the picking.

So Cool Breeze, Delilah, and me sprawl out on the grass behind the church. After Delilah carries on more than an hour about how scared she still is, I decide to tell her and Cool Breeze a little secret. "Wanna know what Uncle Bump has to say when he hands out the food at the General Merchandise Store?"

"Have a nice day?" Cool Breeze guesses.

"Nope."

"What?" Delilah asks.

"Cheese if you please!" I say.

They both split a rib over that. And it's real good to hear them laugh, because under their laughs I can tell they're worried up as me. All three of us know things aren't going to turn out good. The more I think on it, the more I've got the urge to jump. But of course, I don't have my rope handy, so I just use an imaginary one. "Mary, Mary, quite contrary, how does your garden grow?" I say.

"Very funny!" Delilah says.

"The right rhyme for the right time," I tell her. Then I get back to saying "Mary, Mary" all over again. While I jump, I wonder why all the jumping songs are about a girl named Mary. And why Delilah thinks I can't see that every five minutes she scoots an inch closer to Cool Breeze.

By the time Delilah's almost snuggled up beside him, I've got a plan. I let go of my imaginary rope and fall to the ground. "My stomach's rumbling," I say, breathing heavy from all that jumping.

"Same here!" Cool Breeze says. He stands and fetches both our schoolbags out of the ditch. When he comes back, he sits down a whole foot away from Delilah. And I can't say I mind.

Cool Breeze and me pull our lunch sacks out of our schoolbags. I've got a peanut butter and jelly sandwich, but all he's got are peanuts. Delilah didn't bring a lunch because she didn't know what a long day it was going to be, so I give half my sandwich to her.

While we eat, Cool Breeze keeps going over the garden problem like it's a math equation he can solve. "Now white folks always blaming us for their troubles." He cracks a peanut shell.

Then something occurs to me. Something I never thought of before. "Uh-oh!" I say.

"What?" Cool Breeze and Delilah ask.

In normal times, I wouldn't care about talking with my mouth full of food. But I need Cool Breeze to think I'm a real lady, so I take all the time I need to swallow my sandwich down and lick my teeth clean before I share the scary idea.

"There's gonna be a short run on vegetables at the Corner Store, because up till now folks were waiting to get their stuff free from the garden. I hear Mr. Mudge's collards are rotting on the shelf. Now watch. He'll raise prices higher than a cat's back."

I can tell Cool Breeze is impressed I thought of this, because he purses his lips and says, "Now ain't you a real economist."

"A real windbug is more like it!" Delilah says. Then she laughs like she's just kidding.

But I know an insult when I hear one. And when someone insults you and pretends you're too dumb to know it, that's a double insult.

Just before Delilah gets another chance to cozy up beside him, Cool Breeze bolts to his feet again. "All the same," he says, "I'm going down to the Corner Store to get some food before the short run."

And wouldn't you know it, Delilah changes her mind about my theory. "Good idea," she says. "I'll come too. I've gotta stop home for some money."

"Same here," I say. And I reckon right about now's when I'd be getting home from school anyway, so at long last it's okay to show my face.

When I get into the yard, I hear Uncle Bump's harmonica ring out from his shed.

I knock.

Uncle Bump opens the rusty door.

"Guess what!" I say.

But Uncle Bump doesn't guess. He just says, "Listen to this." Then he blows a few raggedy chords and raises up his eyebrows.

"Good. Real good," I say. And one thing's clear: Uncle Bump's been locked in his shed for hours. He hasn't heard a word about what's going on.

"Guess what!" I say again.

"Don't know," he says, and steps out of the shed.

"Delilah told me all about the picking 'cause she was there. Plus," I say, "there's gonna be a real short run on vegetables. Everyone says so." And I don't mean to fib, but I reckon I get a bit carried away with my theory because then I say, "Even the reverend agrees."

"Well, then . . . ," he says. He drops his harmonica into his right pocket, pulls a quarter and two dimes out of his left. "You'd best get over to the Corner Store and load up." He hands me the change.

If Uncle Bump knew how much trouble our folks are in, he'd never let me cross to the other side of town. And even Delilah's mother won't let her go now. Of course, I'm not sure I should cross the tracks either, but something inside's telling me to stop being a scaredy-cat, to be more like the reverend.

So after I set my schoolbag inside my house, I meet up with Cool Breeze out front. Then I *tweet, click, click,* and Flapjack jumps out of the watering can and scampers down the lane beside us.

When we get to the Corner Store lot, I give my coins to Cool Breeze. "Can't go in with Flapjack," I tell him. "So get me one of Mr. Mudge's famous chocolate chip cookies. Plus mustard greens, radish, and make sure you get a button squash."

"What's the magic word?" Cool Breeze asks, and smiles.

Those dimples do it every time. That tingly feeling buzzes through me. "Please," I say real soft.

I stroke under Flapjack's chin. He starts to purr, and I'm relieved he doesn't mind being in this lot after all that happened to him here. And wouldn't you know it, we're just minding our business when we see that fat cat Sugar prancing our way. I reckon Flapjack thinks Sugar's a real fancy lady or something, because soon as she arrives, he follows her into the forest that runs between the Corner Store and Mr. Mudge's farm.

Truth be told, I don't think playing with Worths, human or animal, is a smart idea. I *tweet, click, click,* but Flapjack doesn't come, so I head into the trees to fetch him myself.

Seconds after I march into the woods, I hear Flapjack scurry up behind me. But the second I turn, my pulse jumps. That's because running after my cat, near out of breath, is Honey Worth. And Honey doesn't want Flapjack—she wants me!

"Hey!" she yells. "You wait right there!"

Swimmy-headed, I gaze at the freckles on her chin and hurry through my escape plans in my mind. I could run, lie my way out of this mess, or show Honey respect and make myself sick.

"Raise your head," she says.

I do as she tells me. I look into her searing blue eyes.

Honey scoops her cat from the ground, juts her full neck across her kitty's back. "You and me both know your brother's dead and gone 'cause he wrecked my brother's leg," she says, breathless, her blue eyes icy ponds.

My tongue hangs dry in my mouth. I want to throw a punch right into her stomach and run, but inside my head, a whisper tells me what to do instead. "I'm real sorry for what happened to your brother," I say. I feel queasy as each word leaves my lips. And I hate myself when I say, "Can't apologize enough."

"Now I don't suppose you was at the garden picking down in Kuckachoo today, 'cause you're a good girl and went to school, right?"

"Yes, ma'am," I say. My words are clouds, not really there.

"Well, Sugar and me went to the picking party down Magnolia Row this morning. And you must've heard what happened—the butter bean fiasco and all."

I watch Honey's lips. I expect them to move in tired patterns of hate, but they do something else instead.

"After the picking, there was a meeting at my house," she says. "My daddy and his friend Mr. Tate said they didn't take care of the garden, because Mr. Mudge hired your uncle and some other hands to do it instead." And Honey's not through. "My mama says your uncle's mad at all us white folks 'cause your brother disappeared in the bayou. That's why your uncle planted over our garden with butter beans. My mama says your uncle wrecked our garden to get revenge."

The words, they jumble in my mind. They skip over each other, double Dutch. Butter bean. Uncle. Fiasco. I don't know what a fiasco is, but I know it doesn't sound good. And one thing's certain: through all this hate, I've been warned. It's like Honey couldn't help herself. Some goodness seeped out.

"They're gonna get him!" she says. "Y'all better run!"

Run I do.

I've got no time to tell Cool Breeze where I'm going. I just flex my toes to keep my sneakers on my feet and race through the woods. Flapjack dashes beside me. I shove the low branches out of the way. Sticks scrape my shins as I tear past elm, oak, pine, and hickory.

Then a strange light stops me cold.

It's silver. Sun gleaming on silver. The silver moves. I see it's a shovel. From way back here, through the leaves and branches, I make out a man in an overcoat. It scares me to see anyone at all, though, because Elias and me have crossed through this forest loads of times, and we've never run into a soul.

The man's back's to me. He's digging a ditch. He throws something in it.

And I see Flapjack. He's right next to the man! He claws the trunk of an old oak. There's an enormous bird's nest up on the branch. *This is no time for lunch, Flapjack!* I want to yell. But I don't have to.

"Scram!" the man screams at my cat. He's madder than a wet hen!

I take off running through the forest. My hungry cat races up beside me. Together we tear across the pumpkin patch, through rows of sunflowers, and across the tracks. By the time we turn onto Kuckachoo Lane, my breath scrapes inside my lungs.

I ram open the door to Uncle Bump's shed, but the shed's empty, so I race across the yard into my house. And I can't believe it. There he sits at the kitchen table, dealing a game of solitaire like it's just an ordinary day.

I gather up his cards.

"Hey, put my game back!" he says.

"Something 'bout butter beans," I tell him. I'm not thinking about my words, choosing the ones that sound best. "Hide!" I yell. I yank his arm with both my hands, try to pull him up.

"What's got into you? Where's them vegetables?"

"Honey Worth . . . They had a meeting . . . Come on!" Tears collect in the corner of my mouth. "They're coming to get you. Honey said!"

Uncle Bump stares at me like I'm speaking Latin.

"They say you ruined the garden."

His eyes narrow. "That don't make sense."

"It don't got to make sense." I pace across the kitchen. "You've gotta go somewhere."

Uncle Bump shakes his head "no."

Just then Mama bursts through the door. Thank goodness! Mama won't let Uncle Bump stay home sitting on a pile of danger.

"What're you doing here, Bump?" she screams. She throws her pocketbook on the table and hits Uncle Bump on the back with both hands. "Ain't you heard what they saying 'bout you? 'Bout us? Let's go!"

He stands and nods like he's working out a problem. "I'm not running on account of some words from a little white girl," he says. Then his backside hits the seat again and sticks there, batter on the griddle. "I ain't a coward," he says.

"Course you ain't a coward, Bump. But last I checked, you wasn't no idiot neither," Mama shrieks. "Don't you remember what happened to . . ." Mama looks at me, changes her mind about something. Then she glares at Uncle Bump. "If my husband could see you sitting at this table, waiting to get yourself killed, he'd kill you himself." Her eyes widen. "You promised Brayburn you'd watch over us."

Uncle Bump yanks his harmonica out of his pocket and starts to blow.

Next thing I know, Mama storms out the side door.

So here I sit at the table, trying to reason. But Uncle Bump won't have any part of my logic. He's lost in his harmonica tune. While he plays, his eyes half close, but in the open parts, I see a glint I've never seen before. The glint in his eyes is like glass that glitters on the side of the road. You expect it to be clear, from a bottle of soda. But you bend down to pick it up and it's not. It's blue. Or it's green. You wonder where it came from. A white lady's shattered jewelry box? A broken bottle from a fight down the juke joint? Each shard of glass is small as a thumbnail, but in the burst of color, you know there's a whole story waiting to get told.

Now I can't go saying what the story inside my uncle is, but I can say this: it's new and it's ugly and it's strange. And I wish I never saw that glint in his eyes at all.

Uncle Bump never does budge from his seat before Mama returns with Reverend Walker at her side. "Addie Ann, you come with me," she says. She grabs my hand and pulls me through the kitchen, out the side door.

Mama and me hunker down on the steps only seconds before she starts to bawl. "They have it in for us Picketts," she cries.

By the time Reverend Walker creaks open the side door, I reckon Mama's run right out of tears. "I know it's not easy," the reverend tells us, "but I know you'll both agree. There comes a time for a man when his dignity's worth more than his life." He rubs his thumb across his beard. "This is Bump's time."

CHAPTER 22

October 15, 1963, Late Afternoon

When the reverend goes back inside our house, I try to make Mama feel better. "After a couple days the sheriff will forget all about the garden," I say.

Mama just sits there on the side steps and looks at me like I'm too innocent for this world. Then she reaches over and sets a strand of my hair behind my ear. "That man won't forget. But maybe the reverend will talk some sense into your uncle. Bump's gotta leave the house before—"

The bark of a dog cuts off her words. Mama and me stare at each other, too terrified to move.

The reverend appears at the side door again. "You'd best get out of here," he says.

Mama grabs on to the rail, pulls herself upright. Her knees tremble, and I can see she's holding that rail so she won't collapse. "We're not leaving Bump," she cries. Then she shouts through the side door into the house, "Come on, Bump! Time to go!"

But I don't hear Uncle Bump push back his chair. I don't hear his angry steps as he walks outside to Mama and me.

Now Mama bends down beside me so we're eyeball to eyeball. Then she squeezes my arm like she's trying to break it. "Don't you move," she tells me. Next she lets go my arm and flies past the reverend into the house. The reverend follows.

Sitting out here on the side steps alone, I don't know what else to do but try to listen for my brother. I shut my eyes tight and wait for the yellow and orange glitter. But behind my eyes it's nothing but black. I try to feel the rush of water in my belly crashing over the rocks on the riverbed. But all I feel is sick. *Come on!* I say to myself. *Come on!* I need to hear from Elias more than ever. I wait for my breath to get steady and even, but the longer I wait, the shorter it gets, till it almost sounds like the pitter-patter of Flapjack scurrying down the path. No matter how hard I listen, all I hear is that barking dog getting closer and closer and folks yelling inside the house.

It seems even the reverend doesn't know if the Good Lord can deliver us through, because I hear him shout to Mama, "Get Elmira. She'll help."

But Mama shrieks, "I'm not leaving!"

Then I hear Uncle Bump. He yells so loud it scares the

bejeezus out of me! "I told you, Maisy. I'm not running. You're her mama. Get her out of here. Right now!"

Mama crashes through the screen door, face puffed, holding back an explosion of anger and tears. She grabs my hand, yanks me down the side steps. I *tweet, click, click.* Flapjack hurries to meet us.

Just as we race round to the front of the house, we hear the barking hound again. That dog's pulling the sheriff and his gang of men down the lane straight to us.

I'm wild with fright but Mama's wilder. "Not again!" she shouts as we run down the lane. "Please not again!" By the time we reach Elmira's place, Mama's babbling nonsense. I pound on Elmira's front door. The second she opens it, Mama falls into her arms.

"Lord have mercy!" Elmira says.

Elmira's house is small as a sewing thimble. Two rooms. Candles and potted plants everywhere. Hardly space to move. Elmira and me drag Mama through the kitchen to the bedroom and set her on the bed.

Then I tell Elmira all about how Uncle Bump's getting blamed for the butter bean fiasco, how he won't leave our house, how the sheriff and his men are at our door, how we're all praying she'll work magic. All the while, Mama's blubbering. And the only thing Elmira says is "Mercy! Mercy!"

Then Mama shrieks, "I've got to help him!" She tries to jump out of bed, but she doesn't get too far, because Elmira and me pounce on her. Elmira sits right on Mama's legs and pins Mama to the bed with her hefty bottom.

"We'll help Uncle Bump," I tell Mama. "You stay right here."

While I talk, Elmira reaches round to the windowsill, pulls off a jar of oil. "You wanna help Bump?" Elmira asks.

Mama nods.

"Then do as I say." She opens the jar of oil and holds it under Mama's nose. "Sniff."

Somehow the scent of the oil makes Mama's body relax into the bed. Soon Mama looks like she'd rather rest than run. That's when Elmira stands up, and I touch Mama's legs to make sure they're not broken. Thank goodness they feel like they're holding together fine.

Next Elmira holds out a teaspoon of medicine. "Swallow," she tells Mama.

After Mama swallows, Elmira whispers, "She'll be sleeping in no time." Then she plucks out a bunch of grass growing in a box on her window, wraps the grass in a ball round her finger, and presses it into the soles of Mama's feet. By the time Elmira finishes her foot work, Mama's eyes flutter.

I wipe the hair off Mama's forehead and tuck it behind her ear. "I love you, Mama," I whisper.

My words seem to help Mama's eyes close all the way.

"She'll come through," Elmira tells me.

Of course, the second I hear Mama will be okay, the rest of the nightmare hurtles to the front of my mind. When I talk, my voice is a thin line. "What can you do for Uncle Bump? A spell? Something?"

"Well, I'm sure I can," Elmira says.

And I'm sure she can too. That's because Elmira was

born gifted. For the past twenty-three years, she spent her days cooking in Old Man Adams's kitchen, but nights she came back to the Negro side and worked as the hoodoo doctor, curing ladies of the flu by sprinkling elderberry on their foreheads, helping gentlemen find love by fixing violets in their shoes.

Elmira waddles past me into the kitchen to find her mojo bag and roots. "Sit here," she says, and pats an empty seat at her rickety kitchen table.

Beside the kitchen table sits the Dutch oven she got from Old Man Adams. And believe me, with Elmira's spacious bottom and enormous bosom plus the new oven, there's not much room left to move.

But I squeeze into the seat and watch Elmira search through her cluttered cupboards for the right materials to cast a spell. There's her mojo bag, the candles, the herbs, a cat-o'-nine-tails, and some colored stones.

"Where's my lavender? Lavender!" Elmira mutters. She fumbles through her materials.

For all she's trying to help my uncle, this magic's taking far too long. And I know I can't wait. So I shut my eyes and whisper, "Where to?"

This time I don't wait for the orange and yellow glitter to come to me. I go after it. I call the crowbar gleaming in sunshine right into my mind. And the river. I don't hope it chooses to meander my way. I imagine that river and dive right in. Even though I don't know how to swim, I'm not pulled under. I float, I float. My back against the water, I blow my breath into the open sky. Gooseflesh splashes over me. I hear a voice, it's soft but it's clear: *Follow me.*

I open my eyes and trail the whisper to the door.

"Where you going?" Elmira asks.

"To help," I tell her, even though I'm not sure how.

But Elmira nods like she understands.

And I chase my brother's voice out her front door, into the dusky sky. Flapjack darts out from beneath a bush. Together we bolt round the bend and down the lane.

CHAPTER 23

October 15, 1963, Evening

Flapjack and me are only halfway home when burnt air scrapes inside my nose. My skin aches. My whole body throbs. Soon enough I see a mob of neighbors in the lane. Then I see my house and Uncle Bump's shed are one fiery blaze.

Anger boils inside me, more than I can take.

I weave through the people to the fire. The men in the Reverend's Brigade race from the well with buckets. They inch to the flames, dump the water.

"Reverend!" I shout. But he can only see the runners with buckets. He can only hear the crumbling clapboards. He can't see me standing here. He can't hear me cry.

"Uncle Bump!" I scream. I chase a flame up the porch

steps. But just as I reach out for the front door, someone tugs my hips. I fall backward down the stairs.

Here's the reverend, holding my face next to his. "What're you doing!" He's crazy with fear.

"Where's my uncle?" I yell.

"Git on down the lane."

"I'm not running!" I tell him.

The reverend glances past me to the flames. "What's with y'all?"

"Where is he?" I yell.

The reverend looks back at me. "I'ma tell it straight," he says.

I swallow.

"Sheriff bombed the house. Smoked me and Bump out. Bump's in jail. Sheriff says he'll take Bump to court come morning." The reverend sighs. "I'm sorry," he says. Then he leaves me here on the ground.

By the time Bessie comes and wraps her fingers round my wrist, it's dark. "Let's go," she says, and pulls me up. "Somethin' important." And I wonder what could possibly be more important than my house burning to the ground, Uncle Bump in jail, Mama going mad.

I follow Bessie down the dirt road, while the truth comes clear in bits and pieces. My map? Gone. My swing? Gone. My jump rope? Gone. The television? Gone. The television! I don't know why a broken-down television I can't turn on matters. But it does. It matters for everything.

When we get to the end of the lane, I stop and hunch over, heave the smoky air into my lungs. But Bessie doesn't care I can't breathe. She's still grabbing on to my wrist, leading me through stalks of milkweed.

"Shut your eyes," she orders. "Go on!"

I don't want to do what she says, but my eyelids, they fall anyway. And the next thing I know, I hear the milkweed stalks rustle and Bessie run off.

I'm alone.

At least I think I am. But then a shirt against my face clears my nose. And a mixed-up scent of baseball and autumn helps me breathe.

What happens next makes no sense at all.

Something about the smell and the heavy arm round my shoulders takes me home, even though I know my home's gone. And all of a sudden, the sheets Mama sewed with suns and stars, the kitchen table, my map, my swing, my jump rope, and even my television don't mean a thing.

When at long last I get up the guts to open my eyes, I can see my home, it's right here with me. My brother's beside me! Here, under the bright full moon, I cry and shake and I can't stop. It's like I've dropped a sack of potatoes I carried for ninety-six days. All this time I made myself believe he was okay. Now I can't be strong another second.

Everything turns dark.

My head hurts.

I hear a groan.

And I realize that sound, it comes from me.

"I never meant to shock you," Elias says. He rubs the

top of my head, while I take a few minutes to put every-thing back together again. Me, here in the milkweed. Smoke in the sky. I try to speak but my throat's charred.

My brother scoops his arm under my neck, helps me sit. "Drink," he says. He hands me a canteen of water. But I'm crying and drinking at the same time, so there's more water going out than coming in.

"I hid out here in the milkweed till dark. Then I covered my face with this kerchief." Elias pulls a bandana out of his pocket. "I saw Bessie at the back of the crowd, so I hid be-hind a tree and threw a rock to get her attention. At least she ran right over and hugged me up before she went woozy—unlike you."

"Sorry," I say.

"If I knew girls were gonna be fainting at my feet, I'd have come back sooner," he says.

But I don't think it's funny and my brother can tell.

"I sent a message so you'd know I was okay," he says, "but Bessie says y'all never got word." Elias pulls me into his chest, hugs me tight.

And that's when I see his brand-new sneakers. But I don't want to ask questions. I just want to stay here in his arms. It's a miracle he's back and Uncle Bump's alive, but truth be told, a piece of me's spitting hammers and nails. Here all this time Elias was safe while Mama, me, and Bessie filled the well with our tears.

"He didn't want anyone to trace the note back. He slipped up," Elias says, his voice deader than ash. "I over-heard the driver in the shop. He was talking 'bout the but-ter bean fiasco, saying they're blaming Bump. Second I heard that, I knew I had to risk being seen. When the driver finally left the shop, I bolted home."

"Who slipped up?" I ask, and pick a pod of milkweed off a stalk. "What're you talking about?"

"I'll tell you later. Right now, we've gotta take care of Uncle Bump. It seems if some folks get their way . . ." Then my brother gets that faraway look in his eyes, and I see there's something he doesn't want me to know.

"What?" I suck in my breath.

"They'll put him under the jail, not in it."

"What?" My brother isn't making sense. "The reverend said Uncle Bump's in jail. He'll go to court come morning," I tell him.

"Not if they kill him first," Elias whispers.

I tear apart a pod of milkweed. All the feathers inside fall on me. Then I look up at my brother and wonder if he's gone mad.

"There's something Mama and me been needing to tell you a while now," he says. "We've been waiting till you were old enough. I can see now's the time."

While Elias talks, all the lies my family told me collapse on me like a pile of bricks. They press on my chest. I can barely breathe. I'm afraid I won't breathe. Afraid I'll die. Because this truth, the truth Elias tells me, it might just be more than what I can take. My brother tells me all about Daddy—that Daddy didn't die of pneumonia like Mama always said.

"You all right?" he asks.

I go ahead and nod. But how am I supposed to be all right with the fact that my daddy was murdered? How am I supposed to be all right when my family didn't even trust me with the truth?

"I can't stay out here long. If the wrong folks see me, we'll have double trouble," he says. "So you've gotta talk. You've gotta tell our story."

I dig my fingernails into the dirt.

"The story of our family. The real one. When folks hear it, they'll remember what's at stake for Uncle Bump. For us all." Elias swipes under his nose, but his tears fall anyway. "Can you tell it?" he asks.

The sparks catch inside me. They burst into a river of flame. "Yeah," I whisper. "I can. And I will."

When I hear that whisper, I know whose it is. Before this moment, I would've sworn that whisper belonged to my brother, who's always sure where to go, what to do. But when I hear it now, so clear, so close, I know that voice. It's my own.

CHAPTER 24

October 15, 1963, Night

I leave my brother in the milkweed and race back to the lane. My neighbors are still fixed on the flames. Shadows flicker on their faces. And one thing's clear: we can't stand here and watch our lives burn. This isn't just about Uncle Bump. This isn't just about us Picketts. This is about all of us. Who we are. What our future holds.

Now I'm madder than a rare-roast devil. I grab a bucket set on the porch of a nearby house, lug it to the lane, turn it over, and climb on top. Then I scream louder than I thought I knew how. "Listen!"

All of a sudden, I remember what that man from the

NAACP said: *When it's your time, you'll know. You won't be able to sit on your rumps and watch. You'll feel it in your bones. You won't have a choice but to get up and . . .* There's no doubt about it. "This is our time!" I shout.

And what do you know? Cool Breeze Huddleston is the first to hear me shout hellfire and brimstone. He's the first to turn and stare.

"You really Cool Breeze?" I yell.

He nods.

"Then prove it!" I shout.

Cool Breeze glides toward me like he's under my spell. "Now I want you to run faster than Jesse Owens in training," I tell him. "Get Mrs. Jacks. Tell her this is the big test. The final exam! We need all our people from Weaver to meet us down the jailhouse. We need them to help save Uncle Bump. We need them to help save us all!"

When I say it, I know it sounds real good. And I wish Mrs. Jacks could see me taking charge of the madness, trying to make a dream come true in a matter of hours while others spend their whole lives.

After Cool Breeze runs off, a few more neighbors turn from the dying flames to listen. To listen to me!

"Delilah," I yell.

She pushes through the crowd toward me.

"You be my special helper. I want you to get to Bramble lickety-split."

I'm expecting her to say "Thrills, chills, and charges!" I'm expecting her to turn away, not to help. But Delilah just stands, eyes wide.

"I know you can do it!" I tell her.

Then Mr. Montgomery calls, "C'mon, Delilah!" and he runs beside his daughter all the way down the lane.

Smoke swirls above the empty lot where my house, Uncle Bump's shed, and my swing used to be. My eyes sting. I swipe under my nose and this time it works. The tears, they stay inside. One by one, my neighbors turn from the flames to listen. To listen to me! And one by one, I send them off through the county to call on our sisters and brothers, our teachers and preachers for help.

Then I jump off the bucket and follow the reverend while the brigade stays behind to finish off the fire. We're a thundering herd of feet trudging along the dirt lane, off to the jailhouse to make sure Uncle Bump survives the night. The second I turn round, one thing's clear: the reverend and me are leading a march every bit as powerful as the one in Washington, D.C., that Reverend Walker told us all about.

Our neighbors follow us across the tracks. While we walk, I tell the reverend that I know my family story and I want to share it. The reverend looks at me. His eyes glisten, and I've got a feeling he knows my family story too. He wraps his arm round my shoulders, gives me a squeeze. When we turn down Main Street, white folks back up against the nearest buildings, shocked to see us coming through.

As soon as we arrive at the jailhouse, the reverend motions us to circle it. And before the sheriff can figure out what's what, a human shield surrounds the concrete building.

❦

Hours later, when the sheriff's tired of yelling, he decides to aim his shotgun at the crowd. But it's too late to scare us away. That's because under the bright moon, we see folks from Darwiler, Titus, Hominy, and Jigsaw pouring into town. Young and old, they're coming to stand beside us.

The reverend and me, we climb onto a boulder beside the jail. From up here, I can see Curtis Bertrand Huddleston rolling down the road on the back of a flatbed truck, proving he really is Cool Breeze after all. A hundred folks from Weaver follow. And there's Delilah marching in from Bramble, followed by more girls and boys than ever trailed her at the schoolhouse.

A lightbulb hangs from a wire outside the jail. A patch of light falls on the reverend. "Y'all," he shouts. He waits till everyone hushes. Then he says, "We're going to spend the night arm in arm like a chain that can't be broken. Folks coming in from throughout the county, we welcome you to join our circle. The time has come for the Negroes of Thunder Creek County to stand up and fight! Too many of our sisters and brothers have been injured, killed. We can't let this go on another day. Another hour. Another second. The fate of Bump Dawson is the fate of us all."

"Amen!" folks shout. "Glory be!"

Then the reverend's eyes get fixed on something far away. And I see what. My lip wiggles worse than ever. There are four Klansmen dressed in white sheets and pointy hats. They creep closer. One holds a rope noose.

My head gets light. Brother Babcock's eyes go swollen. Delilah lets out a bloodcurdling scream.

Then a raspy voice in the crowd starts to sing. *"Oh freedom!"*

The second I hear that voice, I know Mrs. Jacks is here, helping us rise above.

Our voices bond together. They rise up like a force that can fight. *"Oh freedom over me!"*

When the Klansmen get to the rim of our circle round the jail, the reverend motions for us to part the way. And I can't imagine what's going on. Does the reverend want us to let them through? Through to Uncle Bump?

Our voices ring strong as people separate.

But the Klansmen don't tromp down the clearing to the jail. Instead, they huddle.

I feel I might collapse.

Then the Klansmen turn away and march back down the street, the one on crutches trailing behind.

And I don't know what's gotten into me, but I start jiggling all over the place and hallelujahing and raising my hands up to the sky, like the Good Lord's entered my body and soul.

One thing's clear: our large crowd of Negroes scared the jeepers out of those Klansmen. By parting the way, we let them see just how many of us are here, all in one place, together! We've ruined their plans for Uncle Bump. At least for now.

"Bump!" the reverend calls toward the jailhouse window slit.

I imagine Uncle Bump slumped in the corner of a four-by-four-foot cell.

"A thousand folks are here for you," the reverend shouts.

Then Mrs. Jacks sings, *"This little light of mine, I'm gonna to let it shine."* And our voices ring out for hours.

There's hundreds of friends plus hundreds of strangers, but it feels to me we're all part of one big family.

Once the sheriff gets tired of our singing and leaves, the reverend calls to the crowd from on top of the boulder. "Now I'd like y'all to sit and listen," he says. "I'm going to ask Addie Ann to tell you folks her family's story. As you'll see, it's not unique. But it's why we're here. To change the course of history. What happened to Addie Ann's father is part of our common past. And what will become of Bump Dawson is part of the future we share. It's our job to make sure Bump lives free!"

Then the reverend touches my shoulder. And it's like tag, I'm it.

Here I am on the boulder, looking out at these people. They've come to help my uncle. They've come to help themselves. My breath is slow. The fire's inside me. And all I can do is tell my story.

The first part's easy. It's what Mama's told me time and again, the history I've always called my own. "My daddy was Brayburn Pickett," I say.

"A little louder," the reverend whispers.

I nod and call up the same voice I used on that bucket, the voice I used to get these folks here in the first place. "Uncle Bump was just a teenager when his big sister married my father," I say. "Uncle Bump and my daddy met every morning for coffee at the diner. One day, an extra-pretty lady waltzed into the diner. She came from Hornet, Mississippi. She was visiting a friend who lived in Nashville.

"In case you're wondering, Nashville is the capital of Tennessee," I say. "Nashville's where my parents and Uncle

Bump lived. According to Mama, it only took one pretty lady. Then Uncle Bump was fast on the track to the Mississippi Delta."

All of a sudden, Uncle Bump's deep laugh tumbles out the jailhouse. It fills my whole heart. It helps me go on. "Uncle Bump got settled in Hornet, Mississippi," I say. "Then he sent word to my parents in Nashville, Tennessee. Uncle Bump told my parents that Negroes down in Hornet could use my father's carpentry skill.

"Daddy couldn't stand to build another pretty home for white folks in Nashville, so lickety-split he packed up the family and set off for a new adventure in the Delta."

I close my eyes and imagine Daddy driving down the highway, top of the car down, wind flying through his hair, Mama beside him, three-year-old Elias in back. I take a deep breath. "Soon as my father got out of Nashville, he saw the go-on-forever fields. He saw the go-on-forever sky. He fell in love with the Delta. In love forever."

That part was easy. But now my legs turn froggy, because I've got to tell the rest. The part I just heard for the first time. The story I can't believe is mine.

"Daddy . . . ," I say. It's a good thing this crowd is silent, since I don't have the strength to talk loud as before. "I used to think Daddy died of pneumonia, but now I know that's . . . not true. The truth, it's ugly. . . . It's worse."

The reverend nods like I should go ahead, keep telling what I know. So I close my eyes and look for the river, feel the river, am the river. Am the water crashing over the rocks on the riverbed, rushing so fast, not stopping, not stopping, while I tell the story. The story Elias told me.

My story.

My story.

My story.

"We moved to Hornet," I say. All I hear is a nightmare. A nightmare full of colors and smells. "My daddy wanted to build the Negro side of Hornet into a place where real human beings could live happy. From the way I heard it, folks across town got mighty hot when some of our houses looked better than theirs. And Daddy didn't want to build homes for white folks, no matter how much money they offered. Then . . ."

I don't want to tell them, just like Elias didn't want to tell me. I don't want the children here to know things like this can happen. But I've got no choice. Elias said by telling our history, we might change the future for Uncle Bump—and for us all.

So I draw in a breath. "My daddy," I say, "he had ideas of his own." For a minute, I stop and wonder what my life would be like if Daddy had just followed the rules.

I'm tossing that over when the reverend whispers, "Go on, Addie Ann. Go on."

I take another breath. The river curls in waves. "My daddy didn't want to depend on white folks to earn money," I say. "And that, I reckon, was the problem."

I look out at the people and see their eyes glow in the moonlight. I wish I could snap my fingers and say, "I'm kidding, y'all," but now I know I've got to tell the rest. The whole truth. The most horrible part.

"Daddy turned down an offer to build a grand house for Hornet's white mayor. That was it. The next night a couple hooded Klansmen on horses trotted up to my family's house."

Then I can't help it: I speed through the story like it's happening again. "Those men grab my brother, Mama too. Yank them out of the house. Keep a pistol aimed at Daddy. Force him to stay inside."

Inside me fire rages, through my legs, and round my head, lighting the dark. "The men throw a firebomb into the house. The house bursts into flames. Mama grabs Elias by the wrist, races down the street, away from the sight. But my brother pulls free, runs home.

" 'Daddy! Daddy!' Elias yells. But no matter how many times he calls, Daddy won't come on out. Out of his burning home."

I bury my face in my hands and picture Uncle Bump playing gin rummy at a friend's, someone bursting in with the news. Uncle Bump running out fast as he could, cheeks covered with tears, muscles itching to swing.

Now the reverend hugs me. "Can you finish?" he asks.

It's all I can do to nod.

The people wait like they would wait a hundred years.

But a wild rage fills me.

A rage that falls behind words.

That gasps between breaths.

That poisons my tears.

"A couple days later," I say, "the *Hornet Herald* published an interview with the mayor of Hornet. The mayor said he hired my father to build him a new home. He said he paid my father for the job in advance. Then he said my father spent all the money but refused to build the house.

The mayor said that when he ordered my father into court, my daddy was so full of shame he . . ."

The truth burns inside me. And I wonder if sometimes it's better not to know.

I open my mouth to speak but I can't. My lips are parched. Someone carries a jug of water to the boulder.

I sip the water down, a drip down my throat into my chest. To the river. The river. That one sip is too much. The river spills its banks.

It floods.

Floods.

Floods.

The truth floods out of me. Out my heart. Out my mouth. Out to the people. To the old folks who've heard it before. To the children who will never want to hear it again.

"The mayor said Daddy burned himself up in his own home. But my daddy hadn't ever . . . hadn't ever taken the money. It was all a lie."

There's gooseflesh over me.

"Mama," I say, "she was left alone with my brother, only four years old, me on the way, Daddy dead and gone, our home nothing but a pile of rubble. That's when Uncle Bump, Mama's brother, moved us from Hornet to Kuckachoo. That lady from the diner never did turn into his wife, so we were the closest family my uncle had. Uncle Bump used whatever money he earned to buy our food and clothes. Though he never went past fifth grade himself, Uncle Bump made sure I got all the way to seventh grade and my brother went all the way to high school."

When at long last I get to the end of my story, folks break out singing:

> "Go down, Moses.
> Way down in Egypt's land.
> Tell old Pharaoh,
> 'Let my people go.'"

I climb down from the boulder and sprawl out on the ground. No blanket, no pillow, no nothing. I've never been so tired in all my life. I stare up at the dark sky and wonder what was the last thing Daddy ever saw. I hope it was something nice. Maybe a photograph of him and Mama at their wedding. Maybe a picture Elias drew.

CHAPTER 25

🌱

October 16, 1963, Early Morning

Gray clouds trot across the sky: ugly, uglier, ugliest. I'm stiff all over. I can't believe I slept here on the ground till morning. And I can't believe how big our crowd still is, how many folks left their homes, their beds, to fight for Uncle Bump. To fight for our future.

Sirens scream through the air. I push myself up, only to see the sheriff's blue car with red lights fixed on top. It shoots round the bend to us. Another blue car follows.

Reverend Walker climbs onto the back of a flatbed truck parked outside the jail. Seconds later, the sheriff drives up beside the truck, opens his window, and yells, "Get out of my way!"

But the reverend says, "We'll let you into the jailhouse, Sheriff, on one account."

"Move!" the sheriff shouts.

"We'll move if you swear to transport Bump Dawson to the courthouse. Without harm!"

The sheriff jumps out of his car, slams the door, opens the trunk, and pulls out a billy club.

But something about the lot of us Negroes staring back at his little club seems to make him change his mind. "All right," he shouts. "I swear. Without harm. Now let me through!"

True to his word, Reverend Walker tells the crowd to part an aisle down the center and clear a path to the jailhouse door. Three deputies follow the sheriff into the building. Then Reverend Walker orders us to surround their cars.

A few minutes pass till the sheriff and his deputies lead Uncle Bump out the jail. Uncle Bump's hands and feet are shackled. He wears a pale blue shirt and pale blue pants. When he gets closer to me, the knot in my belly tightens. Now I can see someone beat the hound out of him. And I have no doubt the sheriff's knuckles fit the bloody handprint on my uncle's right cheek.

The sheriff shoves Uncle Bump into the backseat of his car like he's throwing in a sack of dirty laundry. With so many folks surrounding the car, Uncle Bump doesn't see me. I want to knock on the window, but then I wouldn't put it past the sheriff to handcuff me too. So instead, I walk beside the blue car all the way to the courthouse, watching my uncle, wondering if he'll ever be free again.

When at long last we arrive, the sheriff yanks Uncle

Bump out and pushes him up the seven courthouse steps—seven, not six.

Then I climb those same steps behind Bessie and Elmira. My legs, they're heavy like a woolly mammoth's. I've got the collywobbles. And I know if I don't get some bellyache root soon, all this will get even messier.

Inside the courthouse a sign with white letters on it says Rows 1–8 White. Rows 9–12 Colored.

I follow Elmira to the ninth row. As we wait for the judge to arrive, she leans close and whispers in my ear. "While y'all was down round the jailhouse last night, your mama was sleeping sound in my bed. In the middle of the night, there's a knock at my door. I go get it. I jumped a mile!"

The funny thing is, even though my uncle's handcuffed in this very court, the whole while Elmira talks, I'm happy as a May magnolia.

"He was more miracle than I could ever conjure to cure what ailed your mama! Oh, dear! I'm afraid I pinched him rather hard to be sure it was him in the flesh and not a visiting ghost. Once I got convinced he was here body and soul, I took him to my bedroom to wake your mama. Then I left them alone."

By the time Elmira finishes her report, there isn't enough room in the courthouse for a grasshopper to jump inside. All the rows are full, and Uncle Bump's supporters have crammed into the central aisle.

A skinny white man slumps to the middle of the floor like this is just another day at the office, nothing unusual, no big deal. He starts to talk and I'll tell you one thing: his nose could use a good blow. "In the case of the State of Mississippi versus Charles 'Bump' Dawson, the court is now in session," he says. "All rise. The Honorable Judge Cogswell presides."

Everything in me trembles. And all the good feelings I got from Elmira's story slide off me and onto the floor like an old snake's skin. I can't believe I'm about to watch Uncle Bump fight for his freedom, and there's nothing I can do but stare like I'm watching a Shirley Temple film on television.

Up front, there's a platform. On the platform, an empty black chair. When everyone sits down again, a sturdy man in a black cloak sits in that chair. I reckon he's the judge.

"Order in this court!" the judge says. "The preliminary hearing will begin. Now then, will the attorney for the prosecution please identify himself."

A pale man with sprouts of black hair stands and wraps his overgrown mustache round his index finger. "Mr. Hickock here," he says.

Next the judge asks if Uncle Bump has a lawyer. But everyone knows we Picketts don't have the money to hire one.

So when a white lady with a suitcase calls out, "I represent the defendant," I wonder if I'm so tired I've started to dream. But there she is, standing beside the witness box in a red dress with short sleeves.

"Who are you?" the judge asks.

"Sylvia Gold, Your Honor," she says. Her singsong voice bangs up against the sharp angles of her face. It echoes off the arched ceiling and sounds like the high notes on Uncle Bump's harmonica.

"Where you from?" the judge asks.

"Right now, Jackson, but I grew up in New York City," she says. She drops her suitcase to the floor beside Uncle Bump. "I'm with the NAACP Legal Defense Fund," she says.

Even from back here, I can see the judge's scraggly eyebrows crawl together to form one line. When at long last they separate, he says, "Uh-huh. The National Association for the Advancement of Colored People. Well, I've heard you Yankee lawyers make trouble in the cities. But what, pray tell, brings you here?"

"We got a phone call telling us Bump Dawson is in need of representation," she says.

I reckon most lawyers roll up their shirtsleeves to prepare for a hearing, but not this one. Miss Gold takes the elastic out of her hair and shakes her head. Her red curls tumble down her back like a sunset. Then she whispers in Uncle Bump's ear.

Soon enough the judge bangs his hammer. "Our first order of business is to determine if there's enough evidence to hold a full-fledged trial," he says.

The second I hear it, I pray the judge will end this stupid case here and now.

The judge asks Mr. Hickock, the lawyer fighting against us, to explain why my uncle would spend his time ruining the community garden.

Mr. Hickock stands and twirls the bristles of his mustache.

"I'm afraid this is a simple case of family revenge," he says. "Clearly, Bump Dawson was seeking revenge for the disappearance of his nephew, Elias, who is missing and presumed dead."

And me? I try not to roar with hilarity. I saw my brother last night in the milkweed. He breathed. He blinked. He talked. If that's not alive, I don't know what is!

Mr. Hickock finishes his nonsense. Then the judge says, "After examination of the criminal law of Mississippi, as well as the allegations before me today, I've made a deliberate and carefully considered judgment."

The breaths hopscotch down my throat.

"There's ample evidence against Charles 'Bump' Dawson," he says.

Evidence? I didn't hear any evidence.

"This case *will* go to trial!"

Applause louder than the Jackson-bound train chugs through my head. I grind my teeth back and forth to the rhythm of the claps. I just hope I don't crack one of them, because even though we Picketts have a lawyer, we sure don't have a dentist.

"Now to the arraignment," the judge says. "Bump Dawson is charged with grand theft of the town's property, trespassing, vandalism, and disturbing the peace. How does the defendant plead?"

"My client pleads not guilty," Miss Gold says.

"Very well then," the judge says, "a jury will hear this case in five days."

"Five days?" cries Miss Gold. "Five days isn't enough time to put together a case!"

"Welcome to Kuckachoo," says the judge, "where five days is plenty!"

Miss Gold's eyes bulge out of her head while the judge turns to the lawyer fighting against us. "Mr. Hickock," the judge says, "the citizens of Kuckachoo will look to you to prove beyond a shadow of a doubt that Bump Dawson is the guilty man."

"Yes, sir!" says Mr. Hickock like he's a soldier saluting his commander.

"And, Sheriff," the judge says.

The sheriff stands before his front-row seat. "Yes, sir?" he asks.

"I'm holding you accountable for keeping the defendant safe till trial."

"Well, of course, Your Honor," the sheriff says like he's too sweet to squash a bug.

CHAPTER 26

October 16–21, 1963

The sheriff throws Uncle Bump back in jail, and I run across the tracks to find Mama and Elias. When I get near Elmira's house, I take in the still-smoky air, and I reckon Mama must hear me coughing because she hustles outside.

"Oh, my baby!" She pulls me tight to her bosom.

"Where is he?" I whisper.

"Shhh!" Mama says. "What happened?"

It hurts me to tell Mama that, yes, Uncle Bump's case is going to trial after all. And I think the only reason I do tell her is I'm more than dying to see that brother of mine.

Mama clucks her tongue. "As expected," she says.

Then she leads me through Elmira's house to the bedroom, where the curtains are shut so no one can see inside.

"We've got to be extra careful now," Mama whispers.

"Where is he? You seen him, didn't you?" I ask.

That's when she pulls a chain out of her pocket. At the end of that chain is a gold watch. A grin so wide comes over Mama's face, I reckon her cheeks might crack. And my heart, it's warm as porridge knowing after all these days crying and praying, at long last she's seen her son.

"Last night when you all was down round the jail-house, your brother was right here in this very room," she whispers. "He told me, 'Mama, you take this now. It'll help you remember I'm still ticking.' " She squishes up her lips and kisses the face of the watch like she's kissing the face of her son.

She tells me she could hardly stand to part with Elias early this morning, but she had to let him go. "He slept here in my arms before he left this morning. He was sure the case would go to trial. Said he wanted to meet Bump's lawyer back at the office in Jackson to help prepare. Now don't even ask me how your brother knew Bump had a lawyer—a lawyer all the way from Jackson!" Mama shakes her head. "Well, I reckon that brother of yours knows just about everything."

And I can't believe the way this is turning out, that at long last I've found my brother alive, but he can't stay and talk to me because he's got to go. Not just down the road a piece, but all the way to the state capital.

Mama and me stand in Elmira's bedroom till her smile

fades and both of us choke on our fear. And I've got to admit, I'm mad Mama would lie to me about my daddy. Probably more mad than I've ever been in my whole life. I know I am. But even though I know it, I don't feel it. I can't. Not when my family's still in danger.

"Come on, Mama," I say. "We've gotta keep some faith."

For the next few days till Uncle Bump's trial, Mama and me stay at the Montgomerys' place, because they've got more room than Elmira. We don't do much but sleep and talk to our neighbors. But everyone says the same things: "Chances aren't good." And "Evidence don't mean a thing." And "Even with all proof he's innocent, a Negro will end up in jail or dead."

Each morning, me and Mama wake up worried and downright miserable. I miss out on a whole bunch of school, and neither me or Mama go to work, even though Mrs. Tate could fire us and then where'd we be? But Mama says given the shape we're in, we wouldn't be any use anyway. She says with all that's going on, Mrs. Tate won't be the least bit surprised when we don't show. And we've just got to pray she'll understand once all is said and done.

Each night, Mama and me rest on the Montgomerys' couch, her head at one end, mine at the other. I wear the pink nightgown I borrowed from Delilah, and Mama wears the giant blue robe Elmira lent her. The tick of the gold watch in Mama's robe pocket lulls me to sleep. And each night, in my sleep, I replay the same vision, half memory, half dream.

Flapjack and me, we're darting through the forest. Branches tear up my knees. Honey Worth's grainy voice echoes in my mind. "Y'all better run!" Then a swash of sunlight on silver stops me in my tracks. I see a shovel, then the back of a man. He's digging a hole. Flapjack and me sneak up close. We want to see who the man is and what he's doing. But dark clouds gather. The sky turns purple-blue. In the hazy light, the man plays tricks. He's a haint. A monster. A hooded Klansman. Then all of a sudden, Flapjack hisses. Startled, the man shouts, "Scram!"

That's when I wake up.

That's when I always wake up.

Then I get to thinking about the trial.

I can't say I know just who planted over the garden with butter bean seeds, but I've got to admit, it could've been a Negro who was right mad the white folk stole our land in the first place. And it scares me twice to death to think it could've been Uncle Bump. What with all his feelings stuffed inside and his anger about Elias, I can't help but think it's more than possible he exploded. Then, in a flash bright as lightning, I hate myself for even wondering if Uncle Bump had something to do with this butter bean crime.

❦

Each night after supper, Mama and her friends gather at church to pray Uncle Bump will be proven innocent in court. While Reverend Walker's service provides some comfort, just today, the day before the trial, Mama decides she can't rely on prayer alone. So Mama and me go to see Elmira for some hoodoo fixes. And I wonder, if God really is all that and then some, why does Mama need magic too?

As soon as we get to Elmira's, the smell of mint growing in the windowsill pot springs right up my nose. Mama and me sit down at the rickety table beside the Dutch oven. Then Elmira squeezes into a kitchen chair and reaches across to grab our hands.

"Thank you, Elmira," Mama says. "You've already helped me so much. I hate to ask for more, but I don't know what else to do."

"Now, now," Elmira says, and pats Mama's hand. "I aim to see this trial done right." Then she reaches behind her, opens a cabinet.

Mama and me wait a good long while till Elmira locates all her tools: an empty jelly glass, a bowl of sugar, a kitchen knife, a brown candle, and matches.

"We've got to sweeten up that judge so when he sees Bump at trial, he'll only feel love in his heart," Elmira says.

I always feel warm around Elmira. And it's good to be beside her again in a kitchen.

"Addie Ann, we're counting on you to write the name of the judge here," she says. She unscrews the lid off the empty jelly jar. Then she hands me the sharp knife. "It's for the writing," she tells me. "I ain't got a pen."

But it's hard to write on the slick surface. I hold on to the tip of the knife like it's a pencil. I've got to scrape it against the metal lid over and over to get each letter to show up. And while I carve Judge Cogswell's name, Mama and Elmira watch like I'm performing some sacred act, like I'm fixing the outcome of the trial here and now.

Once I finish, I set the knife on the table. Then Elmira lights a match, melts the end of the candle, and presses the candle onto the jelly lid. "Favor the case of Bump Dawson," she chants. "Favor the case . . ."

"Better say 'Charles,' his given name," Mama says.

"Charles 'Bump' Dawson," Elmira repeats. She strikes another match and lights the candle. "Favor the case," she says. Then she motions with both hands for Mama and me to repeat it.

"Favor the case," we say. I watch the candle's flame shoot up into a point, and pray the hoodoo will ward off the angry spirits that made the members of the Garden Club lie about Uncle Bump in the first place.

Next Elmira sprinkles a pinch of sugar round the base of the candle. "As jelly is sweet to us," she says, "as sugar is sweet to us, so will Judge Cogswell be sweet to Charles 'Bump' Dawson and favor his case."

While we watch the candle burn, any doubts I had about Uncle Bump melt away. I don't need to worry. Squished in here between Mama and Elmira, I'm sure we're going to win.

When at long last the candle burns out, Elmira says to me, "Your mama tells me what a dapper gentleman your daddy was. A sturdy, strong one. He would want to be at that trial to help out, so I'ma tell you how to bring his spirit there." Elmira gives us a spoon and a small sack to do the job.

Three hours after we've come, Mama stands to leave and tries to pay Elmira a quarter. But Elmira refuses. She just says, "What's given, returns."

Mama insists we go straight to the graveyard to follow Elmira's instructions. But now it occurs to me: if Daddy died in Hornet, then how can he be buried here in Kuckachoo?

"After your father died in Hornet, I gathered an urn full of ashes and buried him here the proper way, so he could stay close to us," Mama explains. And I can tell by the way I see deep into her eyes, Mama's telling the honest-to-goodness truth.

Together, we kneel beside the grave that holds my father. I feel funny knowing what really happened to him. And even though I never knew him, a twinge of guilt rips through my chest, because all these years I never pictured him holding me, playing me a song, fishing with me down the bayou. If I'd thought more about Daddy, if I'd known more about him and his story, then all these years I would have loved him more.

Mama slides the spoon and sack out of her pocket and collects some dirt. "You was strong and brave in life, Brayburn. In death, we ask you to help Bump with all your power and strength. Addie Ann and me are bringing this here dime to pay you for your graveyard dirt." Mama giggles and pulls the coin from her pocket. "Though I know you would've given it free," she adds, and sets the coin on Daddy's stone.

While we walk back to the Montgomerys' house, Mama wraps an arm round me, a firm arm, and I can tell she got some hope, some strength, by asking her dead husband to help out.

❦

Tonight at the Montgomerys' dinner table, Delilah and me don't say anything other than "Pass the corn," and "Pass the taters." Mama and Mrs. Montgomery cry into their chicken. Mr. Montgomery says, "Ladies, we need to have . . . to have some hope. You know Bump . . . Bump is strong. He'll make it . . . he'll make it through." But I can just tell Mr. Montgomery doesn't believe a word leaving out his own mouth.

Tonight Mama and me, we lie with our heads at the same end of the couch, Mama holding me in her arms. And I get to thinking about the trial again. *If it wasn't Uncle Bump, who was it? Who would ruin the garden?* But since everyone I can think of is a friend of mine, I decide not to think anymore.

It's strange how when you stop thinking, the answers grow in your mind.

Tonight I doubt Mama sleeps at all. But I do.

Tonight my dream is the same but different.

I'm running throught the forest, same as always, and Flapjack's beside me, same as always, but this time the news reporter for the Delta Daily *is here too. We hide behind a fat pine tree. When I peek out, I spot the man with the shovel. The sky's clear, not dark, and I can see the man's not a haint. Not a monster. Not a hooded Klansman. He's just a man digging in the forest, burying something in a ditch.* "Who is it?" *I ask the news reporter. The news reporter goes out of our hiding place to investigate. He sneaks from tree trunk to tree trunk till he's just feet from the man. Then he yells,* "Hey, you!" *The man's head snaps round. Startled, the man yells,* "Scram!" *But it's too late. The reporter already took his picture with his instant camera. Now he's running back through the woods to show it to me. I take one look at the photograph and gasp.*

I wake up, my breath even and calm.

"Got it," I whisper.

I wish I could tell Elias what the night said, but I won't see him till the trial's through. And if I tell Mama, she's likely to leave me home, thinking this is all too much for a twelve-year-old to bear. So for once in my life, I keep a secret all to myself.

Now I nudge Mama. "Wake up."

"Mmmm . . ." It seems Mama's stuck in a dream of her own.

"Come on!" I tell her. "Today's the day."

Mama can barely get herself dressed, she's got the fidgets so bad. But me? I rush to pull on the orange dress with the yellow iris down the back, the one Delilah let me borrow for courage.

Before I leave for court, I go out to the yard. I see something sparkling in the ashes where my house used to stand. I don't want to dirty my sneakers. But I can't help it. I tiptoe across the charred yard to the glitter on the ground. I pick it up and brush off the black flakes. I know just what it is: the silver knob to change the channels. It's all that's left of my television set. I drop the knob onto the ground and step back across the ashes to the Montgomerys' yard.

Mama, Mr. Montgomery, Mrs. Montgomery, and Delilah empty out of the house. The lot of us stand shoulder to shoulder in a circle while Flapjack twists round my ankles. The old oak is a burnt stump. The swing's gone. The television's gone. Everything's gone but this circle.

We open our palms to the sky while Mama prays for Uncle Bump's deliverance. Then she reaches into her pocket, removes the sack of graveyard dirt, and sprinkles it onto all our hands. When she drops the dirt onto my fingers, it tickles, and I reckon maybe Daddy really is here after all. Then I close my fist round Daddy's dirt and pour it into the back of my sock, so I can make sure he comes with us to court.

CHAPTER 27

October 21, 1963, Early Morning

There's only a handful of us who know the truth: my brother's nothing but alive. Last night he drove back to Kuckachoo with Miss Gold. Now he's hiding in the Montgomerys' pantry—sleeping, eating, and praying the day away—so he can be here when the trial's done. And I don't think it will take too long. Mama says here in Kuckachoo justice is served up faster than a malted at the Corner Store. She doesn't expect the trial will last till noon.

When we get to the courthouse, I bend down and kiss Flapjack goodbye. While my cat stretches out in a patch of sun beside the courthouse, Mama and me climb up those seven steps and head inside.

After we take our seats in the colored rows, twelve white men settle into their seats in the jury box up front. I wish folks like Mr. Montgomery and Mrs. Jacks could be the jurors instead. But seeing as they can't pass that cock-eyed test to register, I reckon Negroes will never decide our own fate in court.

Well, I'll tell you one thing: I can't wait for the truth to leap out of its hiding place and give everyone a good fright.

"All rise!" shouts the court clerk, who's still got a cold.

Folks are quiet while the judge walks to his chair, bangs his hammer, and calls on the lawyer to make an opening speech.

"Ladies and gentlemen," Mr. Hickock says to the jurors, "I represent the great state of Mississippi. We are here this morning to do justice. As you know, a heinous crime has been committed."

And I'll tell you something else: if that lawyer thinks using a big word like "heinous" is going to make us think he's smart, he's wrong.

"Good people of Kuckachoo," Mr. Hickock says, "you planted a community garden for the purpose of feeding your children, but before you could harvest the crop, someone deliberately, viciously, horribly, and intentionally—I repeat, intentionally—ruined that garden by planting it over with butter bean seeds. It's clear that person intended harm, because that person didn't even set poles beside each plant so the vines could grow *up* the way they're supposed to.

Instead, those vines grew *across* the garden like ivy and choked the life out of anything trying to make it on that land. Not even the butter beans came up right. That person took food out of the mouths of your little babies, your children. And that person is here in this courtroom."

It's a good thing Dr. Martin Luther King Jr. isn't here in this courtroom, because I hear Dr. King doesn't like violence, and right about now I'm aching to slug Mr. Hickock's face. And I reckon Mama knows what I have in mind, because she grabs my fist and holds it in her warm hand.

"Today, the witnesses for the prosecution will prove Bump Dawson stole the seeds from Mr. Adams's garden cabin and destroyed property that rightfully belongs to our community," Mr. Hickock says. "Later, the Honorable Judge Cogswell will decide whether to put Bump behind bars for five years. Or perhaps ten."

Mr. Hickock turns my stomach worse than crawfish stew. Now he rocks back on his heels. Then at long last he sits down on his spindly behind.

Next, the judge calls on our lawyer, Miss Gold. Special for the trial she wears a fancy blue jacket and skirt. But Mama takes one look at Miss Gold's too-short hemline and shakes her head. So what if her legs show? To me, Miss Gold looks fetching, kneecaps and all.

"Good morning," Miss Gold says to the jurors. I like how she sounds all sharp and sure like she's ready to fight. "I represent the defendant, Bump Dawson," she says. "As Mr. Hickock has told you, we're here today to see justice is done. To deliver justice means to do what's right and fair. Yes, somebody ruined your community garden, but what's right and fair is to find the true culprit, not just a convenient scapegoat for this crime."

Mama's grip on my hand loosens.

"Today, gentlemen of the jury, I will prove to you that Bump Dawson deserves nothing but your respect. This is a question of character. Not only was my client a faithful servant for more than a decade, but he's also an upright, law-abiding citizen. You'll soon see that Bump Dawson, the man sitting before you, deserves an apology from the entire community, because he's not guilty of any crime."

I have to stop myself from bolting to the front of the courtroom to give Miss Gold a hug. What she says, it's right and fair. And I'm sure as the sun shines that the judge will end this whole trial right now. It's clear as day. There's nothing left to discuss.

So when the judge says, "The case for the prosecution may begin," his words evaporate out his mouth, condense in a cloud over my head, and rain down all over me till I'm soaked to the bone.

Then Mr. Hickock calls his first witness to the stand.

Mama takes one look at the witness and shakes her head back and forth. And I just know that tea is spilling all over again in her mind.

That's because the first witness in Uncle Bump's trial is none other than Honey's mother, the lady with the plastic strawberries on her hat, the one who flunks hardworking Negroes at voter registration, Mrs. Tate's friend, Mrs. Worth.

Today Mrs. Worth's short blond hair is all fluffed out. And she's got on a hat, a purple box of a hat, with a blue feather stuck to the side of it.

While Mrs. Worth rests her plump hand on the Bible, I scrunch my toes in Daddy's dirt to let him know we need him bad, and we'd be more than grateful if anyone else in Heaven could fly down and help out too!

"Do you swear to tell the truth, the whole truth, and nothing but the truth, so help you God?" the court clerk asks Mrs. Worth.

"So help me God," she says.

"Very well then," says Mr. Hickock, "as a most influential member of the Garden Club, do you know that Charles 'Bump' Dawson has tended to the weeding and watering of the community garden, some of the most bothersome tasks in growing vegetables?"

"That's exactly right," Mrs. Worth says. "I originally thought my husband, Harold, and some of the neighborhood men were doing the job. But now I've learned Mr. Mudge hired Bump Dawson and some Negro hands to do it instead."

A sweat breaks out under my dress. My armpits itch. Uncle Bump said he was working part-time mopping the floor and handing out the government cheese at the General Merchandise Store in Franklindale. He never said anything about tending the garden. But come to think on it, he never smells like cheese. Now I can't help but wonder, what if Uncle Bump lied? For a minute, I get stuck in this crazy thinking till I remind myself what the night said.

Mrs. Worth goes on. "All the evenings I thought my husband, Harold, was working so hard on the garden, it turns out he was out with his friends, eating and listening to music down at Roxy's. Now Harold's in big trouble, but I can assure you, I will sentence him myself."

The men in the front of the courtroom laugh.

"Oh, this is no laughing matter," Mrs. Worth says. "The very same person who picked the weeds was actually the criminal who planted the seeds—the butter bean seeds, that is. The butter bean seeds that ruined our garden." Then, sure as God made little green apples, Mrs. Worth points at Uncle Bump. "He did it!" she says. "He's the one!"

"Why would the defendant want to ruin the garden?" Mr. Hickock asks.

"Because Bump Dawson hates you and me both," Mrs. Worth says. "He blames all white folks for the death of his nephew."

Now if that don't beat all! Uncle Bump doesn't blame every white Kuckachookian for what happened to Elias— just a few creeps like Mrs. Worth's son Jimmy and his wicked friend, Buck.

"Objection! Speculation!" shouts Miss Gold. "The witness doesn't know the true feelings of the defendant and therefore cannot state the defendant's motivation."

"Overruled!" the judge says. He bangs his hammer.

Mrs. Worth pulls a tissue out of her purse and wipes each eye. "Bump Dawson wanted to ruin our plans. Ruin our harvest. He planted over our garden with butter beans," she says.

Mrs. Worth grips the iron rail round the witness-box and leans toward Uncle Bump. I want to tell her to sit back and shut her overgrown mouth, but now she's screaming, "We have youngsters here who need more in their bellies and now they're going without!" She grits her teeth. "You want our children to starve!"

I'm at the end of my rope when the judge orders Uncle Bump's lawyer, Miss Gold, to begin the cross-examination.

Miss Gold walks up real close to Mrs. Worth. "You say Bump Dawson and some other field hands have kept up the garden all these weeks. How do you know?"

"What do you mean, how do I know?" Mrs. Worth says. "Everyone knows! Mr. Mudge hired Bump to do the dirty work."

"After the planting did you ever see Bump Dawson in Mr. Adams's garden?" Miss Gold asks.

Mrs. Worth purses her lips and bugs out her eyes like Miss Gold's question is nothing short of absurd. "If you think I've got time to go traipsing through the mud, you're awfully uninformed. I have four children to look after, I register voters at the courthouse, and I call the bingo games at church," she says.

"Well, you may be interested to know," Miss Gold says, "Bump Dawson never worked at Mr. Adams's place after the garden planting. Not even for one day!"

"Creation!" says Mrs. Worth. "If that ain't a bald-faced lie! Everyone knows Mr. Mudge hired a few of the coloreds to tend the garden, Bump Dawson included."

"And do you know the names of the other field hands?" Miss Gold asks.

"Their names? Colored names?" Mrs. Worth puts her hand to her chest and chuckles. "I don't know their names."

"Then are you telling me, Mrs. Worth, that the one and only field hand you can identify happens to belong to the very same family as the boy who broke your son's leg and ruined your son's chance of getting a football scholarship to college?" asks Miss Gold.

Mrs. Worth scrunches her upturned nose. "One matter's got nothing to do with the other!" she says, and scowls. "Bump Dawson oversaw that land *before* Mr. Adams died, and he continued to do the job *after* Mr. Adams died. If you want the names of the other field hands who tended the garden, I'm sure Mr. Mudge would be happy to supply them. Course, he left town after the garden was laid by. Between opening his new shop in Muscadine County and tending his sick mama in Florida, he's been gone from Kuckachoo for weeks."

And I reckon I can't wait to let the cat out of the bag.

"But it doesn't much matter who the other field hands are," Mrs. Worth says, "because we've got the *head* of all the field hands right here! The boss of the coloreds. The one in charge of what they did."

Miss Gold holds her chin in her hand, taps her finger against it. "If Bump Dawson actually did commit this crime, how do you suppose he got access to so many butter bean seeds? Wouldn't that be next to impossible for a man of his means?"

Mrs. Worth takes a deep breath in her nostrils. "I can see you're missing some critical information, so allow me to supply it," she says. Then Mrs. Worth talks real slow, like

Miss Gold's got a silo of wheat between her ears. "I was inside Mr. Adams's garden cabin on the day of the planting," she says. "I can tell you it was jam-packed with a wide variety of seed—more than we could ever use. I'm sure there was plenty of butter bean seeds there too, enough for Bump Dawson to destroy our garden!"

To Mrs. Worth, eveything's clear as raindrops. "Once Mr. Mudge hired Bump to keep up the garden, Bump had plenty of time to break into the garden cabin, haul out the butter bean seeds, and commit this crime," she says. "So if you follow me now, there isn't anyone else it could be."

Miss Gold stands still as a charred hog on a roasting spit. I wonder if she's changing her mind. Does she think Uncle Bump did it? I'm afraid any minute now she'll quit our case and march out the courthouse door.

"No further questions," Miss Gold mumbles.

At long last, Uncle Bump turns to face the viewing gallery. Through his blue uniform, I can make out the bones of his elbows and knees. Sweat runs like sap down his forehead, and I know he's searching the rows for Mama and me. For a second, I can't help but wonder whether the broken-down look on his face, the dead look in his eyes, is guilt. His eyes find mine. I hope he can't see me cry.

Next Mr. Hickock calls Mr. Tate to the stand. After Mr. Tate swears on the Bible, Mr. Hickock asks him how many butter beans it would take to cover Mr. Adams's field.

"To cover it thickly, you would need fifty-eight pounds of seed per acre, so six acres would require . . . exactly three hundred forty-eight pounds of seed," Mr. Tate says.

And I can't believe someone so stupid can do butter bean math in his head.

"Now, how big is Mr. Adams's garden?" Mr. Hickock asks.

"Well, 'bout the size of five football fields," Mr. Tate says.

"Speaking of football, Mr. Tate, the record shows that back in high school you brought the Kuckachoo Kickers to the state championships four consecutive years. I've always wanted to ask, how'd you do it?"

"Irrelevant!" Miss Gold shouts, but the judge over-rules her.

Then Mr. Tate spends forever boasting about how he used to be the best football player in the history of the pigskin. And I don't need to look at Mama to know she thinks Mr. Tate would do better humbling himself before the Almighty than bragging before the court.

At long last it's Miss Gold's turn to cross-examine the witness. Standing beside the muscley Mr. Tate, Miss Gold looks scrawny, but she makes up for it by scaring him a bit. She points a finger at Mr. Tate and waves it in front of his face. Then she pauses beside the witness-box, one hand on her hip. "You and some of the other gentlemen in Kuckachoo told your wives you were weeding and watering when all along you were down at Roxy's?" Miss Gold asks.

Mr. Tate looks down at the floor. "Correct," he says.

"Please tell the court why you abandoned your responsibilities at the garden."

"It's simple, really. The first time we showed up at the garden to do our job, we ran into Sam Mudge at the gate. Sam tells us tending is Negro work. Says we shouldn't let our wives talk us into doing it. Says he'd rather pay his own money to hire Bump Dawson and a few field hands to do the job, instead of watch us humiliate ourselves. Then, since our wives wasn't expecting us home anyway, Sam suggests we go hear Thelma Peacock sing the blues at Roxy's," he says. "The first night Sam bought our meal. We had a mighty fine time, so the next evening when our wives thought we was working down the garden, we went to Roxy's again. That night, if I recall, Mad Johnny was blowing his saxophone like a crazy fool! Soon it just became . . . well, habit."

"I see," says Miss Gold. "So all those evenings you were supposed to be tending the garden, you were listening to the blues down at Roxy's?"

"And munching fried catfish!"

Miss Gold doesn't look amused. "Tell me this. Are you the biggest seed salesman in Thunder Creek County?" she asks.

Mr. Tate stands in the witness-box, holds both hands on his potbelly. "Am now!" he says. Then he laughs along with his audience in the white rows and sits back down.

Miss Gold plants her face up close to Mr. Tate's till his smile gets erased.

"Seriously," he says, "I'm the most successful seed salesman in Thunder Creek County."

"Then please tell the court whether you sold any large quantities of butter beans this year," Miss Gold says.

"Well, there are nine hundred twenty-three butter bean seeds per pound, so let me think. I sold . . . three hundred twenty-one thousand, two hundred four seeds."

I hate the way Mr. Tate talks all polite like it comes natural, when at home he's nothing but a tobacco-spitting lout.

"And how fast do your butter bean vines grow?" she asks.

"The particular variety I sell grows at an alarming rate. Ten inches a week!"

Miss Gold struts back to her seat, opens her suitcase, and removes a green jump rope. She orders Mr. Tate to hold one end of the jump rope while she stretches it across the front of the courtroom. Then she asks the bailiff to measure it with a measuring tape. The bailiff says the jump rope is exactly six feet long.

"For the record," Miss Gold says, "this butter bean vine was clipped from Mr. Adams's field just yesterday."

And that's when I find out it isn't a jump rope at all.

"Now then, Mr. Tate, do we agree that if a vine grows ten inches per week, then at six feet, or seventy-two inches, this vine has been growing seven weeks?" Miss Gold asks.

"Irrelevant!" yells Mr. Hickock. "What does that have to do with anything?"

"Sustained!" says the judge.

"Well, then," Miss Gold says, "let me ask you this, Mr. Tate. To whom did you sell the three hundred twenty-one thousand, two hundred four butter bean seeds?"

Even from back here, I can see sweat bubble up on Mr. Tate's forehead. "Well, I, uh, sold them to Mr. Adams before he died. And Bump Dawson stole them."

"Speculation!" Miss Gold says.

"Overruled!" says the judge.

"And how do you keep track of your sales?" Miss Gold asks.

"Records," Mr. Tate says. He folds his arms across his chest.

"And with your records," Miss Gold says, "I imagine it would be quite simple for you to prove to the court you sold the butter bean seeds to Mr. Adams, the very seeds you allege were then stolen by Bump Dawson to plant over the garden."

Mr. Tate nods.

"Then, Judge, I would like to request that the witness please retrieve his records, so that we can admit them as evidence," Miss Gold says.

But then Mr. Tate changes his mind. He tells Miss Gold he doesn't have time to keep track of each little sale, and even if he did, he wouldn't be able to get his records, because they're in the bedroom where his wife's sleeping. "She was up all night with the baby. You're a lady," Mr. Tate says to Miss Gold. "I shouldn't have to tell you how hard it is to have a baby and your help up and gone to a trial."

Mama and me, we chew up our tongues. And I know if we could, we'd spit them into his beastly face.

Now Mr. Tate's forehead drips like he's hiding something, and I start to wonder what it is. And I reckon Miss Gold wonders too, because when she turns to the judge, she looks like my cat does just before he pounces on a field mouse.

"Your Honor," she says, "I request we stop this trial until the records have been subpoenaed and both parties have had the opportunity to review them. I would like them taken from the witness's bedroom. Immediately!"

"Go on now. Fetch the records," the judge tells Mr. Tate. "No hurry," he adds, and winks.

Then Miss Gold looks at the judge the same way I look at Flapjack after he's dragged a dead mouse in the kitchen.

CHAPTER 28

October 21, 1963, Late Morning

Once the case for the defense begins, Miss Gold tells the jury she's got a witness who can prove Uncle Bump would never wreck Old Man Adams's land. "My witness, Mr. Pinnington, will demonstrate that Bump Dawson is not a man who seeks revenge but a man who seeks justice," she says.

A small white man with a white beard totters to the stand. What with his fancy suit and suitcase, I reckon he's very important. While he wobbles up the side aisle, he checks his pocket watch, and I can't believe it takes me all the way till this little man is sworn on the Bible and locked inside the witness-box to remember who he is: Old Man Adams's lawyer, the man who gave me the television.

Mr. Pinnington is his name!

"Did Mr. Adams ever mention anything about his head servant, Mr. Dawson?" Miss Gold asks him.

"Well," Mr. Pinnington says, "Mr. Adams did tell me it was because he was impressed by the hard work of his Negro hands, and the kindness shown to him by Bump Dawson in particular, that he wrote his will as he did."

"And by the way, just what did Mr. Adams write in his will?"

"It's common knowledge," Mr. Pinnington says. "I reviewed this months ago."

"Remind me," Miss Gold says.

While Mr. Pinnington checks his pocket watch a second time, I start to heat up because I reckon this little man thinks he's got somewhere more important to be.

Then he unlocks his suitcase, pulls out a heap of paper, and reads, " 'I bequeath my gold pocket watch to my head servant, Bump Dawson. To Elmira Grady, my cook, I leave my Dutch oven. To Miss Addie Ann Pickett, my cook's assistant, I leave my television set. I hereby bequeath my furniture, my books, and the remaining contents of my home to my alma mater, Ole Miss. The house itself will be used as a gathering spot for the people of Kuckachoo. I expect the annual Christmas party to carry on without me. Most importantly, I leave my land to all the people of my community. Together whites and Negroes shall plant a garden.' "

When Mr. Pinnington finishes reading the will, a man in the first row roars, "That will. It's a fake!" A lady yells, "Everyone knows Mr. Adams was sicker than a tick stuck in sap." And there's only a handful of folks in this court-room with their jaws still hinged together.

Of course, the judge calls for order, but he's got to bang his hammer six times before everyone settles enough for the trial to go on.

And one thing's clear: if I don't get a chance to tell them what the night said, folks with common sense and ordinary logic will pin this crime on Uncle Bump. And if Uncle Bump spends years behind bars without our family, without his harmonica, I wonder if he'll still have the will to live. It's a question I hate to ask, an answer I dread to hear.

Mr. Hickock folds his arms across his chest. He struts up to the little lawyer, Mr. Pinnington, and says, "Now correct me if I'm wrong, sir, but it doesn't require a stretch of the imagination to believe that when Mr. Adams passed away, Charles 'Bump' Dawson felt he deserved the man's land. As Mr. Adams's head servant, Bump had grown rather uppity over the years. Some who observed Bump say he even acted as if he'd forgotten his color, since he took care of the old man like he was his very own son."

Mr. Hickock rocks back on his heels. "Now, if in fact what you say is true, and Mr. Adams did indeed leave his land to all the people of Kuckachoo, then it stands to reason that when the Negroes were excluded from the sunrise pick-ing, they could have been mad. But Charles 'Bump' Dawson would have been angriest of all. Wouldn't you agree?"

Mr. Pinnington covers his face with his hands and shakes his head like he can't stand to stay in Kuckachoo one more second. Then he sighs and says, "I suppose given the circumstances, yes, it's possible Bump Dawson could've grown angry. But he's just a convenient scapegoat for the injustice that has occurred here."

"What's a scapegoat?" I whisper to Mama.

"I reckon it's someone folks can blame for their troubles," she says.

Now Mr. Pinnington pops up, unlocks the witness-box himself, and hurries out the courthouse door. And I've got another question for Mama.

"Why won't he stay and fight?" I whisper.

"Clean folks don't want to get dirty," she whispers back.

And even though I don't have the foggiest what Mama means, I'm not about to get in a long discussion here in the courthouse, not when Miss Gold's calling my very own uncle to the stand.

Uncle Bump trudges to the witness-box. His shackles clang. He doesn't bother to lift his feet. They just slide along the floor. He doesn't try to stand up straight and proud. His shoulders sag. But when I see his fists clenched at his sides, I get some hope, because hands ready to punch tell me he'll fight for his cause.

You know how you can half close your eyes and everything looks fuzzy? Well, if you half closed your ears, everything would sound blurry and you'd swear you were sitting in church listening to the reverend and Mrs. Montgomery. That's because at church, every time the reverend says something, Mrs. Montgomery always shouts back, "Amen!" Even when the reverend says, "Good morning!" Mrs. Montgomery yells, "Amen!"

And now that's how it sounds with Miss Gold and Uncle Bump.

"Did you ever visit the garden after the planting?" Miss Gold asks.

"No, ma'am!" Uncle Bump shouts.

"After the planting, did Mr. Mudge hire you to weed and water the garden?" Miss Gold asks.

"No, ma'am!"

"Do you hate all white people?" Miss Gold asks.

"No, ma'am!"

"Do you blame all white people for what happened to your nephew, Elias Pickett?"

"No, ma'am!"

"Did you ever break into the garden cabin?"

"No, ma'am!"

"Mr. Dawson, did you or did you not plant butter beans over the community garden?"

"No, ma'am!"

"No further questions," says Miss Gold.

The service is over, and back here in the colored viewing gallery, our good spirits are flying all over the place.

But that's all wrecked the second Mr. Hickock swaggers to the witness-box. "We've already established that Mr. Tate sold the butter bean seeds to Mr. Adams," he says. He straightens his bow tie and turns to Uncle Bump. "After your brother-in-law went and got himself killed, you were saddled with the burden of his offspring, meaning your hands were surely fuller than you wanted them to be."

Mama squeezes my hand so hard I stop worrying about throwing up on the courthouse floor and start worrying my fingers will break off at the knuckles.

"Objection!" Miss Gold shouts. "Leading the witness."

"Sustained!" says the judge. "Redirect questioning, Mr. Hickock."

"Yes, sir," says Mr. Hickock. "Then, to make matters worse, you learned Mr. Adams's garden was supposed to be shared, yet you were not invited to the first Garden Club meeting. Now with all that going on, you will admit that you were an angry fellow, were you not?"

Uncle Bump stares straight ahead at the viewing gallery, but he doesn't say a word, so Mr. Hickock leans over the railing round Uncle Bump and shouts all rough and mean, "Answer me, boy!"

A blue vein bulges down the center of Uncle Bump's forehead.

Now Mr. Hickock yells even louder, "Answer me, boy!"

And Uncle Bump explodes. "I'm a man!" His three words rumble through the courthouse like sentences, paragraphs, books.

"Aha!" Mr. Hickock says. He raises his right index finger. "Indeed you are a man. A very angry man!"

"Objection! Leading!" Miss Gold cries.

"Overruled!" The judge bangs his hammer.

"It's logical to assume an angry man like you would

break into the garden cabin and plant over the entire field with butter beans to get revenge. Correct?" Mr. Hickock says.

Uncle Bump clenches his teeth.

"Speak up, boy. I can't hear you," Mr. Hickock says.

A tear hotter than Mama's iron burns down my cheek. I'm mad enough to slaughter a hog with my bare hands. I see how our case, it's coming apart—how the law, it's not on our side. My throat burns raw as buckwheat. I know what I need to do, but I don't know quite how to do it. How can I, Addie Ann Pickett, get up there in front of all these people? How can I, Addie Ann Pickett, tell them what the night told me?

But now the crickety-crack of a door rings out from the back of the courtroom, and a fuss splashes through the viewing gallery.

"What have we here?" the judge asks. He lifts up his glasses and squints at the back of the room.

I turn in my seat. And what do you know? There's Mrs. Tate with Miss Springer. "If it pleases the court," Miss Springer calls out, "my friend, Penelope Tate, has some rather intriguing evidence to present."

The judge lowers his glasses back down on his nose. "Oh, I see!" he says. "The lovely Mrs. Tate! Come on up!"

Miss Springer gives her friend a gentle push forward. Then Mrs. Tate swivels down the center aisle in her pink dress and white hat. She looks just like a movie star—just like Audrey Hepburn.

CHAPTER 29

October 21, 1963, Noon

When Mrs. Tate arrives at the front of the courtroom, she chats a few seconds with Miss Gold. Then Miss Gold talks to the judge. And before long, Mrs. Tate's resting her palm on the Bible, swearing to tell the whole truth.

"I'm not one for speaking to the public and all," Mrs. Tate says soon as she's settled in the witness-box. "But my friend, Miss Springer, brought me here and my mother's watching my son because I've got something to tell y'all."

"Mrs. Tate, if you'll forgive me," says Mr. Hickock, "you appear on edge. Truly you don't need to testify. We've already heard from your husband, which is good enough for the both of you so far as I'm concerned."

Mrs. Tate closes her eyes like she's trying to erase the ugly sight. But sorry for her, when she opens them back up, Mr. Hickock's still there. So Mrs. Tate says, "Excuse me, Mr. Hickock, but I wouldn't be here if I was just gonna repeat what my husband already said."

It's amazing how Mr. Hickock slinks away.

"Just talking from personal experience," Mrs. Tate says, "I think a lot of you would be surprised to know I was actually quite a good student in school. I've got more going on than what you see. But folks don't seem to want to believe two things—beauty and brains—can go together. What's more—"

"For the love of the Lord!" Miss Springer cries out from the back of the courtroom. "Quit whistlin' Dixie!"

"But I'm not whistlin' Dixie!" says Mrs. Tate. "It's a similar case here. Folks don't want to believe that the person who disrespected you and me and everyone who worked so hard on this garden, the person who doesn't care whether *we* eat or don't eat as long as *he* eats, the person who has our respect but doesn't deserve it, could actually be, well, one of us. Folks would rather believe what's easy: a Negro committed this crime. But the truth is more complicated."

With that, Mrs. Tate reaches into her purse, takes out a sheet of newspaper, and hands it to the judge. "This should help solve the puzzle."

"Looks like a sheet from the *Delta Daily* to me," the judge says. "And the date on it . . ." The judge lowers his glasses on his nose. "July 18, 1963."

"Exactly, sir. If you turn that news sheet over, you'll see

238

that scrawled beside the crossword puzzle is the list of all the seeds that were left in Mr. Adams's garden cabin at the time he died. Mr. Mudge wrote up this list at one of our Garden Club meetings. As you can see, Judge, according to Mr. Mudge, when Mr. Adams died, there weren't any butter bean seeds left in his garden cabin. No butter bean seeds at all."

"And so, Mrs. Tate?" asks the judge.

"And so the idea that someone broke into the shed and stole the butter bean seeds that ruined our garden doesn't amount to a hill of beans," Mrs. Tate says. "But this does!" she adds. Then she digs to the bottom of her purse and plucks out a long slip of yellow paper like it's a quarrelsome buttercup wrecking her lawn. She hands it to the judge.

I crane my neck off my backbone trying to make out what that long strip of yellow paper could be. What a slip of paper could possibly have to do with mud, tears, and vines, I can't imagine.

The judge smooths out the slip with his palm and checks it through his magnifying glass. Mrs. Tate has more to say. "It's like this," she begins. The second she opens her mouth, though, the judge holds up his hand like she should shut it back up.

But I reckon Mrs. Tate is sick of waiting for the judge to figure out what she already knows, because she plows ahead to tell her story. "Just yesterday I'm looking for the perfect outfit for this trial," she says. "I pick out a yellow dress, a two-piece with satin trim. Of course, I wouldn't think of wearing that darling dress without my lemon chiffon hat to match. So I search my closet. I open all my hatboxes, one by one, but no lemon chiffon. And I'm wringing my hands because I don't know where else my hat could be. Not unless I stuck it in one of my husband's hatboxes by accident."

"Objection!" Mr. Hickock calls, and stands. "Irrelevant!"

"Overruled," says the judge. "And don't be rude to the lovely lady."

"So I stand on my tippy-toes," Mrs. Tate says, "and when I pull down one of my husband's hatboxes, I hear a strange rustling sound inside. I remove the cover, and there, where his cowboy hat used to rest in peace, are all these long slips of yellow paper instead. I pull them out, one by one, then by handfuls."

Mrs. Tate stares down the jurors. Then she tells the most exciting part. "I get a closer look at one of those slips and I'll be!" she says. "What I see in my hand is . . ."

"What?" asks the judge. "What did you see in your hand?"

"Oh," Mrs. Tate says, "just the key to the butter bean fiasco." She bats her blue eyes. "If you must know," she says, "it wasn't a Negro who planted the butter beans and ruined our harvest."

The jurors sit still as the butter sculpture at Old Man Adams's Christmas party.

"As you can see, I never did find my lemon chiffon hat, so last minute I had to switch my whole color scheme to this," Mrs. Tate says, and touches the sleeve of her pink dress.

Halfway up the central aisle, I see Delilah. She's sitting

on the courthouse floor, shaking her head in sympathy with Mrs. Tate who tried to dress to match the day but failed.

"In any case," Mrs. Tate says, "it pains me most of all to say this: my husband, Ralph, never sold the butter bean seeds to Mr. Adams. He sold them to . . . to . . ." Mrs. Tate looks down at her hands like she's trying to see if she carried her courage here today. When she looks back up, I can tell by the flash of anger in her eyes that she did. "He sold those butter bean seeds to Mr. Mudge."

The pictures in my mind slide into place like a television show.

"Fact is," she says, "my husband did make this hefty sale, but, Judge, that paper in your hand proves he sold the seeds to Mr. Mudge, not Mr. Adams. That is a receipt of sale, Judge. Receipt of sale! If you look down there at the bottom, you'll see Sam Mudge's signature. Now, Judge, when I was a schoolgirl, I thought all that mathematics I studied was a bunch of hooey. How was all that multiplication and division gonna help me?" Mrs. Tate laughs. "Funny, it's coming in rather handy today!"

"What do you mean?" the judge asks.

"Well, Judge, that there receipt in your hand shows my husband, Ralph, sold three hundred twenty-one thousand, two hundred four butter bean seeds to Mr. Mudge on July twenty-second this year. That was just a few days after the last Garden Club meeting when we'd finally decided what to plant. Now then, we all know that the vegetable garden is six acres, so if there are nine hundred twenty-three butter bean seeds per pound and it takes fifty-eight pounds to cover one acre with thick vines, then you can see that to cover six acres would require . . . well, three hundred forty-eight pounds or . . ." Mrs. Tate rolls her eyes up in her head. When they fall back down again, she says, "Exactly three hundred twenty-one thousand, two hundred four seeds. And if the seeds are sold in fifty-pound sacks, then to cover six acres you'd need . . ." Her eyeballs roll up and down again. "Seven sacks," she says.

I reckon I'm proud Mrs. Tate can do butter bean math in her head too!

But now Mrs. Tate's smile fades. "My husband, Ralph, may not be the cheeriest man in Kuckachoo," she says, "but he is loyal to his friends. And that's why I hope you'll forgive him for standing up for his friend Sam Mudge, who started him out in seed sales in the first place. I know Ralph is so shocked by this butter bean crime he can't come to see the truth yet himself. But we all have a little space in our hearts where the truth resides even if we don't want to look there. And I know eventually my husband will look into that space and be proud of me. Proud I stood up for all of us who planned this garden. And so you might say I'm doing this favor for my husband, sparing him from getting into the awkward position of turning in a friend who has already turned on him."

In the back of the courtroom, Miss Springer applauds. I see lots of hats bobbing up and down. Pink hats. Black hats. Blue hats. It seems all the ladies in the viewing gallery have turned to their neighbors to whisper.

Then a gravelly voice shouts, "Traitor!" and folks go

crazy. Some holler at Mrs. Tate as she leaves the witness-box. The judge bangs his hammer.

And me? I've got to get to the stand. I've got to prove what Mrs. Tate says, it's the no-doubt-about-it, one-hundred-percent, honest-to-goodness truth.

CHAPTER 30

October 21, 1963, Early Afternoon

At long last it's quiet in the courtroom. Now's my chance. I press past Mama's knees, fly down the center aisle, and wave my hand like I've figured out the answer to the challenge problem in school. It all makes sense. My dream, I know it's true. And I know I've got to tell Miss Gold what the night said.

But the judge sees me first. "What on earth is this spectacle?" he roars.

"Please, Your Honor," says Miss Gold. "She's Bump Dawson's niece."

"Get her outta here!" the judge shouts.

The next thing I know, two court officers lunge at me

from both sides. They wrap their fat hands round my arms and lift me up in the air.

Then *thwack!* A loud thud vibrates from the back of the courtroom. I turn my head. There's Mrs. Jacks slamming her walking stick into the courthouse floor. And dog my cats! I reckon even Mrs. Jacks misses school for real important things.

"Your Honor, if you would permit just one more unscheduled witness, I would like to call this girl, Addie Ann Pickett, to the stand," Miss Gold says.

White folks howl with laughter. The judge bangs his hammer again and again, but the shrieking giggles roll on. I shuffle my legs in the air like I'm riding an imaginary bicycle, which is the only kind I've ever had, so I know just how to do it. And the news reporter takes pictures of me with his Polaroid instant camera.

One thing's clear: the judge is good and scared this mess in his courtroom will be tomorrow's front-page news, because at long last he gives in. "Fine!" he yells over the hubbub. "Bring her up!"

When the officers drop me into the witness box, I look out at all the people laughing at me. And the strange thing is I know just what to do. This time I don't need my brother's instructions. I stand up. But I don't look down the way Mama always says I should. Instead I raise my eyes to stare—no, glare—at the members of the Kuckachoo Garden Club. I see blue eyes sinking in pity, hazel eyes tickling with gossip, and brown eyes burning with hate. And I see other eyes, like Honey Worth's, quivering with questions.

The next minute stretches like a forty-nine-car railroad

train. My silent protest swallows up the laughter one guf-faw at a time.

I fix my eyes on Mrs. Worth's.

Right away, she sits up straight and fiddles with the hat on her head.

At long last there's more order in the court than there's been all day.

The court clerk holds the Bible in front of me. I swear to tell the whole truth, so help me God. When I hear those words, I think how much the whole truth can hurt. Lickety-split, it flashes through my mind: a morning not long ago. We were in the middle of a math test. Mrs. Jacks stepped into the hall to talk to the principal. I could feel Jeremiah Taylor's eyes bore a hole into my paper from behind me. When Mrs. Jacks hobbled back in the room, she said, "I presume we've all kept our eyes on our own papers, have we not?" And right then I said, "Yes, ma'am" along with all the others. I reckon you could say I didn't tell the whole truth, because Jeremiah was cheating and I didn't let on. And I wondered if I was a bad person after that. But then, what good would it have done me to tell on Jeremiah?

Now I sit down in the witness-box.

"Is there something you'd like to say?" Miss Gold asks.

Here I am, sworn to tell the whole truth and everything, so I imagine I'm not in a courtroom but in a classroom— Mrs. Jacks's room. I picture myself in school, but after school, talking to the teacher who cares what I've got to say. I open my mouth, and what do you know? For once in my life, a bushel of ripe words falls at my feet. "The evi-dence," I say. "It's in the woods next to Mr. Mudge's farm."

"Blasphemy!" cries Mr. Hickock.

A breeze blows through the open window. I describe what I saw when Flapjack and me dashed through the forest the day Honey Worth warned me to run.

The judge twirls the hammer in his hand. I'll bet he's afraid the news reporter will follow my clues even if he doesn't. And then how will he look if the evidence turns up? So at long last he bangs the hammer down and says, "The lawyers, the witnesses for the defense, the jurors, and me— we're going to get to the bottom of this nonsense once and for all. Officers, see to it no one else moves from this court!" He points to the news reporter. "Jott James, you come along too. I know you'd prefer to photograph the Miss Sweetheart competition, but today we'll need your camera to document the evidence and check the veracity of what this young lady says." Then the judge looks straight at me and says, "Young lady, if what you say is not verifiable, be warned. I can try you for perjury!"

Thanks to Mrs. Jacks and her Latin roots, I crack the judge's secret code. By using the words "*veri*fiable" and "per*jury*," the judge is telling me that if I don't prove what I say is a fact, the law will come after me and I'll face a jury all my own!

A court officer unhooks the latch on the witness-box and opens the gate. Then he grabs me by the arm again, right in the spot where it burns. He pulls me out of the seat. But I shake off his grip. I can walk my own self! I'm not under arrest!

When I look back at Mama, she puts her hand to her lips and blows me a kiss. But it's not a kiss with a smile. It's a kiss with a prayer.

Miss Gold walks with me across the court. We follow the judge through his private room. The shelves brim with more books than I've ever seen in my life. I only wish I could stay here to read them. I wish I could forget my uncle's freedom depends on whether I can find the evidence in the forest.

When we leave the judge's private room and walk out the courthouse into the parking lot, I shield my eyes from the bright sun.

"Do you know exactly where the evidence is?" Miss Gold asks me.

I nod, but truth be told, I don't. Well, not down to a gnat's eyebrow. Here I've left half the county sweating inside the courthouse on account of the fact I'm supposed to turn up evidence to clear my uncle's name. I reckon I might as well make a run for it now, because if I can't make good on my word, Uncle Bump might never come home to our family again. Heck, I might get locked in the jailhouse too!

CHAPTER 31

October 21, 1963, Midafternoon

Miss Gold and me trail the judge, Mrs. Tate, Mr. Hickock, the news reporter, and the jurors down the road to Mr. Mudge's farm. I *tweet, click, click,* and Flapjack scurries to catch up with me.

While we parade down Main Street, Mrs. Tate wobbles in her high heels. I can tell she's uncomfortable in more ways than one. And me? I'm ten thousand times more nervous than I was when I walked to Weaver with Cool Breeze for the first day of seventh grade! With every step I take, I wonder why Mrs. Tate decided to join our side. Well, whatever her reason, now it's up to me to prove what she says is true. If I can't do that, then Mrs. Tate and me, we're both history.

At long last the whole lot of us stumble up Mr. Mudge's walkway. And who do we spot digging up dandelions out front? None other than Mr. Mudge himself! This morning in court Mrs. Worth said Mr. Mudge was out of town the past month. But I know better! And look at him. His overalls are streaked with mud. There's a pile of plucked weeds at his feet. And if tending's Negro work, I don't know why he's doing it himself.

Not surprising, Mr. Mudge is flabbergasted to see us. And I reckon he's stalling for time, because instead of saying "hello" or "good day" to the lot of us, he pulls off his garden gloves one finger at a time, then folds them awful neat before tucking them in his back pocket. Then he pastes on a smile and says, "Finished taking care of my mother in Florida. After that, had to meet with the Coca-Cola folks all the way in Atlanta to place my order for the new shop. Just got back. And can you believe this?"

Truth be told, no I can't, but I keep my trap shut while Mr. Mudge beats the devil round the stump. "They say someday soon they're gonna give me a better price on aluminum cans than glass bottles. Seems we're moving to the future faster than I can keep pace."

I can't help but feel bad for Mr. Mudge, the way he's wiggling round like a worm on a hook.

"Sam," says the judge, "I know you won't mind if we just take a quick look around your property." The judge looks past all the jurors to me. "That Negro girl over there says she's found some evidence for the court."

Here I stand, Addie Ann Pickett, accusing my brother's boss, Mr. Mudge, of doing wrong. Me? I'm nervous as a long-tailed cat in a room full of rocking chairs! The way this is going, it doesn't seem right.

"Look-a-here," Mr. Mudge says to me. "What kind of evidence could you possibly find on my land?"

"Probably none," the judge answers for me. "I'm sorry to do this to you, Sam, but you know if I don't investigate the newspaper will." The judge takes a paper out of his cloak pocket and shows it to Mr. Mudge. "By order of the court, you've got to remain inside your house during the search," he says.

All of a sudden, Mr. Mudge is furious. His mouth falls wide open, his eyes light up, and he looks just like a jack-o'-lantern. "Scram!" he shouts.

And that's when I know for certain what the night said is true.

"I'm sorry, Sam," the judge says. "But you'll have to stay in your house during the search."

So Mr. Mudge says to me, "You're nothing but ungrateful colored trash!" Then he stomps up his steps and slams the house door behind him.

I push against the hot air, try to stay steady, but my legs are shakier than the strings on Mama's mop. I follow the judge past a wheelbarrow and onto Mr. Mudge's farm. When we pass Mr. Mudge's garden shed, the judge picks up a shovel resting against the shed door and hands it to the bailiff.

Flapjack dashes off ahead while Miss Gold asks me to tell everyone what I saw the last time I was here on this land. Part of me, the part deep in my chest, doesn't want to talk. Despite the mean things Mr. Mudge says about Negroes, he's helped my family all these years. He gave my brother a job. And just a few weeks ago, he hired the rest of us for the garden planting.

I remember the time Delilah told Cool Breeze the rumor that his daddy was spotted a couple miles away in Bramble. How Cool Breeze searched for his daddy for days without luck. How the rumor turned out not to be true. And how much Delilah hurt him by passing it on. And I shiver to think I could be doing the same to Mr. Mudge.

I think how I swore to God—to God!—to tell the whole truth in this trial. But my insides are screwed up all over the place till I picture Uncle Bump in those chains, those jail clothes, and the words, they come.

"It was almost a week ago," I say. I lead everyone down a row of sunflowers on the farm, and cross through the pumpkin patch to the edge of the woods. But when I see how many trees are in this forest, my heart flutters in my chest. There's elm and oak and hickory and pine. How will I ever find the right spot? I shut my eyes, remember what I saw. The tree. The shovel. The farm. If I could see the farm, then that place where Mr. Mudge dug his hole can't be too deep in the woods. My eyes scan one tree after the next till at long last I see a gnarled oak, and I know that's the one. I push aside branches, flex my toes in my sneakers, and run straight to it. Then I point my foot on the dirt under the tree. "Right here," I say. "I saw Mr. Mudge bury something strange right here."

"What is it?" Mr. Hickock asks. "What's buried?"

"The something I saw," I say.

Mrs. Tate gasps like a willow. "The *something*?" she cries.

Here Mrs. Tate followed me out the courthouse door, telling all of Kuckachoo she believes I have the evidence to prove what she says is true. She had faith I knew *where* it is, but now I've told her I don't know *what* it is.

Me, I stare a hole right through my sneaker.

"You're old enough to know better than to drag us through the woods on account of *something*," says Mr. Hickock. "We've come all this way and you don't even know what it is that was buried?"

My breath ties up in my throat like a shoelace with a double knot. If I've ever needed Flapjack, I need him now. I *tweet, click, click,* but he doesn't come.

"Did you ever consider, little miss, that Mr. Mudge might've been burying a poor raccoon that died in his trap?" Mr. Hickock asks.

No, I never did think of that.

And one thing's clear: I need to find the something I'm looking for. I need to find it right now! If I don't, the next time I see Uncle Bump, he'll be behind prison bars.

I feel myself dying.

My sneaker's still pointing at the spot beneath the oak tree, so I scrunch my toes and feel Daddy's dirt there. And I reckon I just might make it through this.

"I assume there's nothing but dirt and vines here," says the judge, "but my bailiff will dig one hole—and one hole only—to uncover this so-called evidence. If the evidence isn't here, then I'm afraid the jury will have to reach a verdict taking into account the fact that you misled me and wasted our valuable time."

The bailiff digs up the first six inches of ground. He throws the dirt in a neat pile behind him. While the bailiff digs, I hear jurors mumble. "Rubbish!" says one. "A little colored girl!" says another, who spits on the dirt beside him. The only quiet juror is the foreman. Through the leaves, the dappled sun tickles the top of his bald head.

All the while, the judge whistles the Ole Miss fight song. And I can tell he doesn't care how this turns out. Not so long as he looks good on the front page of tomorrow's *Delta Daily*.

At long last the bailiff drops the shovel to the ground. He stands in a huge ditch, surrounded by nothing but spiders, roots, and dirt. The jurors cackle.

One thing's clear: if they were looking for a village idiot, they found one. My face crumples up like a tissue.

And I reckon Mrs. Tate's more than a tad disappointed in me. She turns to the judge. Her voice quivers. "Well, even if there's nothing here in this forest, surely the bill of sale I showed you proves something," she says.

"All the bill of sale proves, Mrs. Tate, is that Sam Mudge bought butter bean seeds from your husband. It doesn't prove Mr. Mudge planted the seeds, and it certainly doesn't prove he planted them over the community garden," the judge says. He looks at the jurors. "Without any additional evidence, you'll have to use the information you already have to decide if the defendant is guilty beyond a shadow of a doubt."

My heart cracks open like a pecan. Without the evidence I need, we're finished. Uncle Bump's finished. The jury won't have a shadow of a doubt that my uncle's guilty as charged. He'll be dragged away and locked up. For five years. Or perhaps ten!

I *tweet, click, click* over and over. Where's my cat when I need him?

Now Mr. Hickock tells Mrs. Tate, "I reckon that's the last time little girls—no matter what their age—should ever be trusted in a court of law."

And then the most crazy thing happens. The thing I would never expect in all my days: Mrs. Tate busts free from her ladylike manners. She turns to Mr. Hickock and says, "You're a real prize!" Then she slaps her hand over her mouth and giggles.

Mr. Hickock's so mad. His face turns red and puffy. He looks worse than crawfish stew. He looks like a plucked pelican. He tromps away through the forest, the jurors following him.

But every few steps Mr. Hickock turns to glare at Mrs. Tate, who's seemed to shock even herself.

"Please, Mrs. Tate," the judge says. "Let's try to get ahold of ourselves. We need to return to court."

Mrs. Tate nods. But as she walks through the forest with the judge, she giggles again. And again.

But me? I can't move. I'm weighed down by a ton of anger and a barrel of grief. From this day on, Uncle Bump will be called a criminal, and Mrs. Tate a birdbrain, all because I can't find what I'm searching for.

Miss Gold's the only one left with me under this oak

tree. "I know I saw something. I did," I tell her. My voice, it's lower than the drop out my bedroom window. Then I can't help it. I burst into tears.

I'm only at the start of my cry when I hear the most frightening sound: a hiss like a snake's. Miss Gold and me peer over the edge of the ditch, but thank goodness, there's no snake in sight. We hear the hiss again. Now we look toward the sound. And there, a stone's throw away, stand the news reporter, the judge, and Mrs. Tate. They're pointing to something up in a tree. That tree, it's also an oak.

Gooseflesh covers me. "He's never hissed before," I say.

"Huh?" Miss Gold asks.

"Well, only in my dream," I whisper. "We'll need that shovel."

I lead Miss Gold to the other oak tree.

There's Flapjack, up on a branch, swiping his paw at a blackbird nest, the same nest he wanted to pounce on when we bolted through the forest the day of the garden picking.

The mother blackbird caws at Flapjack. And I can't stand to see my cat attack, so I scold him till at long last he comes on down.

Then I set to work turning up the dirt beneath the branch with the nest on it. I reckon Mrs. Tate and the judge think I'm sweating up my brow for nothing at all, so they set off again across the forest. But the newsman stays behind to gather the facts.

I'm all wore out, when all of a sudden I hit burlap.

With his instant camera, the news reporter snaps a picture. Then he shouts real loud through the woods for the judge, Mrs. Tate, Mr. Hickock, the bailiff, and all the jurors to come on back.

When everyone's gathered round the ditch, I pull out seven empty sacks. I rub the dirt off one. My palm gets scratched on the burlap, but it's more than worth it because there on the side of the sack, in big red letters, it says BUTTER BEAN SEEDS, 50 LBS.

Flapjack, a regular hero, purrs at the edge of the hole.

Everyone can see that the butter bean fiasco has grown even thornier. And me? I burn with anger. To think Mr. Mudge almost sent Uncle Bump off to jail without regret!

CHAPTER 32

October 21, 1963, Late Afternoon

By the time we get back to the courthouse, I could drink a lake. We pass through the judge's private room with all the books, and then into the courtroom. As soon as folks see us, they close up their fans and sandwich bags and shuffle back to their seats. I find my way to sit beside Mama. I'm in the middle of telling her what happened when I hear a clang against the floor. And there's Uncle Bump, ankles shackled, moving real slow, like dead lice are falling off him, while the court officers lead him back to his chair.

The judge bangs his hammer. "I believe folks in this courtroom have been waiting long enough," he says. "The prosecution will now close its case."

"Yes, Your Honor," Mr. Hickock says, and stands. Of course, no amount of mustache twirling will get him a victory now, but still, he gives it a good try. "Gentlemen," he says, "we were all young once, and one of the first things we learned in school was that one plus one equals two. I don't have to tell you we learn the basics of life first. Be nice to your neighbors, share your toys, and one plus one equals two.

"Now let's remember that Bump had the *motive* to destroy your garden. He wanted to avenge the death of his nephew, Elias. Also, Bump had the *means* to wreck the garden. When Bump was weeding and watering under Mr. Mudge's direction, he had access to the butter bean seeds stored inside the garden cabin."

Mr. Hickock rocks back on his heels. "Earlier today Mrs. Worth testified that the garden cabin on Mr. Adams's land was filled with seed sacks that were not used at the planting. Sure Mrs. Tate showed you a silly list of seeds that she says were in the garden cabin after Mr. Adams died. According to that list, there were no butter bean seeds in the garden cabin. But with all due respect, Mrs. Tate probably wrote up that list of seeds on a piece of old newsprint just this morning."

I can't believe Mr. Hickock's calling Mrs. Tate a liar! Worse, he's acting like he didn't just see the evidence we turned up in the forest. All of a sudden, I'm seized by the urge to give Mr. Hickock a mustache trim. By hand! I'll yank each hair out one at a time. His eyes will tear up from the pain. And every now and then, he'll let out a howl. I'll just tell him, "So sorry. For the deluxe special trim, it's gotta be done real slow and careful." But the good news for Mr. Hickock is I'll donate my labor for free!

Now Mr. Hickock rubs his hand over his scraggly face. I reckon he's trying to appear like he's thinking real hard, but instead he looks like he's brushing off the crumbs from his breakfast. "So let's remember what our teachers taught us," he says. "One plus one equals two. Bump Dawson had the motive to wreck this garden and the butter bean seeds he needed to commit the crime. One plus one equals two."

Mr. Hickock twists the edges of his mustache round his finger. "One month ago the garden was laid by. There was nothing left to do but wait for the harvest. That's when Mr. Mudge left town to tend his sick mother, and the criminal had the perfect opportunity to strike. He broke into the garden cabin, stole the butter bean seeds, and planted them over the entire garden."

Mr. Hickock smirks like he just cracked an egg on Uncle Bump's head and is watching the yolk drip down. "Jurors," he says, "a few empty seed sacks turned up in Mr. Mudge's forest today. So what! Anyone could have buried those sacks there on Mr. Mudge's land, most especially someone desperate to frame him!"

Everyone in the viewing gallery whispers. It's the first they've heard of the seed sacks. And I wonder if they can understand. Now that Mr. Hickock's turned every bit of real evidence inside out and upside down to tell his tall tale, it's all I can do to pray Miss Gold will rearrange the pieces of the story so the truth will make itself known.

Mr. Hickock saunters back to his seat.

It's Miss Gold's turn. She stands, picks an oak leaf off her dress, and drops it on the courthouse floor. "Jurors," she says, "earlier today Mr. Tate, the biggest seed salesman in Thunder Creek County, testified that butter bean vines grow at a rate of ten inches per week. Mr. Hickock wants you to believe that after Mr. Mudge left town four weeks ago, someone broke into the cabin, stole the seeds, and wrecked the garden with them. But if the seeds were planted over the garden four weeks ago, this butter bean vine would be only forty inches long. Instead, it's seventy-two inches long. Based upon the length of this vine, we can calculate that those butter bean seeds were planted seven weeks ago. Therefore, the scenario Mr. Hickock describes is nothing less than impossible."

All I can say is Miss Gold is one clever lawyer lady!

Miss Gold struts over to Mrs. Worth, who's sitting in the front row of the viewing gallery. I know it's Mrs. Worth because I can see the back of her purple hat.

"If you follow me now," Miss Gold says, "Mr. Mudge didn't want to lose any business from his Corner Store. He simply couldn't stand the thought of Kuckachookians buying their vegetables from anyplace besides his shop, so he devised a plan to destroy the garden altogether. A couple days after the last Garden Club meeting, he got to work by planting the border of the land with fast-growing Indian corn. He told folks that this corn would shield the growing crops from high winds, but really, that corn would do more."

What Miss Gold says makes my lip shake.

"Just after he planted the corn," she goes on, "Mr.

Mudge bought the butter bean seeds from Mr. Tate, exactly as Mrs. Tate attested. But Mr. Mudge didn't keep the seeds in Mr. Adams's garden cabin. If he had, everyone would have used those seeds at the planting. Instead, he kept them on his own property."

"The first evening that the men who volunteered to weed and water the garden showed up to do the job, Mr. Mudge sent them off to Roxy's. He told the men that he had hired Bump Dawson and some others to tend the garden, and these men believed it. But what you must realize is this: after the garden planting, Bump Dawson never came to the garden again.

"Night after night, Mr. Mudge had the farm to himself. After a couple weeks, the Indian corn grew so tall that anyone checking up on the garden could hardly see past it," Miss Gold says. "That's when Mr. Mudge committed the crime."

The courtroom erupts.

The judge bangs his hammer like he's pounding a dozen nails into his desk, but still, folks go hog wild! So the judge stands up. He spreads his large arms wide open. His black cloak unfolds and he looks like a wizard. "By order of the court," he yells, "shut up!"

At long last the voices die down enough for Miss Gold to finish building our case.

"Behind the stalks and in the cover of night, Mr. Mudge planted those butter bean seeds," she says. "First he prepared the soil with his tractor. Then he haphazardly tossed the seeds every which way and waited for the rain to turn them under."

Miss Gold holds up some pictures. "Jott James, the news reporter and photographer for the *Delta Daily,* took these instant photographs today at Mr. Mudge's farm. These photographs document what the jury, the judge, and I saw an hour ago: seven empty butter bean seed sacks buried in the forest next to Mr. Mudge's farm. Addie Ann Pickett witnessed Mr. Mudge burying these sacks last week when he was supposed to be out of town."

Miss Gold stacks the photographs in her hand like they're a deck of playing cards. "While it is true that Mr. Mudge left town to open a new shop in Muscadine County," she says, "on the day of the picking, he panicked. Like so many criminals do, he threw caution to the wind and sneaked back to the scene of the crime to be extra-sure he had hidden any evidence that could possibly link the fiasco to him."

And to think that at the time I was running through the forest, I didn't even know I was watching a crime unfold. Well, I sure do know it now!

Miss Gold chuckles. "Well," she says, "at least he was smart enough to drive the back roads to his farm, because as far as I know, no one reported seeing his truck the day of the picking. But of course, if anyone had spotted him and asked about his sudden return, Mr. Mudge had the perfect alibi at the ready. He could have simply said, 'I heard about the butter bean fiasco, so I came right back to help!' "

Miss Gold paces in front of the viewing gallery. Back and forth. Back and forth. Then she stops, dead center, and stares out at us all. "It was Mr. Samuel Mudge who destroyed this community garden. It was Samuel Mudge who wanted to ruin the crop, so that you would still have to buy your vegetables from his Corner Store. It was Samuel Mudge who stole the harvest from your children," she says.

She turns to face the jury. "You have the wrong man in custody," she says. "And unless you know beyond a shadow of a doubt that Bump Dawson is guilty as charged, you must set him free."

Miss Gold points at one juror. "You!" she shouts. "You might have a hunch Bump Dawson committed this crime.

"You!" She points to another juror. "You might have an inkling he's guilty as charged."

She takes a deep breath. Then her voice gets quiet and even. "I am here to tell you that a hunch or an inkling is not enough," she says. "You need *proof*! If you convict this defendant without *proof* he committed this crime, then *you* are the one who will be found guilty. Not in a court in the state of Mississippi, but in the highest court there is." Now Miss Gold points her finger to the Heavens and roars, "The Kingdom of God!"

A chill rises up my spine.

Miss Gold hands the stack of photographs to the jury foreman, whose bald head is burned red from the sun. And all I can say is I sure hope his brain didn't get burned too, because I need him to be able to think real good.

"The defense rests," Miss Gold says, and returns to her seat beside Uncle Bump.

Next the judge opens his thick black book, reads out some rules, and dismisses the jurors. While the jurors file out of the courtroom, someone shouts clear till tomorrow, "Lock him up and bury the key!"

But we proved our case. The jurors have to believe us. They have to believe the truth. At least that's what I think till Mama rubs the cross that hangs round her neck and says, "Lord have mercy." Then she closes her eyes and stays that way.

After I imagine what each and every member of the jury will say when they meet in the back room, my mind's as tired as my body. My eyes shut too. And it's funny how the Lord's right here in his long beard and overalls waiting to have a word. Mama always tells me to be grateful, so I start out with a big thank-you. The Lord smiles. Then I say, "You can't imagine how much I love Uncle Bump, so please, I'm begging you, don't let them take him away."

I'm just about to finish my plea when Mama chugs me in the ribs. She nods at the front of the courtroom. The jurors file back, silent and serious.

My heart thrashes around in my chest like a squirrel stuck in an upside-down bucket.

But aside from Mama's sniffles, it's quiet as a cemetery here, so the judge doesn't have to call for order. He just looks at the jury foreman and asks, "In the case of the State of Mississippi versus Charles 'Bump' Dawson, what say you?"

The jury foreman's chair creaks when he stands. He makes a face like he just took a big gulp of sour milk. Then he opens up his mouth and spits it out. "Not guilty."

"What?" asks the judge.

Now the jury foreman shouts as if the words stink to high Heaven. "Not guilty!"

The bayou floods inside me. It spills right out my eyes. Mama weeps too. Elmira dances a jig, Mrs. Jacks sings,

"Glory, glory, hallelujah!" The reverend shouts, "Praise the Lord!" And Mrs. Montgomery yells, "Amen!"

I can't say if it was our prayers or Elmira's magic or Miss Gold's words or Mrs. Tate's papers or the empty butter bean sacks that did the trick. But I reckon things in Kuckachoo might be starting to change, because up till now, even if a Negro man had all the evidence on his side, he'd usually end up in jail or worse.

Of course, setting an innocent Negro free isn't the same as locking up a guilty white man. One thing's clear: Mr. Mudge will never pay his dues. But for now, I'm jubilant. And the promise of a future for my family nourishes me like honey cake.

After a court officer unlocks Uncle Bump's shackles, my uncle makes his way through the jeers and cheers right to me. "You saved my life!" he says. A tear slides down his cheek. "You gave me back my freedom!" He pulls me close, my face against his belly.

Inside this hug, it's good. Better than good. Sensational! Uncle Bump strokes the back of my head. And me? I'm filled to the brim.

❧

Of all the awkward moments, the strangest comes when I'm leaving the court. There, in the doorway, stands Mrs. Tate, her legs splattered with mud. I'll tell you one thing: she's going to need a heck of a lot of carbonated water to get the mud stains off her shoes today! Folks stare at Mrs.

Tate, eyes wide. Some nod with admiration. But most are less than cheery.

Mrs. Worth has an all-out hissy fit. "Penelope Tate, I thought we was friends," she shrieks, "but you sold me down the river. Mark my words, Penelope, I will never speak to you again! Never!"

Mrs. Tate blinks back her tears.

I always thought Mrs. Tate wasn't too mean for a boss lady, but till today, I never knew she was brave. Now I see while she stood up for herself, she also burned down part of her community. More than anything, I want to thank her, but I'm not sure how I can talk to her in public without shaming us both, so I pass through the courthouse door and leave my thanks unspoken.

Uncle Bump, Mama, and me walk hand in hand down the seven courthouse steps. At the bottom, I *tweet, click, click* for Flapjack, but after all he's done today, it's no wonder he's gone off to find himself something to eat.

It's only after Uncle Bump, Mama, and me cross the tracks that I *tweet, click, click* again and my cat comes running. I pick him up, hug him tight, and turn down Kuckachoo Lane, where my neighbors shout out congratulations.

Even though I'm twelve, I reckon I just cut my baby teeth. I grew up more in the last four months than in the four years before that. I'd call it something of an inside growth spurt, but I reckon everyone can see it as much as if it was an outside one.

The second we step into the Montgomerys' house, Uncle Bump shouts out, "Not guilty!" We find my brother in the pantry, Bible in his hand, tears rolling down his cheeks. He doesn't even swipe under his nose to stop them. After everyone hugs a couple hundred times, Mrs. Montgomery brings Elias a pillow and a blanket, and my brother curls up on the pantry floor. Wouldn't you know it, in seconds flat, he's snoring into the night.

And soon as Uncle Bump collapses onto the Montgomerys' couch, he falls fast asleep too. Mama and me don't want to wake him, so we take our blanket to the backyard, where we sit in the October night, stare at the ashes of our old lives, and cry. When at long last we're tired out from crying, we lie back on the charred leaves and count our blessings, one for each star in the sky.

CHAPTER 33

October 26, 1963, Morning

Mama says, "We need the money. That's that." And that's how come Mama and me, we've got no choice but to go back to the Tates' house to see if we've still got our jobs.

Mama raps on the back door, fixes her eyes on her feet. I do the same. But Mrs. Tate doesn't answer right away with Ralphie in her arms.

I look up to see tears filling Mama's eyes. She bites her lip, and I know it can't be easy for her to go begging on the white side. She knocks again. Again we wait. "I reckon we better go," Mama says.

But there's no way I'm leaving this place without feeling Ralphie's soft skin or hearing him laugh. "Just wait," I say.

269

And right then, the door pulls open. There's Mrs. Tate, looking all different than usual. First, she's got black spider splotches running from her eyes to her chin. Second, she's not holding her son, ready to push him into my arms.

I hear Ralphie crying like a siren inside the house. I can't wait to kiss his tummy and make him smile.

"Good day," Mrs. Tate says.

"Morning, ma'am," Mama and me say.

Mrs. Tate pushes open the screen door.

My heart jumps inside me. I'm about to run inside and find Ralphie, but Mrs. Tate doesn't step aside to let me through.

And it's like what I'm hearing isn't real. "I'm sorry," she whispers, "but we can't be using your help no more. Wouldn't look right," she says, and sniffles. "As you can imagine, my husband's not very happy with me now, so I've got to do what I can to keep this family together."

Inside the house, I can hear Mr. Tate yelling. Now Ralphie cries even louder.

Mrs. Tate glances over her shoulder, then back at us lickety-split. "I've got to tend to my son," she says. "I'm sure y'all understand."

Understand? I'd like to, but Mrs. Tate still doesn't know how to fix up the bottle real warm the way Ralphie likes it, not too hot to burn and not too cold to make his tummy turn.

My insides scream. I barely hear Mama say, "Yes, ma'am. May God bless you." I hardly feel her grab my arm and pull me down the front steps, the walk, and Honeysuckle Trail.

While Mama and me trudge along Magnolia Row, back to our side of town, all I can see is that little boy lying in his crib, reaching out for me to pinch his nose and make him laugh. And Mama, she knows no matter how hard it hurts her to think about where the next dollar will come from, right about now it hurts me more. That's because the day I started work for the Tates, I took that little one into my heart.

❦

Once we're back at the Montgomerys' place, Mama stirs up chocolate milk, and Uncle Bump drapes a bedsheet across the kitchen window. Then Elias joins the three of us at the kitchen table. Wouldn't you know it, here's my family at long last together and I can't do anything but throw a double-duck fit. Ever since my brother told me the real story of our family, I knew the anger was inside me. But I didn't have time to feel it. Till now.

My lip quivers.

Mama takes my hand. "What is it?" she asks.

I pull my hand back from hers. "You lied," I say. I take a sip of that chocolate milk but it goes down no better than tar.

At long last, my brother breaks the silence. "Some say the truth sets you free and others say hate drags you down, and which one it would be for you, we never were sure," he says.

"You just got old enough to take this all down," Mama says.

And I reckon in the past few months I sure did grow old fast.

"We noticed your new maturity," Mama says. "You're not a baby no more."

Uncle Bump grins. He's been waiting for Mama to catch on.

"I suppose it's all because of that Mrs. Jacks," Mama says.

I take a deep breath. "Mrs. Jacks and Medgar Evers and the man from the NAACP and Martin Luther King and Elias and Ralphie and those kids who marched in Birmingham and those four girls who died there and the burning cross and our burning house and the fire inside me," I say.

After I deliver my sermon, I'm calm enough to drink the rest of my chocolate milk. But it's cold as the ache in my heart. And I've got to confess my own little fib.

I bite my lip and work up the guts to say it, and when I do, it comes out plain, like toast without cinnamon or butter. "I went to the picking."

Mama stares at the table.

"I skipped out on school."

And who could believe after all Mama's been through, she's still got enough vinegar in her veins to get mad at me? But when she looks up from the table, I see it bubbling in her eyes. "That ain't right. That ain't right!" she says. "Look at this mess!"

Sitting here spilling out all our truths really is a mess. "Sorry, Mama," I say. I tell her I didn't do it to hurt her. I went to the picking to stand up for us all.

The more we run over it, the more Mama says she can understand me. "But that don't mean I'm giving permission to disobey, you hear? You got an issue with my rules, you come to me up front, no matter how hard it might be."

I nod.

"Now what're we gonna do?" she asks. "What're we gonna do?"

"Well," says Elias, "I'm thinking of going to Hattiesburg to help with the Freedom Vote. I can finish up high school there."

I picture the map on the wall. My state, Mississippi, and my capital, Jackson. And beneath it, I see Hattiesburg. "That place is south of Jackson, clear across the state!" I say. My lip quivers again, but this time I don't put up my hand to hide it. I don't mind Elias knowing I hate for him to go.

"Just for a while," he says. "Thousands of us are gonna prove that if the court clerks would let Negroes register, we would. We're gonna hold a pretend election. We're calling it the Freedom Vote."

I see how Elias, he's not all tore up about where he's got to go. I can see by the look in his eyes, he's already left Kuckachoo. It's no longer home.

"I reckon we'll always be running," Uncle Bump says.

Then Mama puts her hand over mine. "I'm just not sure we belong here," she says.

"What?" I ask.

"Here, in Kuckachoo," she says. "Maybe we ought to go."

It's hard to breathe let alone speak, but somehow I find

the words. "West Thunder Creek Junior High School," I say. "I need to stay there."

"But we can't stay here in this county," Mama says gentle.

Uncle Bump leans forward. "Your mama wants you to be free to be what you can in this world," he says. "As for me, the law says I'm free, but since when do white folks look to the law to tell what's right?"

"Your uncle and brother ain't safe here no more," Mama says. "They need to get out of town."

And I don't call Flapjack. He knows I need him. He jumps through the window onto my lap. I stroke his back and wet him with my tears.

Mama, Uncle Bump, and Elias look at each other, not knowing what to say next. So I take Flapjack in my arms and head down the hall to Delilah's room, where her parents are letting her catch up on sleep while they visit cousins down the road in Jigsaw. I pull her out of bed. I tell her she doesn't need to wear a dress. Some jeans and a T-shirt will do.

After Delilah pulls on her clothes, I lead her to the window before she gets a chance to start fussing in front of her handheld mirror. And even though it's not the middle of the night, and even though we could just walk right out the front door, we sneak out. It's tradition, and besides, it might be the very last time.

While we wander down to the bayou, Flapjack weaves round my calves and I tell Delilah everything—about Mrs. Tate and Ralphie and Elias and what all Mama said.

And I can't believe it, but soon as we get there, she sits

right down on the dirt. "Now how am I supposed to get on?" she asks.

I hate to think of leaving Delilah at all, but thinking about leaving her back here with Cool Breeze is even worse. I know she'll hold his hand, they'll stroll by the bayou, and one day, they'll get married.

"I'll take the bus to see you wherever you go," she says.

Just speaking one word is harder than lifting a boulder. "Bus?" I ask.

"Wait here," she says, and runs off.

I hold Flapjack on my lap and stare across the water, where I once feared my brother drowned. I see how the cypress roots twist above the surface, and I wonder what turns my new life will take. I used to think I couldn't go on without Elias but I did. Then I lost Uncle Bump for a short time that felt like forever. Now I'll have to create a new life without Delilah. And without Mrs. Jacks. And I can't help but think it isn't fair. Why can't I ever have everyone I love with me at the same time? Why does life only work in pieces, like a puzzle that's never whole?

When Delilah runs back, she's out of breath. She pushes a sack from the Corner Store into my arms. I peek inside it and see the colors of her gift.

"You sure?" I ask.

She nods, but in her eyes I see she's drowning in questions of her own, questions she'll never ask out loud: *What if I can't find another friend to love me like you? What if I never get to model in New York City? What if I've got to raise my children to clean clothes for white folk right here in Kuckachoo?*

So we sit without talking, the way we did the night Elias was gone too long. But this time I hang my arm over her shoulders, and we stay like that for hours till we're both so hungry we drag ourselves back.

While we walk, the sweet times wash through me. I remember Elias pitching his baseball down the lane to whoever would catch. I see Mama embroidering stars and suns on the sheets. I hear Uncle Bump playing his raggedy harmonica tunes.

As soon as we turn onto Kuckachoo Lane, we can't believe our eyes. The electricity's come on! Lights are flickering on and off inside the homes. We're so excited, we run all the way to the Montgomerys' place. I've got to admit, I have a pang in my chest because today's the day I would've been able to watch my television set if it hadn't been kicked in and burned up, and if Uncle Bump had been able to find an antenna for the roof.

But soon as we get inside, I forget all about my television. Much as I'd like to watch a few shows, some things are more important. There's Uncle Bump, Mama, and Elias, still sitting round the Montgomerys' kitchen table where I left them. They're not jumping for joy about the electricity.

Delilah takes one look and says, "I'ma see 'bout Cool Breeze." Then she slips back out the door, leaving Flapjack and me in the kitchen to hear our fate.

❦

Once I sit down, Uncle Bump lays out the plan. "Maybe tempers will calm," he says. "In the meantime, I'll head to

Hattiesburg with Elias and try to find work. I'ma send my money home."

Me? I'm sadder than a sunburned billy goat.

But then Mama says, "You'll finish up seventh grade at County Colored."

And I'm gladder than an escaped farm hog.

And I'm about to tell Mama for the four thousandth time, but I don't have to because Elias and Uncle Bump say it for me: "It's West Thunder Creek Junior High School!"

"You'll finish the school year there. Then we'll find a way to be together," Mama says. "Meantime, the Montgomerys are kind enough to let us stay on their couch."

The kitchen light shines down on all our faces. And I reckon everything looks bright, the same way it does when you leave a dark house and crash into the blazing sun.

All afternoon, Mama, Elias, Uncle Bump, and me sit round that kitchen table making our plans and hashing over every detail of the trial. Even though parts of our talk are nothing but ugly, I'm warmed up the way all of us are at long last together.

Mama sets a bowl of purple hull peas in the middle of the table. We're all reaching in, helping ourselves, when she says, "Who knows where the next bushel will come from?" She grabs a fistful of peas and rolls them down her tongue like bowling balls. "That Mudge, he's crooked as a barrel of fishhooks," she says.

Then Mama really lets loose. "Sure that man hid you, Elias. Sure he saved you from that barking hound when you was hiding in the Corner Store freezer, but don't be

277

fooled. I bet if you got close enough to him, you wouldn't hear no *thump, thump* beneath that pinstripe suit. Just the *kaching, kaching* of his cash register. If he didn't have a good use for you, he would've let you die in that freezer while that hound barked outside it till kingdom come. Mr. Mudge knew if he sent you down to work his stockroom in Muscadine County—"

I reckon someone knocked my head against the floorboard.

"Mr. Mudge hid you?" I ask.

Elias glares at Mama.

"Sure did, that man," Mama says. "Took your brother out the Corner Store freezer, defrosted him, and put him to work as nothing but an indentured servant. That's right. An indentured servant! Your brother lived and breathed in that Muscadine County stockroom, day and night, eating only from Mr. Mudge's extra supply, no cornbread, no nothin'. The only company he kept was his Bible. And go on, tell her," Mama says.

Here Mr. Mudge saved my brother's life, and what did I do? I turned him in. Now I can't help it. I'm bawling a river.

My brother's mouth hangs open. And one thing's clear: Elias didn't want Mama to say a word.

"See, Mama?" Elias says. "Look what you did!"

Elias says he wasn't going to tell me because he didn't want me to feel bad. He says turning up the evidence was the right thing to do, the only way to save Uncle Bump.

But I'm not so sure.

"She's grown-up now," Mama tells Elias. She throws

another set of peas down her throat. "Don't go feeling too bad for her."

As usual, Uncle Bump watches us, takes it all in.

Then Mama turns to me. "Addie Ann Pickett, you're a regular hero," she says. "Don't you forget it. You saved your uncle's life. That Mr. Mudge! Your brother gave him the message to deliver to us so we wouldn't worry, so we'd know he was alive. Did we ever see that note? Nope." Her eyes narrow.

"Mama," Elias says real gentle, "Mr. Mudge likely took the note so I wouldn't worry about y'all worrying about me. Didn't think of it at the time but now I reckon he had no intention to deliver it, because if the wrong person got hold of it, he'd get charged with harboring a fugitive."

"Whatever that means," Mama says.

Then she turns back to me. "It was early afternoon, day of the garden picking. Your brother happened to overhear Mr. Mudge talking to a truck driver who came to fill the Muscadine County stockroom. The driver had just made a delivery to the Corner Store here in Kuckachoo, where he got an earful 'bout the whole mess. When the driver got to the new shop, he passed on the news 'bout the butter bean fiasco, how Bump Dawson was to blame for everything.

"Soon as the driver unloaded his goods, Mr. Mudge took off in his truck. Now we all know he was hightailing it back to Kuckachoo to bury the seed sacks. Meantime, your brother placed a call to the NAACP from the shop phone. Said we needed a lawyer. Then he stole some coins out of the register and caught the first bus down the highway."

"I didn't steal, Mama," Elias says.

"You didn't steal *enough*!" Mama says back. "So far as I'm concerned, that man owes you a whole drawerful of money."

"At least he bought Elias new sneakers," I say.

But that sends Mama wild. "Yeah!" she says. "New sneakers so your brother could work himself to the bone in his stockroom!"

Elias shakes his head like Mama doesn't understand anything.

"Course, your brother couldn't take the bus straight into Kuckachoo in broad daylight, so those sneakers came in mighty handy when he got off all the way over in Laknahatchie County and came running home through fields and back roads. Seventeen miles on foot! Could've been shot dead on the way too! That Mudge knew full well . . ."

Mama's worked herself into a dither, so I put my hand on hers. And I can feel by the way her fingers soften under mine, I do it at the exact right time, just like someone fetching would. "It's okay," I tell her. "We're all here. We're still a family."

"You're right about that," Uncle Bump says.

"You are," Mama agrees.

But Elias stares past us. He's got that distant look in his eyes, the same look he had after Medgar Evers died.

CHAPTER 34

November 3, 1963

I know Elias would be proud to see me walking down Magnolia Row beside Delilah, my shoulders thrown back just like hers. Now that the whole truth has come out about the will, there's a meeting at Old Man Adams's place to figure out what to plant on the land. They put this meeting on a Sunday afternoon so none of us have to miss school or work.

Of course, Flapjack's right here, weaving round my ankles. I wish the rest of my family could come to the big house too. But Mama doesn't want any part of this garden, so she's staying home to rest. She says it'll take her a year to recover from the trial. It's a good thing First

Baptist has taken up a collection for us, because she hasn't even gone out to look for work yet. And Elias and Uncle Bump left for Hattiesburg last week, so they're not here either. Before they went, Mama gave Uncle Bump back his gold pocket watch to sell for cash so he can start over.

I've sworn to Mama I won't tell anyone where they've gone, but Mama didn't have to make me swear. On the Negro side of town, we all know my brother's heart is beating stronger than ever. Lately, whenever Bessie sees me, she winks like we're sharing the best secret in the world. But across the tracks, white folks are bumfuzzled. They're gossiping he might be alive. And me? I can't do anything better than pretend the rumor's nothing but a fool's wish soaked with my tears.

So even though I'm here without Mama, Elias, or Uncle Bump, I'm still full of celebration, because at long last this garden's ours to share. And while I head down Magnolia Row, Delilah can't stop saying how fetching I look. I'm wearing the gift she gave me. "Turn round," she tells me again, and again I spin so she can see the yellow iris that runs down the back of my orange dress.

Then Delilah spots Cool Breeze in the mix of neighbors crossing town. "Come on, slowpoke!" she yells, and I run after her.

We never do catch up to him, but that's okay, because I've been seeing plenty of Cool Breeze. I've even had the chance to study his dimples close-up. That's because ever since my books burned up in the fire, Bernice shares hers with me at school, and Cool Breeze shares with me at home. So every single night, we do reading and math together at his house. Too bad about the electricity coming back on, because truth be told, I don't mind sitting beside him in the lantern light.

Since our books are left over from the white schools, sometimes the pages are missing right in the middle of the assignment. When that happens, first I get mad to think we've got to use hand-me-downs, but then I get glad, because Cool Breeze and me don't have anything to do but talk. And now that Cool Breeze knows all about my daddy, he's started to tell me about his. But trust me, Delilah comes round plenty to make sure we're not learning anything we're not supposed to.

Now Delilah and me walk round the side of the big house. I near about keel over when I see my neighbors pass by the side door and stream through the front. The *front* door! Well, if I do faint, at least I'll look like the sunshine, lying here on the lawn with my orange dress spread right round me in a circle.

I bend down to kiss Flapjack goodbye. Then Delilah and me push on inside. Despite all my time working here, before this very instant I never did notice how pretty the entry looks with the marble pillars on the inside. I mean, sure I saw the pillars, but I never saw them like this. I look up at the blue, yellow, and red specks dancing in the middle of the staircase. The banisters need dusting something awful.

Delilah stands beside me, her eyes popping out of her head, because once and for all she sees for herself what I've been telling her this whole time was the no-doubt-about-it, one-hundred-percent, honest-to-goodness truth. She stares at the deep red carpet, the silver vase in the glass cabinet, the frilly white curtains in the living room.

"That's where Uncle Bump and me watched the shows," I say, and point to the empty space where the television used to be. And I reckon the folks from Ole Miss took the leather sofa for the university library, since it's missing too. But even with so much furniture gone, Delilah's impressed. I leave her staring at the empty living room because I can't wait to see the kitchen.

When I get there, I find Elmira leaning over the sink, shaking her head one way and the other.

"Elmira," I say.

She turns to me, her eyes wet. "It feels so empty," she says.

And even though there's more people in the house than there were for Old Man Adams's Christmas party, I know just what she means.

"That Mudge," she says. "He'll pay his dues."

From the twinkle in Elmira's eye, I reckon she's already cast a spell.

Elmira's not the only one still sour Mr. Mudge never had to show his face in court. We all are. The judge said there wasn't enough evidence against him for a trial. He said someone likely planted those butter bean sacks in the forest near Mr. Mudge's house to frame him. Wouldn't you know it, now Mr. Mudge is supplying free seeds, seedlings, and equipment for the new garden, including the use of his brand-new tractor. So one thing's clear: Mr. Mudge wants to make extra-sure he's not dragged into court later.

"Here the innocent are run out of town and the

criminal flies free as a sparrow," Elmira says. "On the bright side, soon as our community garden comes up right, folks is gonna buy even less from the Corner Store."

And I reckon Elmira's right. Some folks would rather rely on anyone *but* Mr. Mudge to fill their bellies. Even though we're going to grow our own vegetables, unless we take the bus all the way to Franklindale, we'll still have to get eggs, flour, bread, and honey at the Corner Store. And even if we do ride all the way to Franklindale, we still can't get Mr. Mudge's famous chocolate chip cookies there.

I take Elmira's hand, pull her through the big house dining room, past the empty space in the ceiling where the chandelier used to hang. Once we get to the living room, it's real awkward because the reverend and the mayor have set up folding chairs, but there aren't any signs for seating coloreds and whites like there are in the court-house.

So after some milling about and bumping into one another, things sort out in the regular way. The white folks sit down up front, then some Negro folks sit down behind them. And since there aren't enough chairs, plenty of us stand in back too. Why we marched in the front door of the big house but can't take seats up front, I'm fresh out of ideas.

The white preacher stands beside Reverend Walker. Both men wear black suits and somber faces. "Let us bow our heads in prayer," Reverend Walker says.

Several gentlemen take off their caps.

"Lord," Reverend Walker says, "we ask you to spring a well of peace inside these walls as we begin a journey. A journey to plan for the garden the way Old Man Adams intended."

I hear a little boy laugh.

At once I know I was a fool to think Mrs. Tate would stay home with her son today. Why would she miss the most important Garden Club meeting of all? But now there she is, in the third row, her husband by her side. The second I spot Ralphie on Mrs. Tate's lap, my lip quivers. I hold up my hand to cover it. From here, I can only see the shine of his black hair and the curve of his back as he leans into his mama's chest.

"Give us strength, Lord, as we commence the first meeting of the All-Kuckachoo Garden Club," the white preacher says.

Plenty of folks shake their heads when the preacher says "All-Kuckachoo," but everyone says "amen" anyhow, and things get under way.

"With the will in our possession," says Reverend Walker, "it's nothing but a fact that all Kuckachookians will eat from this garden come the spring picking."

"And we'll have half what we ought to," shouts Mrs. Worth from the front row.

"In the garden of the Lord, there's more than enough for us all!" Reverend Walker says.

"Amen!" yells Mrs. Montgomery.

Next, the white preacher asks folks what should be planted this time round. For a minute, everyone's quiet.

Then Mrs. Tate calls out, "I like carrots, myself. If I recall, there are four hundred seventeen rows. I'd like to see at least seventy rows of carrots. They're good for the little ones' eyes and skin."

"Corn!" cries Elmira.

Everyone groans. No doubt they're thinking of the corn that bordered the garden and protected the butter bean criminal from view.

"Not Indian corn!" Elmira says. "Sweet corn. I can cook up a mighty good soup, plus I can make a lotion from the husks."

"Four hundred rows of corncob then," says Mrs. Montgomery.

Mrs. Worth turns in her seat. "Twenty rows of corncob will be more than plenty."

And right here, the All-Kuckachoo Garden Club gets off to a roaring start. People talk over and under and all round each other.

Sometime during the yelling about the rows, Ralphie stands on his mama's lap. Now I can see his little face. His wide eyes. His pinch-of-sugar nose. He looks round at the people while my heart leaps out of my chest and runs over all these folks to that little boy.

Then Ralphie smiles. And I reckon he sees me. He does! I blow him a kiss.

As soon as I do, that boy stretches out his arms straight toward me. But when he can't reach me all the way back here, his cheeks redden like apples. He tries to jump off his mama's lap but Mrs. Tate holds him firm.

Now Ralphie lets out a piercing wail.

Mrs. Tate doesn't realize I'm to blame for her son's

sudden tantrum. She excuses herself and takes her fussing boy outside. The second she leaves out the front door, I can't help but cry.

Elmira turns to me. "It's okay 'bout the corncob, honey. I'll find 'em some other place."

My nose runs too.

"Don't go ruinin' yourself about the rows. You look too pretty in that dress," she says.

But all this fighting about the rows is nothing compared to the fight going on inside me, the fight to stay here with these people when all I want to do is run outside after Ralphie.

I slip away from Elmira, away from everyone, into the kitchen. I'm leaning over the drying rack, trying to find a way to stop the pain in my chest, when I see Mrs. Tate through the window.

She's holding Ralphie out in front of her while he kicks his legs real mad.

I'm not sure how long I stand staring, my face against the glass, when the next thing I know, Mrs. Tate turns to me. It's like we see into each other's eyes at the exact same second in time, and that second gets stuck, and for some reason, I don't look down.

Our eyes, they hold on to each other's.

Then lickety-split, Mrs. Tate waves her hand like I should come on outside.

I unlock the door. Before I know it, I'm in the yard of the big house, near the rows and rows that all them folks inside are hollering about.

"Ralphie misses you," Mrs. Tate says. "Hold him." She pushes her son into my arms.

Ralphie, he's warmer than rain. I sing in his petal ear, *"He's got the whole world . . ."* Slow, real slow, his scream settles into a moan. Then I hold up my finger, and soft as cotton, he wraps his hand round mine.

AFTERWORD

The anthropologist Margaret Mead once said, "Never doubt that a small group of thoughtful, committed citizens can change the world. Indeed, it is the only thing that ever has."

The people who fought in the civil rights movement proved Margaret Mead was right. They protested, marched, boycotted, and demonstrated for many years. With the help of the media and federal courts, the civil rights workers exposed to the whole world the injustices that occurred in the segregated South. Citizens and lawmakers nationwide were disgusted by horrible images of police dogs biting young boys and fire hoses toppling little girls. And they were inspired by the nonviolent resistance of the civil rights activists. So they responded.

On July 2, 1964, President Lyndon Johnson signed the Civil Rights Act. This act struck down the Jim Crow laws and promised freedom from discrimination for African Americans—and for all Americans. The following year brought another victory in the struggle for equality. The Voting Rights Act of 1965 ordered the elimination of literacy tests and other obstacles to voter registration for minorities.

The Civil Rights Act of 1964, the Voting Rights Act of 1965, and other important legislation opened new opportunities for African Americans and all minorities in our nation. People who were treated unfairly and had the courage to bring their cases to court also contributed greatly to the civil rights movement. Today, we can see the results. Now Americans of all colors attend the same schools, play at the same parks, sit together in restaurants, and marry legally. There are more nonwhite leaders representing citizens at every level of government, and the most blatant barriers to voting are gone. Compared to 1963, when Addie Ann's story takes place, there are far more people willing to speak out against racial prejudice.

Unfortunately, discrimination against African Americans and other minority groups still exists. In fact, all these years after the civil rights laws passed, African Americans and Latinos are still the least likely of all racial groups to get basic health care. And today, all these years after the Jim Crow laws were reversed, research has found that if a white youth and an African American youth commit the same offense, the African American youth is much more likely to wind up in the criminal justice system. North and South, many public schools that were desegregated by law are still segregated. One reason for this is that wealthier white parents often buy homes in different neighborhoods from those where poorer minority parents live. In this day and age, here in the richest nation on earth, millions of children live in poverty, and a disproportionate number of them are African American and Latino.

So really, the struggle for equality isn't over. Today, the cost of silence is high. You may be too young to vote for our nation's leaders. But you're never ever too young to speak up for justice and lead by your own example.

CHRONOLOGY OF EVENTS

Many important events contributed to the modern civil rights movement. The following chronology describes those milestones mentioned in A Thousand Never Evers.

1941–1945
U.S. soldiers risk their lives to fight against the Nazis in World War II. African American Medgar Evers is among them. When Mr. Evers and other black soldiers return home, they are treated like second-class citizens. This infuriates many people and contributes to the rise of the modern civil rights movement.

May 17, 1954
In a case called *Brown v. Board of Education,* the U.S. Supreme Court rules that segregation in public schools is unconstitutional and, therefore, against the law. However, many states and school districts resist the ruling for more than a decade. And even today, though not the direct result of law but of other factors, many U.S. public schools remain largely segregated.

August 28, 1955

From 1882 through 1962, at least 4,736 citizens are lynched by angry mobs. The majority of murder victims are African American men who live in the South and somehow have offended white people. In 1955, after fourteen-year-old African American Emmett Till is kidnapped and brutally murdered in retaliation for allegedly whistling at a white woman, Mrs. Till insists that her son's tortured body is shown to the world. This ignites the civil rights movement.

May 2 and 3, 1963

In an event known as the Children's Miracle, young people skip school to protest segregation in Birmingham, Alabama. Some are only six years old, but many are teenagers. City firemen spray young demonstrators with fire hoses, and city police set vicious dogs on them. At least eight hundred students participate the first day, and at least fifteen hundred the next. Despite their youth, hundreds are arrested and thrown in jail. The images and stories captured by the news media appall citizens nationwide.

May 28, 1963

Black and white college students and their Native American professor stage a sit-in at the "white only" lunch counter at a store called Woolworth's in Jackson, Mississippi. For three hours, they withstand an attack by a mob of two hundred white people, including many high school students, who beat the protestors bloody and pour salt and ketchup into their wounds. White police officers watch but do nothing to stop the violence.

June 11, 1963
President John F. Kennedy shows a new level of commitment to the fight for civil rights when he addresses the nation on television and radio to propose a bill that would make segregation illegal in restaurants, hotels, buses, and other public places across the country. The bill also would help desegregate schools and secure voting rights. However, in order for the bill to pass into law, members of the U.S. House of Representatives and the U.S. Senate must vote to support it.

June 12, 1963
Medgar Evers is shot and killed in his driveway in Jackson, Mississippi. The fingerprints of white supremacist Byron De La Beckwith are found on the rifle. Mr. De La Beckwith is tried for murder twice and set free by all-white juries. It is not until 1994 that he is convicted of the crime.

August 28, 1963
About 250,000 people gather for the March on Washington for Jobs and Freedom. They insist on the passage of the civil rights bill introduced by President Kennedy. At the march, Reverend Martin Luther King Jr. delivers his famous "I Have a Dream" speech.

September 15, 1963

The Sixteenth Street Baptist Church in Birmingham, Alabama, is bombed. Four young girls are killed while attending Sunday school. The five suspected killers are members of the Ku Klux Klan.

October–November, 1963

Many whites in Mississippi deny that black citizens want to vote. But the Freedom Vote Campaign proves that this is false. Activists hold a mock election in which 83,000 black citizens register and vote. They show that African Americans aren't voting because they are intimidated into staying away from the polls or are prevented from registering to vote because of taxes or tests.

November 22, 1963

President John F. Kennedy is assassinated while riding beside his wife in a motorcade in Dallas, Texas. Vice President Lyndon B. Johnson is sworn in as president.

July 2, 1964

President Lyndon B. Johnson signs the civil rights bill that Kennedy had introduced into law. Called the Civil Rights Act of 1964, it outlaws discrimination of all types based on race, religion, or the country in which a person was born. The act declares that segregation in hotels, restaurants, parks, and other public places is illegal. However, in segregated states like Mississippi, many white people resist the new law. Some use violence to prevent black citizens from integrating their facilities.

August 6, 1965
President Lyndon B. Johnson signs the Voting Rights Act of 1965. It outlaws literacy tests and other methods used to prevent African Americans from voting. After its passage, civil rights activists keep fighting to make sure the new voting law is enforced.

ACKNOWLEDGMENTS

Some people say writing a novel is a solitary pursuit, but this book has led me to smart, interesting, and generous people from all over the United States. Heartfelt thanks to:

My multitalented agent, Andrea Cascardi, who helped bring Addie Ann to life. She not only critiqued the manuscript many times but also introduced me to my truly brilliant editor, Michelle Poploff. Michelle, along with Amalia Ellison and Pam Bobowicz, asked hundreds of questions and made the suggestions that helped me realize the story's full potential. Also to Trish Parcell Watts for designing a cover that could spring only from the creative well of someone who lived part of her childhood in Mississippi.

The residents of the Mississippi Delta, who lived through the civil rights era, read chapters, and told me the way things really were back in the day: Lela Bearden, Patricia Browne, David

Jones, Elizabeth Kegler, Gyrone Kenniel, Jonett Valentine, Madie Wheeler, Geneva Wilson, and most especially Lillie Clifton and Mattie White. Also, Mayor Johnny Thomas and Superintendent Reggie Barnes, whom I met many years ago. Their passion and enthusiasm inspired this novel.

Fifth-generation Mississippi farmer Bethany Pepper of Blue Bird Acre CSA Farm, who read the entire manuscript, answered hundreds of farming questions, and insisted on replacing broccoli with mustard greens. Billy Barron of Barron Farms, who told me how to heap up the rows, sent me speckled butter beans, and insisted on replacing basil with sage. And Mississippi farmers Allen Eubanks and Dewey Wise, for sharing their wisdom about everything from cotton to corn.

For their specific advice on this book and for the heroic work they do every day, many thanks to: Jan Darsa at Facing History and Ourselves; Clarence Hunter at the Tougaloo Civil Rights Collection; Minnie White Watson at the Medgar Evers House & Museum; and Penny Weaver at the Southern Poverty Law Center.

Also to Fred Belinsky of the Village Hat Shop in San Diego, who informed me that despite the controversy, it was okay to wear a hat to tea in 1963; Sister Cat, who taught me how to cast a spell; Karen Dufresne of the Lone Star Dutch Oven Society, who told me I'd never eaten a biscuit till I'd eaten one cooked in a Dutch oven; and Laila Haidarali, who wrote a fascinating paper on the history of African American modeling called "Polishing Brown Diamonds."

I started writing this book when I was a sixth-grade teacher in Brookline, Massachusetts. Many thanks to my students who taught me a barrel and a heap about writing for young readers and critiqued the earliest drafts: Alison Aird, Ivy Anderson, Dante Castro, Sakeenah Chapman, Genevieve Chow, Shana Crandell, Celine Della Ventura, Aaron Fienberg, Sophie Kaner,

Caroline Lew, Gregory Lew, Adrianna Reca, Samantha Schwartz, Rita Surkis, Anna Swartz, and Phuong Tran. And to the Brookline Education Foundation, which gave me a grant when I was teaching so I could write through the summer.

A huge thank-you to all the writers, teachers, librarians, friends, and family members who nurtured this story in one way or another, including: Stephen Altier, Jeff Amshalem, Geri Belle, Jamie Berg, David Burg, Sylvia Burg, Amy Cohn, Aaron Darsa, Melody Dawson, Mark Dubnoff, Norman Finkelstein, Louise Hawes, Phyllis Karas, Daniele Levine, Mary Beth Lundgren, Carolyn Miller, Joanie Nusbaum, Rebecca Resheff, Rich Rosenthal, Yonina Rosenthal, Lynn Sygiel, David Tal, Gabriella Tal, and Sandra Wright. And to all the skilled reference librarians who staff the Ask a Librarian desk at the Austin Public Library.

Of course, there were many books that provided critical information. Dog my cats if I didn't carry around these two gems for years: *Whistlin' Dixie: A Dictionary of Southern Expressions,* by Robert Hendrickson, and *Month-by-Month Gardening in Mississippi,* by Bob Polomski. Also *Coming of Age in Mississippi,* an autobiography by Anne Moody; *A Dream of Freedom,* by Diane McWhorter; and *Remembering Jim Crow,* a collection of oral histories edited by William H. Chafe, Raymond Gavins, and Robert Korstad.

With great love and appreciation for my mom, Sondra Burg, whose endless encouragement and advice made this project possible. My sister, Rachel Belin, who read the manuscript with a history teacher's eye. My beloved Gramcracker for telling me to call Addie Ann's hometown something interesting "like Kuckachoo." My childhood cat, Sunshine. My son, Rafi, who brings so much joy. And most of all to my husband, Oren, for his sweet love and great ideas about life in Thunder Creek County.

Inspirational Library

Beautiful purse/pocket-size editions of Christian classics bound in flexible leatherette. These books make thoughtful gifts for everyone on your list, including yourself!

When I'm on My Knees   The highly popular collection of devotional thoughts on prayer, especially for women.
        Flexible Leatherette. $4.97

The Bible Promise Book   Over 1,000 promises from God's Word arranged by topic. What does God promise about matters like: Anger, Illness, Jealousy, Love, Money, Old Age, and Mercy? Find out in this book!
        Flexible Leatherette. $3.97

Daily Wisdom for Women   A daily devotional for women seeking biblical wisdom to apply to their lives. Scripture taken from the New American Standard Version of the Bible.
        Flexible Leatherette. $4.97

A Gentle Spirit   With an emphasis on personal spiritual development, this daily devotional for women draws from the best writings of Christian female authors.
        Flexible Leatherette. $4.97

Available wherever books are sold.
Or order from:

Barbour Publishing, Inc.
P.O. Box 719
Uhrichsville, OH 44683
www.barbourbooks.com

If you order by mail, add $2.00 to your order for shipping.
Prices are subject to change without notice.